CHASING PIRATES

BRIAN DELANEY

Chasing Pirates

Copyright © 2022 by Brian DeLaney

Chasing Pirates is a work of fiction. All incidents and dialogue, and all characters with the exception of some well-known historical figures, are products of the author's imagination and are not to be construed as real. Where real-life historical persons appear, the situations, incidents, and dialogues concerning those persons are entirely fictional and are not intended to depict actual events or to change the entirely fictional nature of the work. In all other respects, any resemblance to persons living or dead is entirely coincidental.

ISBNs:
979-8-9852578-2-3 (print)
979-8-9852578-3-0 (ebook)

Dedication

This book is dedicated to my mother, Phyllis DeLaney.

Mom, at an early age, you introduced me to Dr. Suess, Boy's Life magazine, Encyclopedia Brown, and, of course, the local Book Mobile to keep me reading others' adventures. This, in turn, led me to create adventures of my own for others to discover.

For this act and so much more, I love you and am supremely grateful.

Acknowledgments

I would like to thank all my beta readers, and especially my two new ones, Sue Holihan, and Jean Ball for your valuable and honest feedback. Eileene Dillman- Sis, you have weathered rough seas and have come out stronger than ever. Thanks for your suggestions. Here's to sailing in calmer waters. Russ Holihan – Thank you for going through my manuscript chapter by chapter. The seed of this story came while sitting on the beach during a visit to your Florida home. Without you, this story may not have happened. Dutch Ireland- Thanks for your input and not letting me be too obvious. We may not have found real silver or gold in our fifty-plus years of friendship but know that is where the real treasure lies. Jim Puckey- Despite the hurricane bearing down on you, thanks for taking valuable time to deliver talking points. My money is on you, my friend. I always have and will always be there for you to batten down the hatches. Creating the best story possible could not happen without you all and am blessed to have you on my team.

Thanks to my editor Grace Wynter for her constructive suggestions and not letting me take the easy way out. I and my characters thank you for your guidance and input.

To Kimberly Martin from Jera Publishing. Another fine job on formatting and what a cover! I love that you bring my ideas to life!

A shout out to Art "Mad Man" Mehring for sharing his expertise in the world of diving.

Special thanks to all the amazing pirates in my life. I'm so blessed to have sailed along life's journey with you. I love you all.

And last, but not least, to my darling wife, Cynthia. You are my berth, my allotted place. Your love and support mean everything to me.

"If you live to be one hundred, I want to live to be one hundred minus one day so I never have to live a day without you."
-A. A. Milne

An Allotted Place

CHASE PORTER SAT on his regular stool at the King's Berth and finished his second soda of the afternoon. The Spanish Reale coin hanging from the chain around his neck lay warmly against his chest. He wiped the condensation from his fingers, then rubbed the coin between his thumb and forefinger, feeling the familiar outline of the cross covering one side of the piece. He could draw the image in his sleep: the straight vertical line intersecting with the horizontal one, each tip marked in a semi-circle.

"You're thinking about the student again, aren't you?"

Chase looked up at the man who had become his best friend since moving to Key West three years prior. His name was Rick Grande, but everyone called him 'Rio' after the river in Texas and the John Wayne movie.

The friendship had come as a surprise to Chase. Though the two men were about the same age. Rio, with his dark eyes and long hair usually tied in a ponytail, had the women in Key West falling at his feet. Chase's college professor vibe skewed decidedly more conservative with the ladies. Where Rio was carefree, humorous, and spontaneous, Chase was cautious, serious, and thoughtful.

Still, the two had bonded the first time Chase set foot in the King's Berth, or just "The Berth" as it was known to the locals.

"You don't even have to answer," Rio said, though Chase sensed he wanted one. When he didn't respond, Rio gestured toward the Reale and continued. "Whenever you rub that coin, it means you're worrying. Also, it's creepy in a stay-two-hundred-yards-from-an-elementary-school kind of way." Rio tossed aside the rag he'd used to wipe down the counter and leaned against the bar in front of Chase. "Look, man, it's been over a year."

"It still feels like yesterday." Chase shook his head. "I can't get it out of my mind. I wrack my brain of what I could have done differently."

"No one blames you, man."

Chase appreciated the sentiment, but he knew it wasn't true. The coroner listed the official cause of death as *drowning*. The kid had panicked in sixty feet of water, and by the time Chase reached him, it had been too late. Of course, the parents blamed Chase for the boy's death.

The school finished their investigation and although the blame was placed solely on the student, his death hung on Chase like a wet overcoat, the weight making him feel much older than he was. Today would be no different as he slumped on the bar stool and mindlessly kneaded the coin around his neck.

Across the bar, Rio tapped a finger on the polished mahogany.

"Chase? Come back to me."

"Sorry. Spaced out, I guess."

"What's it called again? A Reale?" Rio asked, as he pointed to the coin. "Really? A replica of a Spanish coin and it's called a *Reale?*"

Despite his mood, Chase couldn't help but grin. He had finished classes for the day, waiting for the end of Rio's shift so they could go diving in the calm, blue-green waters off the Keys.

Glancing at the empty soda glass in front of him, he really craved a shot and a beer chaser, but soda would have to do; one of the basic rules of diving: *alcohol and water do not mix.* Chase let go of the Reale, his hand slowly dropping to the bar as if to appear nonchalant.

Rio was wrong about the coin. It was not fake. The original necklace his mother bought him many summers ago was indeed fake. But she had done so on the day he and his father found seven Reales at Vero Beach. Well, actually eight. Chase had slipped one in his pocket: the one now around his neck. The chain had been the last item his mother had given him, making him cherish the gift even more. Chase had taken it apart and replaced the fake coin with the authentic one, being careful not to break the small tines holding the silver coin, his parents unaware of his deception.

Since then, he'd led everyone to believe the coin around his neck was a replica, taking his father's advice about what to do if he ever found treasure. *Tell no one. Loose lips sink ships.* While he hated to lie about it, he found no reason to confess the truth now.

"The coin helps calm me while I work through a problem," he explained.

"I'm sure it does," Rio began. "So, the *not* Reale helps you relax...." He paused, a smirk on his face.

Chase found Rio's humor disarming, and he knew something humorous was on its way. Rio could not help himself.

"Wait, a not real Reale? So, then wouldn't your coin be... an *UnReale?*"

Chase laughed at Rio's joke, and for a few moments, it took his mind off his problems.

"Seriously, man, what do you have to complain about? You're a college professor who teaches coeds history they'll never use, while I'm schlepping drinks inside this cavern of a bar. Besides, you're one of the hardest working guys I know."

Chase picked up his soda, then realizing the ice had melted, set it back on the bar. "You got me. I admit I'm a little concerned."

"Your college career as flat as your soda?" Rio asked.

"How'd you know?"

"Your hangdog look. You should work on your poker face. How bad is it?"

Education had brought Chase to Key West. His three long years in the history department of Cay College lecturing to students who cared more about their lives on social media than social studies were starting to wear him out. It also felt claustrophobic stuck inside all day. The only redeeming feature was the opportunity to work with the marine biology department, allowed to dive the shipwrecks and coral reefs up and down the Keys, which up until the boy's death, had been a joy.

Chase ran a finger up and down his glass. "It's not good. Plagues me. Makes me question what the hell I'm doing here. I can assure you; I will *never* let that happen again."

"You've got to stop beating yourself up, man." Rio used the soda gun to fill Chase's glass halfway. "You can't always do everything by yourself. Sometimes it's okay to lean on other people like I'm leaning on the boss to get here so we can leave," Rio added, obviously trying to lighten the mood. Then he reached down into the ice bin, picked up a cube, and dropped it in Chase's soda causing it to fizz.

Chase took the glass, his finger tracing the Berth logo on its side. The Berth wasn't just another tourist bar, but a refuge for the locals. A large mirror covered the wall behind the bar, reflecting the backs of the liquor bottles and the faces of those sitting at the long mahogany bar. Wide hewn beams reminiscent of those used in old wooden ships laced the ceiling in rich brown hues.

"Shit fire!" growled the owner of the Berth as he entered from the back room. "Place is empty."

Sam King was a large, barrel-chested man with long graying hair and a bushy beard peppered with specks of gray. King was an imposing figure who could quiet the bar with a growl or brighten it with one of his hearty laughs. No one wanted to get on the man's wrong side.

When Chase first asked about the name of the bar, the owner barked at him. "My allotted place."

"Relax, Boss. They're coming," Rio admonished. "You say the same thing every day and every day I remind you shifts change around this time."

Chase knew Rio had a firm grip on the bar business. He'd seen the pattern himself, beginning with the regulars. The town workers in dirty lime vests with regular seats at the bar, their drinks set in front of them before their asses touched the stool. Next were the maids, looking for their Margaritas. Finally, both the wait and bar staff would meander in after the lunch crowd, their clothes still reeking of fish or fried foods.

"Shit fire!" King repeated. "No diving today." King did not speak much, but when he did, he always said something interesting. Today being no exception. "Dark soon. Never get out to a site in time."

"We're going to try," Chase said, as he got off his barstool. "We have enough daylight."

"I don't know, Chase. If King says we aren't diving, then I'm gonna take his word for it."

Rio shook his head. "How about we try again tomorrow or the next day?"

"No. I'm going anyway." Chase was adamant, even if it meant breaking another dive rule: *never dive alone.*

As Chase walked toward the door, he heard Rio say, "Boy, is he stubborn."

"Atonement," King replied, and Chase knew King referred to the drowned boy.

"That too." Rio shook his head again. "That too."

THE FIRST OF MANY
STORMS TO COME

KING HAD BEEN right. It turned out to be too late to dive by the time Chase had reached the marina, the dive boat captain telling him he should have listened to King and stayed at the Berth for a real drink. Instead, Chase had gone home in order to get a good night's rest. It didn't work.

The next morning, after dragging himself through two classes, he stepped into his office and dropped himself into his chair. Unlike the spacious offices most of his colleagues enjoyed, his had more of a stark closet look; cramped with no windows for light. No matter, Chase reminded himself, *I could work in a cardboard box if necessary*. His office felt pretty damn close.

After grading papers, he began to prepare a lecture on seventeenth-century new world trade routes and the shipwrecks those routes had claimed. Chase liked to add spice to his class in an effort to keep the students engaged. Talk about the old European Powers' quest for riches to supplement their wars and the student's eyes would glaze over. But add ships laden with treasure sitting on the sea floor right off the Florida coast and you grabbed their attention. His students wanted more than facts. They wanted excitement, danger, and adventure. Chase wrapped all three elements into his lectures. No wonder his classes were always full. Well, full *before* the diving accident. Afterwards, enrollment in his classes began to sink like his attitude.

As he struggled to write the lecture outline, his office door opened and the department chair, Christopher Faulk, walked in with a female he did not recognize. Chase stood up. *This can't be good.*

Faulk, a large man with ruddy cheeks and a fading hairline, had a penchant for wearing clothes which fit a little too tightly. He had never really gotten along with Chase, the chair complaining how Chase kept bending the rules and changing the curriculum to fit his fancy. And why couldn't he be more sociable with the rest of the department employees? Chase couldn't argue too much about the man's complaint, because it was true. After what the school called *the incident*, Chase began skipping the faculty events. He despised having to make idle chit-chat with people who he knew did not want to be associated with him.

His classwork had suffered as well. He became short with students who did not sufficiently prepare for class, giving them lower grades than usual out of frustration. Soon, he began to get frowny faces from anonymous students posting on the college's professor rating social media site.

Recently, he'd received a reprimand for flunking a student whose father happened to be a significant contributor to the school. A decision which had not gone over well with Faulk. But handing out grades for students who did not do the work went against his core beliefs. Chase foresaw another reprimand on the way and his back stiffened to prepare for it.

"Chase," Faulk began, "this is Gail Drescher from Human Resources." Chase put out his hand but was met with silence as

Gail sat down in the only other chair in the office. Chase also sat while Faulk remained standing.

"We're here today for, um...." Chase noticed sweat droplets forming on Faulk's forehead as he pulled on his too-tight blazer. "What I mean to say is-"

Gail interrupted. "Mr. Porter, the committee has met to discuss your behavior since the unfortunate diving incident ...."

There was that word again. *Incident.*

"Although you were not at fault in this matter, they have decided the event might be causing you angst or anxiety. And as such, we will not be renewing your contract for the next calendar school year."

"Wait! You're firing me?" Chase said, taken aback. He had always known it would be a remote possibility, but was still shocked by the announcement, even more so by the absurd notion the committee was doing this for *his* benefit. If Chase had not been anxious before, being out of a job would surely do the trick.

"Now, Chase, we all feel a change of venue would be beneficial to you, the students, and the school. We want to begin the healing process," interjected Faulk.

Chase noticed once the actual firing had taken place, Faulk had miraculously found his voice. "The semester is almost complete. You can either finish it, and we hope you do, or we can get a substitute to finish out your term. You'll be paid either way." Chase also observed the coward was no longer sweating.

"You'll need to sign this waiver indicating you will not take any legal action against the institution. This is a normal procedure," Gail said, placing the waiver on the desk and pushing it toward him with her finger. Chase looked at the document but did not touch it. His shock had turned to anger.

Unwilling to hide his contempt, he used his pencil to push the sheet back toward Gail as if the paper itself was covered in something distasteful. "Yea, not going to happen," he said. "I'll finish the semester for the students." Then pointing to the offending document added, "This paper is for you to shove up your ass. *My* normal procedure. Now please get the hell out of my office. I have work to do."

Faulk began to bluster at the insult, but Chase stared at him while pointing his finger at the door before ending the conversation. "What are you going to do, asshole, fire me?"

Anne Braun was a girl on a mission. She had just come from her last job feeling fortunate to be through for the day. Working several jobs in this town had a way of exhausting a person, especially in the hospitality business where Anne spent most of her days on her feet. Today's weariness faded as she hurried up Southard Street, smiling at the thought of her destination. She blew a strand of auburn hair out of her face as she power walked.

Anne smiled a lot these days. Gainfully employed and living rent-free in beautiful Key West would give anyone good reason to be happy. She had one more reason to smile: her new man, Chase Porter. Her college professor boyfriend was smart and handsome. He also had lofty goals and dreams she hoped aligned with hers. She was reminded of the saying, "Behind every successful man, is a strong woman." What a crock of shit, she thought. *I will not stand behind any man. We stand together through life ... or else.*

Or else what? asked the voice inside her head, testing her resolve.

"Or I'd rather walk alone," she replied aloud, hoping she would never have to. She'd done the 'single thing,' and while she wasn't one of those females who needed a man or to be in a relationship, she knew a good thing when she saw it. Chase was different from all the other guys she had ever dated. Correction, *met.* His gentle nature appealed to her as well as his ability to listen to her, really *listen.* Being easy on the eyes and a good kisser just happened to be bonuses.

At the Berth's entrance, Anne pulled at the heavy oak door and struggled to slide through the opening.

"Hey, Teach, how was your day in class?" She recognized Chase's sandy blonde hair as he sat at the bar. He turned to look at her and at once she realized something was wrong. His eyes gave her the first clue. Depending upon his mood, they turned to a different color from his normal hazel. Today they appeared a sad blue.

"What is it?"

"I loss my job. At the end of the semester, I'll no longer be a *perfesser,*" Chase slurred.

Anne pressed her lips tightly as her face flushed with anger. This behavior, so unlike Chase, caught her off guard. As a bartender, she saw her fair share of drunks. Although she did not have a problem with tourists having a good time, the last thing she wanted or needed was a drunk boyfriend. After dating guys who liked the drink too much, Anne did not want to repeat the horror.

Taking a deep breath, she pushed aside her anger, not wanting to come across as insensitive. Still, she did not want to come across as fake either. "OK, soldier. Sitting on a bar stool isn't going to get you moving forward after one lousy setback. What's the next plan?"

Chase stared at her, eyes blinking lazily. "Drink!" he said. "Then drink s'more." Turning towards the bar, he downed a shot, followed by a long swig from his beer bottle.

Conflicted between sympathy and empathy, and knowing how bad Chase felt, Anne shot a gaze of disapproval toward the bartender.

"You could always go work for Jasper," Rio said, and Anne saw that as an attempt to deflect the attention away from himself and back onto Chase.

Jasper Cobb was the preeminent tour operator in town, which also made him one of its top employers. He'd made a name for himself building Cobb Enterprises from the ground up, owning several ventures catering to tourists. Although Jasper might have been under the impression the Key West community respected his business acumen, *that* impression was not shared by those sitting at the Berth.

"Bite your tongue, Rio. Chase is bigger than that and a much better man," Anne said, momentarily doubting herself as she watched Chase do something most self-respecting bartenders hated. He wriggled the bottom of the beer bottle noisily against the bar top, signifying to Rio he wanted another.

Trying again, her anger returned. "So, what do you really want to be when you grow up?"

"Ouch. I see we're not againse using sar … casmm," Chase slurred. "Well, lemme see. What *do* I wanna be when I grow up? Mmmm. Good question."

Anne's patience began to run thin as the sarcastic side of Chase emerged bordering on the caustic. He held a finger to his jaw in mock contemplation. "A pirate," he said. "I think I wanna be … a… PIRATE!"

Anne frowned, then attempted a gentler approach. "C'mon, be serious. You could get another teaching job at any of the other schools around the Keys."

"I'm also drunk. And as far as getting another job, there ish no plan, Anne." He grinned at his rhyme. "See what I did there?"

Anne's frown reappeared. This evening wasn't going the way she'd planned. She decided on a firmer stance. "Not on my watch, mister. I think it's time to take you home." She reached for his arm, but he pulled away, surprising her.

"Whoa, I'm not ready to leave jus yet. Bartenner, would you be so kind and set me up with an-oth-er?" Chase again clanged the beer bottle loudly against the bar. Rio grabbed the empty and pulled it away, shook his head but obliged.

"What is *wrong* with you?" Anne stared at Rio. "Obviously, he's had enough to drink. Why keep feeding him?"

"Anne, love you girl, but this is a bar. I'm the bartender, and what I do is serve my customers." Nodding towards Chase adding, "He's my customer." To emphasize his point, Rio not only gave Chase a beer but he also poured another shot and slid it in front of his friend.

Raising his glass to Rio, Chase made a toast. "Thank you, my good man." After a sip of beer, he looked at Rio and asked. "Do you want to be a pirate with me?"

Chase was now acting like an ass, so Anne just shook her head in disgust. The hell with sympathy *or* empathy, she did not need this nonsense. Frustrated, she turned to leave but did not get far. A loud noise made her stop and turn around. Chase had fallen off his barstool. He landed on his knees and began to laugh, but it was short-lived. A look of confusion crossed his face before he gagged trying not to vomit, but there was no stopping the eruption onto the dusty hardwood floor.

When Rio peered over the bar, a sheepish grin spread across his face aimed at Anne, indicating to her he was asking for help to clean up the mess.

She shrugged. "As you said, Rio, he's your customer. You deal with him." She again struggled opening the large door but had no problem letting it bang shut behind her.

An Unwelcome Apparition

 He water was *calm and clear, perfect for diving. Black fins propelled the divers slowly as if in a synchronized dance. Each movement choreographed as bubbles from regulators formed a slipstream in their wake. Colorful fish added an intricate dance of their own around the colored coral littering the seascape and breaking up the monotony of the sand-colored sea floor.*

Chase looked at his dive computer to confirm the depth. For some reason, he either couldn't read it, or he didn't recognize the numbers. Only then did he notice the boy in the distance frantically heading to the surface, his mask falling past his ascending body, arms outstretched seeking to break the surface to gain access to the fresh, life-saving air awaiting up there.

The boy spit out his regulator as Chase attempted to swim towards him, but no matter how hard he struggled, Chase couldn't move, his arms were heavy and unresponsive, his fins stuck to the sea floor as if mired in quicksand. "Don't panic, don't panic," he said to the boy, hearing the words clearly despite the depth and distortion water normally caused.

Chase began to tire as he continued his futile attempt, watching as the boy no longer struggled. His body went limp as it began sinking towards the sea floor, floating silently downward towards the coral and fish waiting below.

Chase bolted upright in bed, panic-stricken and sweating profusely. His heart pounded as if he had just finished a strenuous jog. He took in a deep breath of fresh air, tasting sweet and welcoming after the nightmare. His panic slowly subsided, replaced by the head-pounding pain caused by the alcohol from the night before.

His arms and legs no longer weighed down by the dream, Chase swung his feet over the bunk, kicking off the light blanket before opening the bunk door leading to the galley. Home was a thirty-one-and-a-half-foot Hunter sailboat moored at Conch Harbor Marina, purchased in response to the high housing prices in Old Town. It was not a large two-story like those 19th century homes adorning Key West streets, but he owned it free and clear. The name *Brains and Brawn* was stenciled in blue letters across the stern, the moniker from the previous owner. An old superstition claimed it bad luck to rename a boat. With the luck he'd been experiencing lately, Chase decided not to tempt fate.

Opening the bunk door, he found Rio sitting in the galley on one of the two cushioned bench seats separated by a small table, sipping a cup of coffee. Another sat on the table, the steam rising telling him the coffee had been freshly brewed. A bottle of aspirin sat next to the waiting cup. Chase grabbed the aspirin first and dry swallowed three.

"Morning, sunshine. 'Bout time you got up … times a-wastin'," Rio said as Chase picked up his coffee cup.

"Ugh, my head," Chase complained before taking a sip and groaning as the dark, bitter liquid hit the back of his tongue. "Why did you let me drink so much last night?"

"You asked for it; I delivered. Now c'mon. We need to get in the water."

Chase drank the hot caffeinated beverage as the last emotions of the nightmare drained away. A chill made his body shiver in his sweat-soaked T-shirt. Stripping it off, he tossed it back through the open bunk door behind him.

"Another nightmare?" Rio asked, softening his tone.

"Yea, same one."

"It's not going to get in the way of our dive today, is it?"

"No. It won't. I'll be ready as soon as I finish my joe."

Changing into a fresh T-shirt and swimwear, Chase had an out-of-the-blue thought. *The dead boy was lucky in a sense. He no longer had nightmares.*

Key West is a small island. Most people do not own cars because everything is within walking or biking distance. Chase needed a vehicle to drive out to the college near the airport. Well, *needed* would soon be an outdated word by the end of the semester.

The two men loaded their diving gear into the bed of Chase's old Ford F150 and drove to the docks where the *Mastery* awaited them. A local salvage company owned the ship, which had famously discovered and owned the salvage rights to the *Atocha* and the *Santa Margarita* shipwreck sites. The owner found the wrecks in 1985, and his team had already harvested over four hundred million dollars' worth of artifacts and treasure in the years since. Both Chase and Rio were investors in the company Loyalty Program, which allowed them to dive the debris fields in search of treasure.

Mark Stanton, captain of the Mastery, greeted them when they arrived at the docks. Captain Mark had befriended Chase when they met at the Berth. Between beers and diving tales they'd become fast friends.

"Today's the day!" was shouted as the trio walked aboard. Every Key Wester worth their salt would be familiar with the cry coined by the man who used it daily for sixteen years before finally finding the wrecks off the coast of the Dry Tortugas.

"Chase? You don't look so well. You sure you're up to the dive today?" Captain Mark asked, concern etched into the deep lines along his forehead.

"I'm fine," Chase responded, trying to sound chipper. With his head still thumping, he wasn't so sure.

"C'mon inside. I want to show you something we found."

Captain Mark led the two towards his onboard office. Weighing in at one-hundred-twenty-five tons, the craft was a sturdy eighty-one-feet in length driven by twin 12-71 Detroit Diesels and twin disk transmissions. It was equipped with a three Anchor Mooring System, ten horsepower electric winches, motor brakes, and twin prop wash deflectors to move sand from the bottom of the ocean. Additional features included four-by-twelve-foot airlifts powered by a CP120 air compressor, Bauer 20cfm SCUBA air compressor, and Aqua Pulse metal detectors to pick up the faintest hint of metal. The vessel was well-suited for the arduous task of finding and recovering treasure on or under the ocean floor.

When they reached Captain Mark's office, he opened the door and led them in to stand around a metal table bolted to the floor. "Check this out." He waved a hand over some maps strewn across the table and held down by a large bronze paperweight. Chase and Rio exchanged puzzled glances.

As if reading their minds, Captain Mark pointed at the bronze piece. "If you think this is a paperweight, you'd be mistaken."

"It sure looks like one," countered Rio.

"This artifact wasn't expensive during its day, but it *is* a part of history." Captain Mark lifted the metal object and handed it to Chase. "What you're holding is an Admiral's bronze seal. This artifact would have been stored in the Admirals Quarters. It's a great find!"

"Why is that important?" asked Rio.

Before Captain Mark had a chance to reply, Chase answered, "Because the Admiral's quarters were near the Captain's, both located on the *Atocha* sterncastle, correct?"

The captain nodded at Chase. "Excellent, Mr. Porter. You get a gold star." Pointing to an irregular arc on one of the maps, he added, "We found the seal here, about fifty yards from a reef."

Chase leaned in for a closer look. The arc resembled two scars along the sea floor: one long one and a smaller one towards the eastern edge of the larger. Tiny dots around the scars looking like aerosol paint splatter signified locations of specific artifact finds.

"We discovered it along with other gold pieces and jewelry, but we haven't found any emeralds in the area ... yet."

Rio looked puzzled. "I don't get it. A seal and some jewelry, what's the significance?"

Captain Mark walked over to the door and closed it, before returning to the table.

"There are stories of a letter written in 1623, which claimed its writer had helped the Admiral smuggle sixty pounds of emeralds aboard the *Atocha*. These were known as the Muzo emeralds and they were kept off of the ship's manifest because the smugglers didn't want to broadcast their plan to the Spanish government for tax reasons. The Admiral's quarters were located at the ship's stern where the emeralds would have been stored for safekeeping. The sterncastle to be exact. We found the seal and believe we're on the right track to find the sterncastle and the smuggled un-manifested emeralds." Captain Mark paused, a gleam in his eye. "The worth is estimated to be several hundred million dollars."

"Wow," said a stunned Rio. "So, where is this sterncastle?"

"That, my friend, is the several hundred million dollar question." Captain Mark raised his voice over the *Mastery's* diesel engines as the ship got underway. "We haven't found *that* either."

Chase left Captain Mark's office in awe. *Smuggled emeralds.* The thought mesmerized him. By the look on his face, Chase surmised Rio was equally impressed. The two brought their gear to the back of the ship's dive platform and secured it in lockers. No matter how Chase tried to concentrate on the task, his mind wandered towards what lay around the site they were approaching.

Loyalty program members either dove to the debris field or stayed aboard sifting through sand brought up from the sea floor by a giant vacuum. Program members were also eligible for the division party, an annual gathering held in May for all members who, in line with their financial contribution, would receive a portion of the year's discovered treasure. Since Chase and Rio did not have large stakes, their ability to get a decent payday would have to be determined by a substantial find.

As they donned their wet suits, the two discussed Captain Mark's recent disclosure. Chase was anxious to help find the sterncastle and the gems it held within.

The dive plan directed them to follow a path in a linear grid pattern along with the other divers. That way, they would be able to cover more territory as they searched for artifacts which fell along the same debris path as those recently found.

Chase held his mask against his face and waited for the dive master to announce, "The pool is open!" indicating the all-clear to fall backward into the water. Bubbles from his entry soon dissipated and Chase's vision cleared as he and Rio swam the fifty-five feet down to the debris field and what treasure might lay ahead.

Chase marveled at the *Mastery* crew's continuing discovery of treasure in the debris field, plucking coins, silver and gold bars, jewelry, and other artifacts from the sea floor. He found it exhilarating these items would see the light of day for the first time in over four hundred years and even more so … how those finds were cataloged and stored by the deck crew, essentially turning the treasure hunters into treasure *preservers*. Proud to work with a company which placed preservation before profit, he knew history would show this crew worthy of the distinction of archeological expertise.

Once in the debris field, Chase and Rio swam three-to-four feet apart, following their lines along their grid path looking for any anomalies on the floor surface. A mound located where it shouldn't be. A misplaced indenture. Anything shiny in the faint sunlight coming down through the water's lens.

Chase waved his hand to stir up the sand, hoping to reveal foreign objects along the seafloor. He kept a close eye on his depth and oxygen supply, understanding the equipment they used allowed them to go just so deep, staying below the surface between forty-five minutes to an hour. Not long enough to find much before they had to return to the ship to change tanks. When the time came, Chase motioned to Rio, and they headed back to the dive platform.

Back on board, Rio mused, "Sure wish we could use the air hoses the other diver's use. They get to stay down longer."

"That would be more convenient," Chase agreed. "There are only so many lines, and Captain Mark's divers need them. I already asked him about it."

"There has to be a better way," Rio said just before putting on his mask and slipping back into the emerald-green water.

Chase agreed. He made sure they each brought along four tanks, providing them four dives apiece. After three tanks had been exhausted, the pair took their final plunge of the day.

Swimming along the grid, Chase noticed a coral reef in the distance, one hundred yards off the grid pattern, standing up from the ocean floor five feet or so in height and approximately twenty-five feet in length. Captain Mark mentioned finding the Admiral's seal close by. A thought tugged at him; *take a closer look.*

Breaking from his assigned route, he swam toward the reef, watching a variety of fish swimming in and out between gaps. A small school darted out of one gap as if spooked by a predator. As he passed by, Chase looked inside to see what could have scared off the fish. He spotted what looked like a dive mask laying on the sandy bottom. *That's odd,* he thought and decided to retrieve it. *No one should even be over here.*

When he reached into the gap, he grabbed only sand. The mask had vanished. He shook his head in astonishment almost losing his own mask. *What the hell? How could that be?* Chase searched but could not find any trace of the mask. It was gone. Shaken, Chase swam to the other side of the reef. There he found nothing but coral and fish. His first instinct? Check the oxygen level. Lack of oxygen played tricks on the mind, and if not corrected, could cause hallucinations. Left uncorrected for too long, meant the divers death.

Checking his gauge, he felt relieved to find the oxygen mixture level showing normal—still plenty left. Scanning the reef again, he decided what he'd seen must have been an optical illusion. He turned, about to head back to Rio's position when at the end of the reef he noticed a pair of flippers disappearing behind the reef's southern end. Shaking his head again, he wondered ... another diver? *But he wasn't there the first time I looked.*

Chase pursued the diver, his heartbeat rising to the point of hearing it thump against his temples. Rounding the reef, he found nothing. *Divers, like masks, didn't just disappear.*

Somehow this diver had. He swam all the way around the reef until he found himself back to the point where he first saw the mask. Chase began to slow his breathing, about to turn around when movement caught the corner of his eye. A Fish? An eel? Or something else? He had the strange feeling he was being watched yet couldn't find the responsible party.

His hands began to tremble, and despite the chilly water surrounding him, perspiration began beading above his upper lip. *Don't panic,* he told himself and sunk both hands into the sand to try and stop the trembling. Disappearing masks and flippers needed an explanation. He'd even accept an insane one.

The thought of ghosts occurred to him. There were plenty of stories of ghost sightings on land *and* underwater. With the number of shipwrecks in the area, why not have spirits inhabit the places where they perished? It made sense that ghosts couldn't drown. Especially the spirit of the poor boy who drowned on his watch.

Chase shook his head to clear the thought. He had never been prone to ghostly beliefs and tried to stay calm below the water, but today's dive was anything but ordinary.

Take it easy, slow down. Closing his eyes while digging his fingers deeper into the sand to ground himself, Chase willed his breathing to slow. When it did, his heart rate followed. *That's it. Keep digging.* The action did the trick as he worked his way back from panic mode to calm; a good trick to have when fifty feet or so below the surface.

He continued the digging motion deeper as his respiration and heartbeat returned to normal, which was when his finger stroked a smooth, solid surface. Curious, Chase dug around the small object then tenderly lifted a stone from its resting place. Examining it further, his heart began to race again realizing this was no ordinary stone, but a Bezoar stone.

Bezoars were smooth stones resembling eggs. This one, encased in four ornate gold strips lead to a small cross on one end and a small ring on the other. The stone, believed to be an antidote for poison, would have had a chain attached to the ring so it could be dunked into a drink with the intention of neutralizing the poison. The rare artifact would not be owned by a sailor but by a wealthy traveler or senior officer ... *Like an Admiral.*

Chase reached for his diver's sack to secure the stone, the artifact too important to leave on the sea floor, when a tug on his shoulder startled him. He spun quickly, arms and fins forcing him backwards like a crayfish escaping a predator, causing the stone to fall back to the ocean floor. His only thought was to get as far away as quickly as possible. As he thrashed frantically, he saw the diver floating ahead of him, but not pursuing. And this one had a mask and regulator, the bubbles escaping and heading to the surface. Reason took over and Chase stopped his struggling.

Rio's head cocked as if to ask a question, giving Chase the OK sign.

Recovering from the initial fright, Chase returned the hand signal. Rio turned to swim back towards the grid on the debris arc, oblivious to the Bezoar stone below him.

Before following Rio, Chase rethought his earlier position on bringing the Bezoar stone to the surface. If this artifact wasn't in the debris field, perhaps there were other artifacts nearby.

Remembering the heavy Admiral's seal find, it made sense that a heavy stone like the Bezoar would also fall nearby. He buried it in the sand and marked its coordinates on his dive computer to recover later. Swimming back, he looked over his shoulder every so often for any new apparitions.

Forty-five minutes into the dive, Rio gave Chase the signal to ascend. Their oxygen levels were close to depletion. Chase put up his hand, signaling his request for five minutes more. He wanted to see if he could catch another glimpse of whatever was by the reef. Like a gambler, who lost everything but his last dollar, Chase wanted one more chance. Despite his ghostly thoughts, finding the stone so far from the debris site had intrigued him.

Rio was having none of it. He grabbed Chase by the arm and aggressively pointed upward. His dive partner did not take much seriously on land, but when it came to diving, Rio took *everything* seriously. Disappointed, Chase began his ascent.

Today would *not* be the day, much like most days in the life of any treasure hunter. Chase vowed to keep the images he'd seen to himself, hoping it might have been a trick of the mind caused by stress or remnants from last night's binge. *A pretty scary trick*, he pondered as he broke the surface.

Because the *Mastery* and her crew planned on staying out at the dive site, King came to pick up Chase and Rio in his Grady-White Canyon 376. Once loaded with gear, the men headed back to Key West.

Chase rubbed his UnReale as he thought about the stone he'd found and what it could mean. The Bezoar stone should not have been near the reef. Yet there it was. And if the stone was discovered away from the arc pattern, what else could they find as they went further away?

A theory began to form centered around the possibility the sterncastle wasn't where the crew of the *Mastery* conducted their search. He vowed to do more research on his theory and on the equipment which would allow him to stay underwater for more extended periods. During future dives off the *Mastery*, he would need more time to explore. And hopefully, without any supernatural company.

A Pirate Pact

THE BRIGHT MORNING sunshine enveloped *Brains and Brawn's* galley as Chase poured himself one last cup of coffee before heading off to the Cay Community College campus. He had decided the sightings during his dive had been a peculiarity. *I've got to stop drinking the night before a dive.*

Drinking also did nothing to stop the nightmares. Another had come to him last night as remnants continued to make their presence known long after he awakened. An image of the dead boy's face would flash in his mind, a blank expression before fading into the opaqueness of his dreamscape. The feeling of struggle and helplessness causing him to wake sweat-stained and exhausted.

Chase pushed those thoughts away by thinking of his soon-to-end teaching job. He dreaded the upcoming slog through the last month of classes before the summer recess and wondered what was next in store.

Setting the coffee cup in the sink along with the other dirty dishes, Chase realized he would be late for class if he did not leave soon. He grabbed his keys, about to open the hatch when someone knocked on it. Puzzled, he opened it to find Anne on the stairs, her hands holding a cigar with a bow around it.

"Did someone have a baby?" he asked, happy to see her. Since she had not returned his phone calls or texts, her showing up had to be a good sign.

"No silly. It's a peace offering … for the other night."

Chase accepted the gift. His girlfriend knew he loved cigars, but she did not like it when he smoked around her. She claimed to hate the smell and as a deterrent, refused to kiss him.

Knowing the present had been difficult for her, he kissed her on the cheek to show his appreciation. "A peace offering?" he asked. "Shouldn't I be the one with a gift for you?"

"Do you have a gift for me?" she asked.

He shook his head, feeling a little embarrassed for mentioning it.

"So, you meant to say, *Thank you*, right?"

Chase bowed. "Thank you, the gift is most appreciated."

He saw her smile falter as she said the words no man wants to hear. "We need to talk."

Chase tried to deflect. The last thing he needed right then was to get into a serious conversation about their relationship. "Now is *not* a good time. I have to get to class and have a full day of stuff to do." He did not explain how the *stuff* dealt with his new theory on how to find the sterncastle.

They walked off the dock towards Chase's truck without a word between them until she broke the silence. "When will be a good time? Can you tell me?" Anne lowered her head, and he thought she might cry, but when she lifted it, he saw no tears … just determination.

"Look, if we're going to be a couple, let's be a couple. I know you're going through some issues right now, but I cannot help you if you don't talk to me." Her tone softened. "Please don't shut me out."

"Anne, it's not a good time to talk. I'm deep in the weeds at work and—"

"If you have time to dive and drink at the Berth but do not have time to speak with your girlfriend, perhaps you don't really *want* a girlfriend."

He took a step back. He liked this woman … a lot. Smart and funny, she possessed a quick wit and expressed strong views. She had a good moral compass reminding him of his mother. The last thing he needed was to have another person in his life leave. "Ok, you're right. How about we discuss this over dinner?"

"Nope!" she shook her head, "I'm riding with you to campus. When we get there, I'll take a rideshare back home."

Chase had to chuckle. How he loved her fire. Surrendering, he opened the passenger door, and she slipped inside. They drove a short distance toward campus before she spoke again. "I don't wanna come across as insensitive, but we need to talk about the other night at the Berth."

"Yea, I got a little tipsy. I needed to let off steam with all that's going on," he responded, a little irritation creeping into his voice at being called out.

"I get that, we all have to let off steam sometimes. It was *how drunk you got* that bothered me. When I asked you to leave with me, you chose to stay and continue to drink. Do you know how that made me feel?"

"I can imagine. Look, I'm sorry. It was a bad night."

Anne thought for a moment, and Chase could see her hesitancy. A look of concern came over her face. "It's not just about you," she began. "Drinking runs in my family. My grandfather was the nicest person in the world…until he drank. He didn't know when to stop."

Chase listened in awkward silence unsure of how to respond. He decided it would be wiser to keep his mouth shut until she finished having her say before offering any condolences.

She continued, "He was a mean-spirited drunk and took it out on my grandmother. By the time he died, he'd left her with nothing except bad memories. So, can you see why I'd be upset?"

Chase answered the question with a couple of his own. "Your paternal grandfather? The one whose house you live in?"

"Oh, god no. He was a peach, and I loved him. No. On my mother's side. To this day she doesn't even think I drink."

"We all know better than that." Chase tried to lighten the mood, but the look Anne gave him caused his immediate regret. "Sorry."

"I do like a drink, but never to excess. And that's why it angered me. I realize it was the first time I'd seen you act like that. It reminded me of some pretty nasty times. I vowed I would never go through life as my grandmother did."

"I get it. But in my defense, I had just lost my job and the drowning— "

Anne interrupted him before he could go any further. "Chase, I don't want to come off as the nagging girlfriend, but I have to be honest with you. I can't do anything about those things. But you can. Maybe talk with a professional? You need to deal with those issues now, and hopefully without drinking yourself into a stupor. I will not stand by and watch the man I may be falling in love with step into the same trap as my grandfather."

There was a slight pause as the words sunk in. Then she added, "I can't tell you not to drink, but can you do so in moderation?"

Chase, taken aback by her candor, thought it sad to think her grandfather had caused her family so much pain. On the other hand, the last part of her argument sounded pretty promising. *May be falling. She even used the L word. Were they getting serious?* He smiled at the thought as he pulled into a parking spot and shut off the engine. Turning to face Anne, he took her hands in his while looking into her eyes. Chase hoped his sincerity came across. "I apologize for my behavior. Moderation it is. I did not know about your family issues. Can I take you to dinner tonight? It's *my* peace offering."

Anne watched him for several seconds before he released her hands so she could open the car door. Turning back to him with a seductive gaze she said, "Sure, but if you don't smoke that cigar today, there could be something more satisfying in your future after dinner."

Chase picked up on her meaning. "Here," he pulled the truck key off the ring and handed it to her. "Pick me up at three."

He patted the cigar in his pocket while walking to his office. He was oblivious to three facts: he was still smiling, had forgotten his briefcase, and now he was late for his first class. *May be falling in love.* Nothing else seemed to matter.

The next day Chase sat at the Berth sipping a beer, conscious of his discussion with Anne concerning her grandfathers' alcohol issues. He had decided to hold off on any shots because he needed to have a clear head to think around Anne.

Scribbling notes on a bar napkin, he asked Rio a question without looking up. "How long do you want to bartend?"

"Um ... hadn't really thought about it."

"Don't you want to live the life of the bold? To seek adventure? To chase something larger than yourself?"

"Chase, I get it you're upset you'll be unemployed soon, but you'll get another job."

"That's just it. I don't want to go back into the classroom. It would prove too easy. Listen, once, when forced to enter my grade school science fair, I told my mother I wanted to do something easy. I remember the way her expression shifted from happy to stern in a matter of seconds before she began to lecture me. 'You were not raised for easy. Ordinary people do *easy* because they have no ambition or imagination. You have both. Now go back to your room and come up with a challenging idea that will make you learn something. And will leave everyone else's *easy* project in the dust.'"

Chase relished the memory. "She was tough. But she was also right. I finished the project and won first prize."

"Just outta curiosity," Rio asked. "What was the project?"

"I made a replica of a sunken ship's debris field using an aquarium, a model ship, and an air hose to show how wave patterns move debris over time."

"Man, *that* was ambitious."

"I'll never forget the way my mother looked at me when I showed it to her. It was like ten Christmas mornings. She hugged me and told me I could do anything as long as I put my mind to it and worked hard." Chase paused, thinking about his mother's words and how he had handled the last few years. Floating along when he should have been swimming. "Maybe now's the time to take that advice again."

Rio shook his head and stroked the ponytail hanging over his right shoulder. "Look at us. We're young, living in the Conch Republic, and have the pick of all the gorgeous females who work on this glorious slice of paradise called Key West. Besides, if I quit here, I have to move out." Rio shared a house on Olivia Street, near the cemetery, with other bartenders from the Berth. It was owned by Sam King, as inexpensive rent control offered the bar owner a way of retaining bartenders.

"We wouldn't want that. Where would you take all your Mrs. Ex-Rio's?" Chase teased.

"I like the fairer sex in quantity. What's wrong with that?" Rio's brow raised in mock indignation.

"It's not fair to the rest of us. You get your unfair share of the fairer sex is all I'm saying."

"It's a curse." Rio shook his head, his broad smile saying otherwise.

Rio was a good-looking guy with a great sense of humor which made women find him easy to be with and so much fun. Since he was not interested in settling down anytime soon, the same women also found him difficult to *stay* with. As far as Chase could tell, it did not seem to bother Rio. To him, women were like words in a book. Turn the page, and there would always be more from which to choose. For Rio, Key West would always be full of new books with plenty of pages to turn forward, but never to re-read.

"So," asked Rio. "As we conclude today's philosophical discussion on not taking the easy way out, let me ask you ... what more do you want?"

"Everything," Chase replied. "I want everything."

"Let's start with the basics. Whaddya got cooking in that brain of yours?"

"This is a tourist town, right? So why don't we offer something no one else is willing to do?"

"As in?" Rio asked as he placed another beer on the bar.

"What do you think of taking tourists out on a pirate ship where we show them how buccaneers lived during The Golden Age of Piracy? We could tell stories of pirates more realistic than they're portrayed in films."

Plenty of companies took tourists fishing or snorkeling or watching dolphins. There were sloops offering sailing tours and catamarans offering sunset booze cruises. There was also a number of tourists who dressed as pirates while they made the rounds on Duval Street. What Chase had in mind required more imagination and ambition than all of them put together.

"OK, how do we do that? You're the history professor. Give me a history lesson."

"Sure, do you know how many sets of teeth George Washington had?" Before Rio could respond, Chase provided the answer, "Four. Who invented the dumbwaiter? Hint, another American president."

By the look on Rio's face, Chase knew he'd have to give that answer as well.

"Thomas Jefferson."

Chase may not have liked the confines of teaching in a classroom, but he loved educating, sharing obscure facts which caught his students off guard. It delighted him to see the surprised looks on their faces as they learned something new and interesting.

"You know a lot about presidents," Rio jumped in. "Whaddya know about pirates?"

"More than you think. But we'll need something more powerful to pull off this idea."

"What's that, Teach?" Rio asked.

"Research. I'm extremely good at research. Learned the skill from my father. What about becoming unreal pirates?" he asked Rio while pulling on his coin. "Let's do something bigger than all of us!" Even from the grave, his mother's words still resonated with him. There would be nothing easy about this project, and he realized he had not been this excited in a long time. Building a business where he could still teach, have fun and best of all, control his destiny.

Chase pulled several napkins from the square bin on the bar. He jotted down ideas about buying a boat, getting a tourism license, and how to entertain tourists out on cruises. What they might need to stand out from other water tours was a twist. A facet so different and interesting as to lure customers, show them a grand time, and make them want to spread the word to others.

"Yea, but what would be so different?" Rio asked.

"We entertain *and* educate."

In truth, Chase had been toying with the idea for a while and being able to share it with Rio felt like a release. "I'll use the skills I've learned as a professor to research pirate lore then I can develop entertaining stories based on fact. The pirate crew would not only entertain the tourists but teach them as well. To give them the ultimate pirate experience. No tour company is doing anything like that. It would be like a floating museum and movie all in one!"

By the curious expression etched across Rio's face, Chase knew he was more than just interested. "So, *we* play the characters?" Rio asked, confirming Chase's suspicion. "Do I get to be a pirate, too? Look, I already have the ponytail."

"You'd be one of the stars in the show!" Chase knew this appealed to Rio's ego.

"And save damsels in distress?"

"Does a one-legged duck swim in circles?" Chase replied with laughter.

"I'll take that as a yes. I'm in!" Rio paused before adding, "Ya know who would make a perfect Blackbeard? He's already got the beard, and that voice is enough to put the fear of god into any tourist. Talk about realism."

"You're talking about King?" Chase liked Rio's idea.

"Yup. He'd be perfect. Would there be booze?"

"Of course."

The two friends tossed around ideas, the details bringing the idea into focus.

They'd hire hospitality workers to play secondary pirates during their off shifts. Chase would come up with stories about enough pirate adventures to keep each tour a little different and ensure repeat customers. Now came the hard part. Where would they come up with the money to get the startup off the ground? Chase was waiting for Rio to make a joke about robbing a bank or enlisting a wealthy matron when he heard King's voice.

"How about a third partner?" he growled as he leaned over the bar.

Chase had not noticed King entering through the back door and listening to their conversation. But to his surprise, instead of being angry as to why his best bartender might quit, King looked eager to jump in on the new business venture. Chase knew King to be a shrewd businessman with a successful bar and a rental property that kept his bartender attrition rate low. It now seemed as if he had the desire to improve upon this success.

"Got one thing you two don't," King stated flatly.

"What would that be?" Chase asked the burly bar owner.

"A bar for collateral."

Chase and Rio exchanged a look of confusion. "Why would you put up your business on a risky venture like this?" Chase asked.

Rio also chimed in, "Yea, if they both failed, I'd have nothing to fall back on."

King scratched his beard before speaking. "Bored."

Chase took a swig of his beer. "Boredom. That's the reason you want to put up the Berth and risk everything?" Again, he knew King to be a good businessman but had not considered the bar business, although lucrative, could also be wanting for lack of excitement. *Schlepping drinks* was how Rio described it.

"Plus," interjected King. "I want to be a pirate, too."

"Watch this," Rio whispered, directing a question to his boss. "Which one did you have in mind?"

King took a deep breath and puffed out his chest. He exhaled his response as if auditioning for the part, "Arrgh. Blackbeard, o' course!"

Chase spit his beer onto the bar and laughed, wiping his chin.

"What did I tell you?" Rio grinned as he wiped off the bar.

"Well, if you're really sure?" Chase questioned, giving King the opportunity to back out. He did not. King bobbed his head. "It's adventure time. I'm in."

"What's the next step?" Rio asked.

"We need a pirate ship," announced Chase. "Other tour boats are tri-hulls, sailboats, or water taxis. If you want to put on a great show, you need to have the right stage."

"Authenticity!" stated King.

Rio chimed in. "A stage we can find. But one on an eighteenth-century wooden ship in the twenty-first century? Now that might be a problem."

King brought out his laptop so they could scour the internet. They started looking at *Sloops*, but reasoned they were too small to accommodate enough paying customers. *Brigantines* were larger, but none looked authentic for their tastes. And then there were *Frigates*. They were fast, maneuverable, had massive firepower, and used by pirates such as Blackbeard, Gentleman Jocard, and even the British Royal Navy. They could not get more authentic than sailing in a frigate.

"How 'bout that one!" said Rio, pointing over King's shoulder. "It's a replica of Henry Morgan's flagship, *Satisfaction*. And it's for sale...." Rio's voice trailed as his enthusiasm waned. He scrolled down the web page, his shoulders sagging in disappointment. Unfortunately, the price tag looked a little steep for what the men had planned.

"Keep looking!" King commanded, while he put out three shot glasses and a bottle of rum on the bar.

As the three scrolled in search of the right vessel, Anne struggled with the door to enter the bar.

"If this is a meeting of the minds, you're all in trouble!" she joked, sauntering up to a bar stool next to Chase and kissing him. "King, can I have a beer? I can't drink the hard stuff until after my next shift." A minute later, Sam King placed a beer with a slice of lime in front of her. Anne looked at the rum bottle and the three shot glasses sitting on the bar. "Drinking hard this early in the afternoon?" She directed the question to Chase. He shook his head and moved the shot glass in front of her. "We have a business plan for our own water tour business," he blurted out. "But we've hit a snag. There is a replica of Captain Henry Morgan's pirate ship, the *Satisfaction,* we keep coming back to because it would be perfect for what we need. It's also pretty damn expensive."

Anne took in the idea but showed no visible reaction. After a moment, she put her palm to her forehead and ran her fingers through her hair. "A pirate ship?" she asked. "Does this coincide with your earlier wish to become a pirate?" Her right eyebrow raised in suspicion.

Chase's hand automatically reached for his UnReale. "Yea, I guess it does."

"Is this more important to you than teaching college?"

He did not hesitate. "Much more important."

"And these guys are in on the deal as well?"

Both Rio and King shook their heads.

Anne tapped her chin. Chase took this as a sign she was contemplating the pros and cons of giving up a stable career for a risky venture where he could lose everything, He hoped that she would see this as him controlling his own destiny. Would she support him?

"Let me get this straight." Her eyes went from Chase to Rio and on to King. "You don't think you'll get all the money from the bank, and you don't have enough collateral from the bar to buy this ship. Do I have that right?"

"Yeah, It's where we're stuck right now. Do you have any ideas?" Chase looked hopeful.

She did. Anne grabbed the rum bottle and spun it around. "I believe I can help you there. If you three are intent on captaining a pirate ship, shouldn't we bring some rum along for the ride?"

The three men shared quizzical expressions before turning back to Anne.

Anne explained how a cousin of hers worked in the marketing department of a rum company and she had an idea of how to get them to sponsor their tours. If successful, the sponsorship agreement would show the tour company to be a legitimate business and the initial funds could go towards purchasing the frigate, reducing the amount needed from the bank.

The dam of fresh thinking broke open and ideas flowed from the four to find other sponsorship revenue. They bounced around from one subject to another and hammered out what they agreed upon as part of the tours. They even came up with a retail store for customers to buy high-end items at the end of each tour.

Chase delegated assignments to all, including Anne who was added as a full partner, prompting her to invest her small nest egg into their enterprise. *Everyone needed to have skin in the game, no matter how small.*

"I won't quit my day jobs just yet. But I cannot wait for that day to come!" she squealed with delight before kissing Chase on the lips. To celebrate their new partnership, King filled up the three shot glasses.

Chase turned to Anne to assure her, "Just this one!" She pushed the glass in front of Chase and nodded while King put another beer on the bar in front of her. After all, she did have another shift to work.

SATISFACTION

THE FOUR PROSPECTIVE business owners met at the Berth, unusually early for all of them save Chase who had pushed his morning classes off on his teaching assistant as he prepared for the meeting at the bank. The past few weeks had been hard on all of them. In between their regular schedules, they had worked on the plans to launch the new enterprise. Vendors had to be contacted, contracts negotiated, and potential crew members interviewed. Now they were down to the last piece of the puzzle … securing a ship.

Anne placed the professionally prepared business plan onto the bar with a slap startling a dozing Rio. "We can't ask for seven hundred thousand dollars with a napkin, can we?" she told the men as she admired her handy work.

"We could use the napkin to wipe your tears when they decline us." quipped a groggy Rio.

"Don't even joke about that," scolded Anne, proofreading the document one more time.

Chase was impressed with how quickly and efficiently Anne had secured a short-term deal with the rum company, contingent on them receiving approval for financing the ship. The name of the enterprise would be Captain Morgan's Piracy Tour Company as a tribute to the pirate, Henry Morgan.

With the business plan, the sponsorship check, and King's title for the Berth in hand, the four headed to the Bank of Key West. They were all excited about the prospect of working for themselves and being in charge of their own futures. Their joy pleased Chase to no end.

Harvey Dent, the loan officer, ushered the crew into a conference room and after the pleasantries, the room became quiet as Dent read the business plan. Chase could feel the tension. Excitement mixed with a tinge of fear.

When he finally looked up, the banker said, "I don't believe it's enough. The plan is sound, but I'm afraid you'll need more collateral for a venture this big. The risk is too high for this bank."

Chase looked at Dent and then at his partners. The air felt sucked out of the room as they all slumped in their chairs feeling the disappointment. He addressed the banker. "We have operating capital, earnest money, collateral, and a sponsorship agreement in place. What else do you need?"

"Look, it's a fine idea and a good plan, but the numbers don't lie. Your ticket sales projection is too high considering the competition. What happens if the sponsorship deal goes south? What if something happens and the ship needs major repairs? If you went into default, the bank would become owner of a bar and a tour ship. We're not in the bar or touring business. We're in the *lending and getting the loan paid back with interest* business. I'm sorry. I can't loan you the money for *this* business plan."

Chase picked up on the emphasis Dent put on the word *this*. Glancing over at Anne, her wink gave him hope.

"How much would you be willing to lend?"

"The loan committee may believe seven-hundred thousand is too high a risk. We could be more comfortable around the five-hundred-thousand range. Or the bank would need more collateral in the range of two hundred thousand."

"That's all we have!" Rio snapped back.

Chase turned a squinted eye toward him to express displeasure at the outburst. King and Anne followed suit.

"I guess we have more planning to do, don't we?" Chase asked.

"I guess you do. See what you can do on your end. I'll see what I can do on mine."

With that answer, the meeting ended. The four walked out of the bank, heading for the Berth to regroup.

"Why did you give me a dirty look in the conference room?" Rio challenged Chase.

"In a negotiation, you never tell the other side what you *don't* have. It's not the end. It's only the first of many negotiating ploys. We've worked too hard and come too far to quit now."

"I'm with Chase. We have to put our heads together and come up with the extra collateral before we go back to the bank," said Anne.

"From where?" King shook his head.

No one had an answer … not yet, so they all walked back to the Berth in silence. Chase was determined to move forward. He needed it all to come true, more than he was willing to admit to the others.

Chase's parents taught him the value of perseverance. "Giving up is the easy part, that's why so many ordinary people do it. Success comes to those who keep searching for the answers, keep pressing on, despite the odds." Both father and mother had drilled this lesson into him and it stuck. Chase saw this as a minor setback in a business he felt sure had many more to come. If they didn't overcome this bump in the road, what would happen when a considerable obstacle lay in their path? By the time the four reached the Berth, Chase Porter knew he'd come up with new ideas to solve the problem.

Sitting around the bar, King passed around beers. Anne pored over the business plan for something she may have missed. Chase glanced at Rio. The bartender sat with a sour expression on his face.

If he cracks a joke now, I might crack him back. He felt relieved when Rio remained silent, but it didn't mean *he* had to. Chase knew it was time to lead. Giving his UnReale a squeeze, he spoke to the group. "Guys, we're not done yet. Do you know anyone with something of value we can add to our collateral list? Something in the two hundred K range?"

"My folks have one of my siblings already in college and two more to follow, so we can't go there." Anne shook her head. "And don't even think about my house, it's been in the family for years, and my dad intends to keep it that way."

Rio added, "My dad will be working until he's seventy. He has nothing of value. How about Daniel?"

Chases' father had a job as a full-time high school history teacher, and a part-time one as a treasure hunter. Neither made him rich. "Nah, my Dad's too close to retirement. He sold the house after my mom died and now lives in an apartment. He offered me some cash when I told him about our plans. It wasn't a lot, but I refused. I told him once we got the business in the water, he could take part in other ways. The guy is a whiz at historical accuracy and can put together a research paper...."

Chase stopped for a second, still rubbing the UnReale, and repeated, "Paper."

"He's got something," Rio said, sliding to the edge of his barstool. "I've seen that look before. My boy has got something!"

"Chase?" Anne asked. "Are you okay?"

Chase reached into his pocket for his phone. "Paper. Guys, we're looking at this problem the wrong way. We may already have the money. What if the owner would be willing to hold the paper for us? I don't know why I didn't think of it before!"

Chase dialed Mr. Knight, the gentleman who owned the frigate they wanted to buy. He lived in Marathon and had put the boat up for sale, though he'd initially told Chase he didn't want to sell. But his wife had taken ill, and he needed to care for her more than he cared for the frigate. Chase did not want to capitalize on someone's misfortune, but his idea might actually help Mr. Knight and his wife.

"Mr. Knight, how is Mrs. Knight?" Chase wanted to be as caring as possible while cautious his intentions would not be perceived as opportunistic.

After a few minutes of small talk, Chase cut to the matter at hand. "Right now, we can only come up with five hundred thousand dollars. Yes … that's right, Mr. Knight. I know your price is seven hundred." Chase listened for a moment before interrupting the man. "Wait, wait. No, I'm not asking you to drop the price. I have another proposal which might help get this deal done. What if we gave you the five hundred thousand now, then you held the paper on the other two hundred? It would be like an annuity. You'd receive a check each month."

Chase gestured to Anne and she quickly used her phone's calculator to figure out what the interest would be on the amount. Chase kept nodding as he listened to Mr. Knight's response before answering. "The prevailing lending rate would be around four and a half percent, Mr. Knight. Is that rate within your comfort level?"

Anne raised six fingers showing what she thought the business could handle.

"How about five and a half? We'll give you an extra point above prime."

Chase could sense the collective breath everyone held in the room. Getting the ship's owner to finance the outstanding amount had been a brilliant idea. He hoped it showed his new partners, with Chase Porter around, there would be no problem they could not solve.

Finally, he smiled and heaved a thumbs up, letting the others know it was okay to exhale. It now appeared as though they would get their ship. Still, the next roadblock loomed.

Would the company be successful enough to repay the debt?

The answer to the question began with a visit to Marathon to take possession of the craft and sail her home to Key West. It had taken a few weeks, several more bank meetings, and a typical mountain of paper to get the loan approved. Now the new owners stood captivated in front of the ship, marveling at its beauty and elegance. Mr. Knight was there to greet the hand-selected crew which included twin brothers Tom and John Garrity, a retired coast guard licensed ship captain Carl (Crunchy) Western, and Chase's father, Daniel.

When they began interviewing in Key West, Chase had been amazed at how many hospitality workers made themselves available between shifts to sign up as a crew member. But then again, who *wouldn't* want to fill their few spare hours playing the life of a buccaneer? Chase and company would be quick to oblige.

Mr. Knight attempted to explain a few items. "She's about two thirds normal size..."

Standing in front of her in awe, Chase paid no attention to anything but the ship before him. "She's magnificent."

"... Oh, you'll love the captains' quarters, although the bunk space is a little tight..."

Its long bowsprit pointed proudly upward, two crows-nest baskets towered above the vessel, the rigging spun like a spiderweb from the deck to the top of the masts.

"Look at those sails!" added Anne.

"Of course, that Liaz 6-cylinder diesel engine will keep you moving with no wind…"

The main deck was wide enough to hold one hundred and fifty tourists or more at a time. Bench seating on either side just below the rails masked modern items such as life jackets and fire extinguishers necessary for following Coast Guard regulations.

"Shit fire," whispered King.

"Well, she's got a flame retardant coating, so there's that…"

The ship wore a rich, dark-brown hue. A thin white line of paint encircled the railing just below the spindles and another along the base above the water line. A much wider band of white stretched under the Captain's quarter windows of the stern running along the cannon hatches to meet at the bow.

"Looks like it sailed out of an Errol Flynn movie," commented Rio.

"All in all, I hate to part with her, but…"

Daniel put his arm around Chase. "Son, you've done it. I'm proud of you."

Mr. Knight had nothing more to add as he joined in the admiration of the ship that now belonged to another.

Chase had arranged for the crew to have a few days of hands-on experience before heading home under the direction of Crunchy, making sure everyone knew their jobs in order to sail home safely. Daniel was in his glory. Chase knew his father had often imagined what sailing aboard an eighteenth-century pirate ship might have been like, and knew the reality made his imagination pale by comparison.

After two days of practice runs, they were ready to sail home. On a bright, cloudless morning, Crunchy guided the frigate out of the harbor. With the wind at their back and adventure before them, the crew set sail for Key West.

"She handles like a dream," Crunchy said to Chase.

Chase pondered his statement. His life had changed dramatically. A few months ago, he taught college history and merely floated through life. Now as the owner of a frigate about to embark on an adventure re-creating the past, he was swimming. No life jacket to save him from the risky venture, so he would have to learn to swim strongly.

"Like a dream come *true*," Chase responded. "A dream come true." He looked out across the ocean from the quarterdeck of his new pirate ship and felt the cool ocean breeze in his face. It made him feel free for the first time in his life.

The trip back to port proved glorious, yet uneventful, and when they arrived in Key West, the crew moored the *Satisfaction* at Conch Harbor Marina in an oversized slot by the harbor's mouth. Someone needed to stay aboard their new ship at night for security reasons. Since King lived above the Berth, Anne had her own home, and Rio was not about to give up his rent-controlled digs, they all decided Chase should move from the *Brains and Brawn* into the *Satisfaction's* captain quarters.

The ship had been retrofitted by the original builders to accommodate a present-day captain. There were additional sleeping quarters for a crew of six as well as a galley, head, and common area.

At first, they began with simple three-hour tours around the keys with dolphin tours and the requisite sunset cruise in the bay off Mallory Square. Next, they added a day-long trip to the Dry Tortugas, thirty-five nautical miles off the Key West coast. Because of the limited sleeping quarters on board, they made no plans for taking tourists out for extended stays on the water.

Chase had been pleasantly surprised when Rio came up with several good ideas. One of the first came from a simple question, and although it had not actually been an original idea, the concept emerged due to his childlike inquisitiveness.

Rio wanted to know, "What should we call the tourists on board? Pirates didn't use the term, *tourist*, did they?"

The professor in Chase kicked in as he pulled out a factoid. "That's easy," he began, "Lubbers. Pirates would call non-sailors, *land lovers*. The term soon morphed into *landlubbers* and finally into just *lubbers*."

Always quick with a marketing angle, Anne added, "They'll remain *Lubbers* until they get through with one of our tours. Then we can elevate them to a higher standard. Make them feel as if they earned something along the way!"

"Like what?" Rio asked. "A rank? Like Boatswain? It's kinda clunky."

"No," Chase countered. "How about ABP? As in *Able ... Bodied ... Pirate*. We give them a rank and a certificate with a free ABP flag to take home."

Anne raised a hand, showing she had another idea. "On the back of the certificate we'll have a coupon for ten percent off at our retail store where they'll pick up the flag ... an instant traffic builder. I'll make a note to contact our existing sponsors; surely, at least one would love to supply one more piece of swag with their logo on it."

"And," Chase concluded, "before each cruise, the lubbers can walk up the gangplank greeted by a camera operator who takes their picture which they can then buy at the gift shop afterward. Another way to get them into the store."

"Are you always one step ahead of everyone else, Chase?" Rio wanted to know.

"When you're chasing a dream, it's always good to be looking ahead."

"Bigger feet, longer strides," deadpanned King.

To keep the tours fresh, Chase made sure the principles had various parts to play. On one tour, Chase would be the captain while two of the others had supporting roles, granting the fourth partner the day off. They would then rotate the parts the next day and repeat the process throughout the week.

Chase did most of the research. His expectation was for the others to come up with fresh ideas and stories about the pirate life on their own. Role rehearsals came between tours and then performed during a Monday through Saturday rotation. On Sundays, everyone took the day off.

"Since when have you become religious?" Rio asked. "Because the only house of worship I've ever seen you in is this bar."

"I'm not religious, but we don't need to burn out. Besides, tourists are late risers, and business is less brisk on the Sabbath. If we close one day per week, why not make it the least profitable one?"

"And also, so you can dive, right?" Anne smirked.

Chase smiled. She knew him well and his unwillingness to surrender his love of diving, especially if it meant hunting for treasure. "Guilty as charged," he confessed.

During the week, King had an employee open the Berth at noon to accommodate the regulars. As the tours proceeded, word of mouth spread, and thanks to Anne's expertise, the website traffic grew. Within a year, Captain Morgan's Piracy Tours, CMPT, had become the number one requested tour ship in all of Key West. Everyone from the crew to the investors were pleased with the success and the return on investment which followed. Especially Mr. Knight and banker Harvey Dent.

"I'm tracking the movements of a storm off the African coast headed our way," Chase said, studying the report on the Berth's

TV. The team had put a lot of effort into their company and didn't need a major storm to come through to damage the *Satisfaction and* their livelihood.

"Rio, aren't you from Galveston?"

"Sure, why?"

Do you have any contacts there?"

Rio eyed Chase. "What ya got up your sleeve?"

"Well, what if we take a small crew and sail to Galveston out of harm's way. Think of the money to be made running a few rum cruises."

"You know, that might not be a bad idea," said Anne. "I'll look into getting a tour license from the state of Texas. We get a vacation with no revenue loss. Chase, you're a genius!"

The team completed the plan to take their ship out of the path of the incoming storm, deciding for the away port of call to be Rio's hometown. King would play Blackbeard during one of the rum cruises as a special guest. Chase would have to research pirates from the area to make the stories coincide with the region.

Anne added, "I have an idea for another stowaway to surprise the guests."

Chase marveled at how they all worked well together. An idea or question from one would turn into a discussion usually resulting in a plan.

They were all still working on ideas when King turned to the TV as a new development unfolded. "Have to wait for the next storm."

Chase focused intently on the story. "It looks like the concern amounted to nothing. This so-called storm petered out over Bermuda, and the most we'll get is rain with thunder and lightning. Nothing to worry about this time."

"You sound disappointed," said Rio.

"Now that we have a fun contingency plan, I am."

They all clinked their glasses to their new plan, as Anne announced, "At least you don't have to think about the storm issue anymore."

"No. He'll find something else to give him a reason to fondle that UnReale," Rio joked.

It was getting late, so Chase decided it was time to leave. With a busy week of tours coming up, he still had work on the new Blackbeard story, research a pirate named Woodes Rogers, as well as pirates from the Gulf of Mexico before he could bed down for the night.

Yea, never worried. Just need to stay one step ahead… only one step. Chase headed for the door, his hand reaching for his UnReale.

LUBBERS WELCOME

"**W**ELCOME ABOARD THE *Satisfaction,* you lubbers!" bellowed Captain Chase Porter to the delight of the Monday afternoon tour guests. "This craft is a frigate, one of the fastest ships of its time. It can out-gun any craft on the high seas." Chase liked to give a brief lesson on the large wooden vessel to set the mood before the two-and-a-half-hour journey.

"The *Satisfaction* is one hundred-forty feet in length from the tip of the bowsprit to the far rail of the stern. She can run with a crew of ten, has thirty cannon below, and eight smaller swivel cannon topside: four on the foredeck, four on the poop deck." He always got a giggle from the children when he mentioned the name of the small area above the quarterdeck. These were the beginning of many laughs during the few hours of each tour. After all, the *Satisfaction*'s crew worked in the entertainment business.

"I'm Captain Porter and I dare any sovereign nation like the Spaniards or the British Royal Navy to venture upon us this day, for that would be a grave mistake on their part." Chase knew he made a striking figure dressed in black, knee-high boots and a sword strapped to his hip.

"British Royal Navy?" shouted Rio as he came up from the belly of the *Satisfaction*, a bandana wound around his head and his hand on the hilt of his own mock sword, ready for action.

"Yes. The British Royal Navy," repeated Captain Porter. Both he and Rio looked to one side and spat on deck in sync. It was a faux spit, no moisture with a lot of noise, mostly air.

Chase gave Rio credit for the little slice of theatre after he had employed the faux spitting impromptu during a show to demonstrate his disgust. Chase followed suit, and the crowd loved the bit. The act had become a part of every tour. And now, everyone on the crew spat at the mention of the British Royal Navy.

"This here's my first mate, Rio. He hates the British Royal Navy." They both spat again. "Arrrgh," Rio growled, much to the crowd's delight.

"He doesn't bite," Captain Porter cautioned before adding, "Much."

More laughter filled the air.

The lubbers loved the experience and told their friends, who told *their* friends which in turn grew the company's reputation. Those tourists also raved about the company on popular vacation-review websites including the CMPT company site, and it all multiplied the attention they received. Soon tours were being booked months in advance, the business stayed so brisk it kept the crew extremely busy.

"Before we make sail, let's be sure you're all sufficiently lubricated. Do we all have our rum? The reason I ask is twofold. One, when out to sea, our pirate forbearers used fruit to eliminate the dreaded disease, SCURVY. But now, a new disease is afoot and must be vanquished. It is called A.P.E."

A few lubbers looked confused or worried, others snickered at the acronym, knowing anything could happen at any time on this ship.

"A.P.E. stands for Acute Parched Esophagus." The crowd laughed, and Chase continued.

"This disease can spread quickly if we're not careful. Fortunately, the cure is on board in the form of rum punch and beer!" Pointing to the lubbers, he added, "I see a few severe cases in the crowd today so drink up me hearties before your esophagus becomes parched beyond repair!"

Mugs were raised, and cheers went up. Chase waited for the noise to subside before beginning a toast. He'd discovered how a toast brought the tourists and crew together, making the lubbers feel as if they were a part of the crew.

"To all ye mates, we're headed into uncharted waters. There will be danger and excitement. Stay alert for the unexpected. But mark my words, this will be a day ye shall remember, so lift your glasses to the meanest, orneriest bilge rats to sail the high seas. Beware world, we've come to pillage and plunder! Let's hear a huzzah!"

The crowd responded in kind. Chase was pleased, finally shaping his own future, and having fun all the while. *This is what I was meant for.*

As the *Satisfaction* left the mouth of the marina and entered the bay, the Captain turned to the crowd and lifted his mug to say, "A drink, mates. To adventure!" The crowd reacted with howls, mug-clanking, and pats on the back. Captain Porter put his hand on Rio's shoulder.

"Looks like we've got a lively bunch today, eh?"

Rio nodded as Crunchy yelled to his crew, "What are you waiting for, ya freebooters? Lift those sails and let's be underway!"

Once out to sea the real theatrics began. The crew members showed the lubbers how to do specific tasks such as tie knots, steer the vessel with Crunchy, or climb the rigging onto the crow's nest with the Garrity brothers. Some crew members were adept at playing musical instruments and often coaxed the guests to join them in pirate songs. Still, the best part of the tour proved to be the pirate lore as told by the Captain of the day.

Today's topic started with Chase coming onto the main deck with two cutlasses in hand, prompting First Mate Rio to shout for the lubbers to gather round for a demonstration in the fine art of swordplay.

"This is a cutlass or short sword," began Chase. "The weapon of choice for pirates as well as the British Royal Navy." On cue, everyone on staff performed the faux spit to the side.

"As you can see, the cutlass is short, thick, and slightly curved. Perfect for running through your enemy like the Bri—" Captain Porter stopped short of mentioning the enemy and it caused laughter to abound.

"Anyway, today we shall give a demonstration on its use. Rio, step up here and let's have a go, eh?"

"No, sir," Rio cowered in trepidation. "The last time, you nearly cut me bloody arm off!"

"Well," said the captain, looking out at the audience. "Are there any volunteers?"

Chase walked around the crowd as a sea of hands raised in the air, but he stopped to look at one lubber who had both arms firmly by his side. "You, then. Have a go? No? Don't worry about Rio. We sewed him up good as new."

Rio lifted his right shoulder and let his arm dangle. Looking sad he said, "And that's me good arm."

The crowd erupted in another round of raucous laughter.

As the Captain walked into the middle of the ship, a young man in a baseball cap raised a hand. "Now, here's a young chap unafraid to spar with, unarguably, the best swordsman on the land, sea, or anywhere else for that matter." Then pointing a cutlass at Rio, Chase said, "Don't you say a word, or we'll be sewing up more than an arm!" He continued over the crowd's laughter. "Come, youngster." The Captain handed one cutlass to the young man, took his stance, and announced, "Let us start off slowly."

The young man turned his cap backward before taking a half-hearted swing at the captain's sword. Chase deflected it. "Not so hard. Use more control. Slowly at first, use patience then look for your mark. Try not to kill yourself in the process if possible?" More laughter erupted.

"Like this?" asked the young man. He proceeded to thrust and parry with more precision as the two went back and forth. They picked up the pace and soon, the captain realized it had become challenging to handle the young man's advances.

"What's this? Am I being played? It looks as if you've had a lesson or two already."

"Why, I've had a few," claimed the young man.

Both were now engaged in a free-for-all, sparring along the deck and around the masts as the crowd made way. While Chase was a skilled swordsman, the young man was able to hold his own. Back and forth they went as the crowd alternately gasped and cheered.

"Where did you learn your swordsmanship?" Chase called out.

"From a little old lady in Venice," answered the young man. Laughter arose right on cue.

"Surely you jest?" Chase responded.

"You don't think the Venetians are fine swordsmen?"

Chase tried again. "How long did you study in Venice?"

"A week," came the reply. The crowd laughed even harder.

"You don't mean to tell me … you learned to be this good in one week?" Chase stopped, hands on hips showing fatigue.

"Oh no," said the young man, clearly toying with the captain. "We spent the rest of the time in Rome!"

The crowd went into hysterics.

Finally, Chase stopped the fight, bowed to his adversary, and said, "Young man, what a shocking surprise for me today. You are indeed a fine swordsman."

"I do have one more surprise for you, sir, for I am NOT a swordsman at all." Removing the baseball cap, a full head of lustrous auburn hair fell to Anne's shoulders. "But I am a fine swords*woman*." She added a curtsey for effect.

The crowd gasped in surprise. When they quieted, Chase took center stage with his newfound swordswoman and announced incredulously, "A female pirate? Unheard of!" He paused momentarily. "Or was it? Ladies and gentlemen, I apologize for the deception. This is one of our crew, Anne Braun. She is here to tell you the tale of not one, but two notorious female pirates." Chase gestured with a sweeping right arm. "Anne, the deck belongs to you."

"Women aboard a pirate ship were supposed to be bad luck," Anne said, eyeing the crowd. "As you can see by the swordplay, the captain needed all the luck he could muster!" She paused to allow for crowd laughter before continuing.

"That did not stop *Calico Jack Rackham* from enlisting not one, but two females to join his ranks. *Anne Bonny* became the first to sail under his flag and acted as his lover as well. A beautiful, yet fiercely independent woman, Anne was way ahead of her time for a female living in the 18th century. During an era where men made the decisions, Anne took it upon herself to make her own and live her life as *she* wanted. Attracted to the swashbuckling *Captain Calico Jack*, the two raided many a merchant ship. Anne showed to be a keen fighter and so well respected by the crew, they even added a second female by the name of *Mary Read.*

Alas, a pirate's life span is short. In 1720, the British Royal Navy ..." Anne paused for everyone to faux spit on the deck. "Attacked Rackham's ship, *Revenge,* as it lay anchored in harbor. Rackham's crew, celebrating another haul from a Spanish merchant ship, partied a bit too much, rendering all hands inebriated, save Mary Read and Anne Bonny, the only two to fight back." Anne leaned forward and spoke directly to the females onboard. "Ladies, does this sound about right?" Again, Anne paused for laughter before continuing her story.

"The captured pirate crew were taken to Port Royal, Jamaica, where they were tried for piracy and ordered hanged. Perhaps having women aboard Calico Jack's ship proved to be bad luck after all… for him." Anne brought her right hand up to her throat and made the hanging gesture, complete with tongue sticking out.

"Once in Port Royal, the jailers discovered the true identities of those two women, thus sparing their lives. Mary Read died in prison shortly afterwards. But what of Anne Bonny?

Because she was with child by Jack Rackham, she gained her release when her father arrived and paid the ransom. No one really knows what happened to Anne Bonny after that. For all we know, the hot-blooded, independent Irishwoman's ghost might be sailing the high seas to this day looking to avenge her lover's death."

Anne put her hands on the railing and looked out over the horizon as if in search of a ghost ship. Lubbers followed her gaze in solemn respect.

Rio seized the moment and jumped to attention. "Let's hear it for our own good luck charm of the high seas, *Miss Anne Braun!*" The crowd gave her a hearty round of applause.

"Now, let us hear from the ship's cook as he tells the tale of the delicacies pirates consumed while out to sea."

Daniel Porter brought out a table from the cook's mess. Other pirates brought several dishes and assorted spoons and placed them on the table.

Chase gazed at his father with pride. As far back as Chase could remember, history had always held Daniel's interest. Chase certainly knew where his own love of the subject sprang from. Even now, Daniel spent his free time diving into textbooks or websites to learn something new or fresh about a time long since passed.

When Chase had given his father a spot on the crew, he had been delighted and told Chase he would spend hours doing *pirate research* because he loved the period in history. While the Civil War or Second World War held other history buffs attention, Daniel Porter fancied the wealth of the new world discoveries, prompting the rise of *the Golden Age of Piracy*. Different periods had their moments, yet one thing that particular time period offered more than any other: *Treasure lost then lay waiting to be discovered today.*

Now, as his father took the stage, Chase knew the only treasure Daniel sought at the time was the reaction he would get from the lubbers after sharing his culinary tale.

"Gather round, and I shall fill your minds with stories of how the pirates filled their plates at sea," Daniel opened his tale. "Right out of port, there were fresh produce such as plantains, yams, oranges, and pineapples. There were meats, olives, and other such foods. The longer the crew spent at sea, the more they had to rely on what they brought onboard to provide sustenance. Pirates were also fishermen able to catch all types of fish, turtles or dolphin. They made up a salad called *Salmagundi,* similar to a chef's salad, with cut-up fish, pickles, olives and if they had them, hard-boiled eggs. It also goes by another name, *Solomon Grundy.* Would anyone like to try it? We caught the fish fresh this morning."

Daniel proceeded to scoop the Solomon Grundy into small paper bowls and hand them to the lubbers who quickly devoured the samples as he began the downside of his talk. "After being at sea a while with no refrigeration, fruits, and vegetables spoil...

or worse. The food gets infested with bugs." He paused here to see the reaction from those still chewing the Solomon Grundy.

"Not this salad though, made fresh this morning," he said reassuringly to the worried looks from the lubbers.

"When they ran out of meats, fruits, and vegetables, they still had one food which did not spoil during long voyages. A square biscuit by the name of *Hard Tack* sustained the crew until they reached land to resupply. No, Hard Tack did not spoil, but it did get infested with small beetles called *weevils*." Again, Daniel paused to see worried expressions.

Chase enjoyed the lubbers' reaction and beamed at his father as he wove his tale. "This development was as disgusting to the pirates as it is to you now. What was a hungry pirate to do? I'll tell you. They would eat their Tack in the dark so as not to look at the offending weevils."

The crowd groaned and grimaced at the thought.

"Another option would have the cook soften the Hard Tack by cooking it in a brown sugar and rum mixture the consistency of porridge. The pirates would then PLUCK the dead weevils from their meal. Or eat them if they needed more protein. I have a bowl here if anyone would like to try?"

Daniel held out the wooden bowl filled with porridge. Scattered on top were what appeared to be dead weevils. As the lubbers shrank back from the offer, Daniel shrugged and said, "Suit yourself." He took a spoon and, making sure all eyes were watching, scooped up the porridge and placed it into his mouth. Groans of disgust erupted from the crowd as he chewed vigorously and swallowed.

Smiling, Daniel said, "Delicious! Anyone else care for some?"

Of course, there were no takers, and Daniel did not let on the weevils were, in fact, only raisins. Using his ploy to shock the audience always brought their attention front and center and taught them what a pirate had to do to survive any length of time at sea. Chase loved the realism his father brought to the enterprise. After they disembarked, the crew had a good laugh at the lubbers' expense.

Even Crunchy had developed his own role. He had taken to wearing an eye patch, which discomforted a few passengers, uneasy at the prospect of a one-eyed ship's pilot. To further play with the lubber's anxieties, Crunchy would often switch the patch to the other eye when no one was looking. Guests who dared ask a crew member about the twist received a standard response, "Go ask him."

Crunchy would listen and then give a grizzled growl scaring the questioner. And although the patch would change eyes several more times during the tour, the embarrassing question was never raised twice.

The last tour of the day would end with a fitting exclamation point at Key West, where every evening a celebration occurred in Mallory Square and on the Bay. The pier was always crowded, and boats of all sizes filled the bay to celebrate the impending sunset.

The *Satisfaction* timed its bay arrival for the daily homage to another glorious day in paradise. The rum punch flowed, music began, and dancing followed. Pirates and lubbers alike mingled completing their comradery with no shortage of laughter. As the sun began its final descent to drop below the waves Chase commanded, "Make ready the cannons!!"

The *Satisfaction* might have been equipped with thirty cannons, but actually there were only six *working*, three on each side. The rest, decorative foam covered in plaster, known only to the crew.

The company wanted to make the experience as authentic as possible, without the added weight which would slow down the ship. Not wanting to fire real cannonballs in the crowded bay, the crew used a special powder mixture for realism. At the precise time the sun dipped below the horizon, the captain yelled out to King, his Master Gunner. "Fire at will!"

Each of the six cannons fired in succession, thrilling those on the ship. But they were not alone. When the last cannon blast subsided, cheers could be heard from the other boats in the bay and from the people along the pier. The cannon firing and cheers signaled it was time for all to head onto the fabled Duval street. When Chase first attempted this salute to the sunset, it became an instant hit. Now, tradition had taken hold of the routine making it a beloved event.

As the smell of gunpowder hung in the air and the *Satisfaction* made its way toward the harbor, the Captain raised his mug one last time to address the happy crowd.

"I'd like to thank you all for sailing with us today. I hope you had an excellent time out on the high seas. You've now been to battle with us and learned *the pirate way*. You've earned your rank as an ABP or Able-Bodied Pirate, so congratulations! Please tell your friends about us and come back aboard soon. I'd sail with you newly christened pirates any day against our enemies." Chase paused and said slowly, "Including the dreaded … British … Royal … Navy."

This time, *everyone* on deck turned their heads to spit.

A Few Unreale Developments

NOT EVERYONE IN the Key West community welcomed the pirate newcomers. The water-tour operators did not appreciate the upstart Captain Morgan Piracy Tour taking a share of their business. Even though each company understood capitalism was based on competition and they had to continually reinvent themselves to succeed, none had seen the overwhelming success of this troupe coming.

Chase Porter had reinvented the tour business. Sure, there were other pirate-rum cruises, but he took the concept one step further. The ship was a virtual theatre on water. As the months passed, the CMPT continued to grow at the expense of the other water cruise operators.

The tourists were drawn to the grand old dame berthed in Conch Harbor. The townspeople adopted *Satisfaction* as their own as well. Her masts could be seen from most of downtown drawing walking tourists to the marina where they slowed to take a closer look at her magnificence. Although *Satisfaction* was a replica, she represented the spirit of Key West: Adventure, history, freedom.

One particular person in town did not share the love for the wooden lady. Jasper Cobb, president of Cobb Enterprises was not accustomed to disruption in his tourist focused business ventures. Which was precisely on his mind one morning as he sat at his desk pondering how to counter Chase Porter. He and his pirate tour boat company had a disruptive effect on Cobb Enterprises.

Cobb's office was located in a quaint, classic eyebrow house on Francis Street with key pine on every ceiling, a pool, and a pool house in the back. At the front, a white picket fence with welcoming pineapple cutouts on every other slat, separating the house from the sidewalk. Two large palm trees stood sentry on either side of the front steps leading into the home.

When CMPT first entered into business, Jasper had not seen it as a threat. In fact, he gave the *Satisfaction*'s crew and their business plan less than ten percent chance of survival in the crowded Key West tourism market. Now, as he skimmed the company's reviews online, he realized he had underestimated both the lure of the ship and their pirate act.

A knock on his door shook him from his thoughts. His daughter and chief financial officer, Ginger, stepped into his office. Smart, blonde, and beautiful, Ginger proved more than competent when it came to business. She had been instrumental in helping modernize Jasper's operation by bringing great marketing ideas to the table. Being a whiz with numbers was a godsend. Having an abundance of energy, not to mention killer instincts she inherited from Jasper made Ginger the perfect right hand in the business.

"Bad time?" she asked, ignoring the wooden chairs Jasper kept in front of his desk.

He favored the uncomfortable stark seats because he didn't want any employees or visitors to get too comfortable and overstay their welcome. "No," he replied. "Just in a bad mood thinking about-"

"Chase Porter," Ginger answered for him. "He seems to be on your mind a lot lately."

She sat atop the corner of Jaspers desk, annoying him. She was Jasper's only child and heir apparent to his empire. He was only fifty-five, she thirty, which gave him plenty of time to maintain his position. Still, she had shown a great aptitude for the business. It would be in good hands when or *if,* he decided to retire. So far, with great relief to Jasper, she showed no signs of inheriting any traits from her mother.

"I don't mean to be the bearer of bad tidings but take a look at the figures from our water tours year-over-year. We're down twelve percent, and I'm projecting it to get worse. We may have to lay off some employees this season."

"Damn!" Jasper pursed his lips to hold back even more cuss words. "There has got to be a way to turn this around. We're the pre-eminent tour company in town, and this upstart comes in and starts taking away our business?"

It was one of only a few times Jasper Cobb had been wrong when analyzing a competitor. *Oh boy, had he been wrong.* While the Captain Morgan Piracy Tours saw reservations extending outward for months, Jasper's reservations began to recede like the sunsets off Mallory Square.

"I could kick myself for not coming up with the idea first." Porters' piracy excursions made Jasper's own tours seem lame in comparison. He hated looking bad in front of the town he felt respected him for his business prowess. What Jasper Cobb hated worse was losing money, and his company was losing a lot. His daughter kept him apprised of that fact every chance she got.

"We have to do something. At this rate, we might have to consider selling a boat or two before the end of the season," Ginger said, frowning.

"That's drastic," Jasper replied, unable to mask his own concern. He'd rarely had to cut back on his interests before, even during a recession. He did not plan on doing so now.

"Drastic times call for drastic action. We can't keep bleeding red ink forever." Ginger paused, a wry smile appearing on her face. "Why not buy him out? We're debt-free, we could take out a loan and pay it down in no time. Have you considered that?"

"Of course, I have. Spoke with our accountant and, as usual, he tells me it's a bad idea to take on any debt. At the same time, Dent at the bank assures me we'll have no problem securing a loan."

"Dad, if we want to grow the business, we have to take a few risks. Can you imagine what we could do with that ship? It would be like printing money!"

Jasper considered his daughter's words. There had been others who had come into town trying to disrupt his business model and take their unfair share of the market. He had either outsmarted them or bought them out. Over the years he had built his reputation as a shrewd businessman and no one to be trifled with. It was time to show the upstart who the top man in town really was.

"I believe it is time to pay Mr. Porter a visit and welcome him to our fair city," he said, smiling at the prospect of how the meeting might end.

"I believe you're right." Ginger rose from the desk and walked toward the door where she turned to him and added, "As usual."

On Sunday afternoon, Jasper walked the short distance from his office to the Berth, surmising he'd find Chase Porter there. Jasper knew the *Satisfaction*'s crew took Sundays off and the Berth had always been their hangout of choice. When he pushed open the bar's heavy door, he saw his deduction had been correct. Chase and his team sat at the bar.

"Welcome to the Key West business community," Jasper called out as he entered. "I must apologize for not coming sooner.

My name is Jasper Cobb, one of the tour operators in town. I wanted to come by to welcome you. I have great admiration for what you're doing."

Jasper extended his hand for all to shake. His smile faded briefly as King, standing behind the bar, leaned back against the cash register in defiance of the outstretched hand.

Jasper folded his fingers back into his fist slowly and slid his arm to his side. His smile returned as he turned towards Chase.

"I have a proposition for you, Mr. Porter. Though my holdings in this business arena are substantial, I would love nothing more than to add your ship to my stable of assets. Would you consider selling me the company and staying on to continue the fine work you've been doing as the entertainment?"

King, Rio, and Anne jumped forward, all talking at once. They shot questions aimed at Jasper, who stepped back, not expecting the degree of negativity.

"What?" Anne yelled louder than the men. "Are you crazy?"

Rio showed his anger as well. "Who the hell are you coming in here like this!"

King growled, "Shit fire!"

Jasper only had eyes for Chase as the young man lifted a hand to his friends in order to calm them down to add his opinion about the older man's proposition.

"We *might* consider selling the enterprise...." Chase raised his hand once more to quiet the three who'd begun arguing again. "For the right price, of course."

"And what price were you considering?"

Chase thought for a moment before answering. "One hundred million dollars."

His partners all nodded, acknowledging the high price. All were smiling as they stared at Jasper. Who was *not* smiling.

"You must be joking?"

"Nope. The offer ends at midnight tonight. It's three p.m. now, so you have a little time to think about it." Chase looked at his watch before adding, "In the meantime, we have official company business to discuss, so if you wouldn't mind?"

Jasper lifted a finger, about to speak, when King leaned forward across the bar and said, "What he means to say is … you gotta go. Now!"

The rudeness stunned Jasper. No one ever spoke to him in such a disrespectful manner. Who did these upstarts think they were talking to? Heat rushed to his face as he spun around and strode to the door. He struggled with its bulk but finally managed to slip through. but not before hearing them all laugh at his expense.

Jasper walked back to his office muttering to himself. Angry at their insolence, yet undeterred by his spurned offer. His mind went to work on ideas of what to do next. If they would not sell him the company, he'd have to take other steps to stop their crew from further ruining his business. He turned onto Francis street toward home. Reaching for the gate latch to his house, he looked up and noticed Ginger sitting on the front porch. Her eyebrows raised as she asked, "What was the price tag when you asked to buy him out?"

"One hundred million," he replied, his scowl deepening.

"Man, the guy does have chutzpah. I'll give him that," she said, as she rolled her eyes.

Jasper bristled at the comment but said nothing. He watched her lean forward, hands clasped, eyes intently focused on him as she continued, "I have to ask you, what are you capable of doing, what depths would you go to in order to stop those guys if this trend continues?"

Her question caught him off guard. First the upstarts disrespected him. Now his daughter challenged him. Not used to such treatment, Jasper fidgeted while pondering her question.

Sitting down in the chair next to Ginger, he studied her. After Jasper had to institutionalize her mother, Janet, he spent his life protecting his daughter and his business interests. Janet had a mental breakdown and became too dangerous to be on her own or even around Ginger. There was no telling what his ex-wife would have been capable of had he not put her away.

Since day one, Jasper vowed to do anything necessary to make up for having to be the one parent in the household. Although he had made his share of mistakes in that department, he was a good businessman. He taught Ginger to take care of herself should anything ever happen to him. Glancing at her again, she studied her hands with a smile on her face. He also had to keep an eye out for signs Ginger might be like her mother. Wondering if daughter might follow the same path as mother leading to insanity was difficult. So far, he had not seen any signs, causing Jasper to feel grateful.

"Perhaps we should go visit the CVB to offer a trumped-up charge to get his license pulled?"

"Sounds like a logical next step," prodded Ginger. "What if that doesn't work? From what I've heard the guy's a friggin' boy scout and clean as a whistle. He does everything by the book. So, then what?"

"Hmmm. While rebuffed at my attempt to buy them out, could a partnership work? There has got to be something they want. Hell, I'm not above resorting to...." He trailed off, not wanting to finish the sentence. Jasper was far from timid when it came to playing hardball. He didn't believe he had to go there. Yet.

But Ginger was adamant. "We have to do something. Get outside the box to disrupt his business before he does something that will really do us damage."

"Tell me, what more damage can he do to us?" Jasper asked sarcastically. "He's already stealing our tourists and profit."

Ginger stood, put both hands on her hips and leaned forward until she was almost in his face.

"He could buy a second pirate ship."

Anne stretched out on the ship's lounge, sipping from a water bottle, and relaxing after the final tour of the day. Sighing, she glanced over at Chase by the table preparing a light dinner for the two of them.

They'd been dating for over a year now and during that time, their partnership had solidified in both business and romance. She was content as they grew romantically stronger but professionally, she wanted more. She had been handling the marketing since they started the company, now she wanted to play a more significant role in the oversight of the financial end. She had a knack for numbers and felt eager to share those ideas with Chase.

"The demand is rising. What do you think about investing in a second ship to handle the overflow?" Chase asked as he brought her a plate with fresh fruit, half a sandwich and a few crackers. "Need more water?" he added, turning back to get his own plate.

"No, thanks," she said. "To answer your question, I know we're on a solid financial footing with the business. But before we do anything else, Don't you think we should consider paying off the note on the *Satisfaction* first?" She thought the idea sound but wanted to temper his enthusiasm with frugality. The demand for their tours was healthy, but Anne had a practical, if not cautious, nature.

She went on to explain, "We don't want to find ourselves over-leveraged with too much debt and not enough revenue to cover the debt service." Anne practiced the ways of her grandfather who had grown up during the Depression era. *If you can't pay for it, don't buy it.*

"You're right, we're in great shape," Chase said. "Ticket sales are strong with reservations extending months in advance. The store revenues keep climbing also, and our sponsorship relationship is vibrant."

"Okay, let's play devil's advocate." Anne mimicked Chase when it came to looking out for any roadblocks. She, too, liked to think of what issues might arise, and what solutions they could conjure to overcome any obstacles.

"What if we needed major repairs to the *Satisfaction* due to a storm or dry rot or any number of issues that could plague a wooden ship? Without the *Satisfaction,* we have no stage. No stage means no revenue. She's like the proverbial basket with all our eggs in it."

"But if we only have one basket, isn't your argument *for* a new ship?"

"One might think so, but if we had two ships to pay for and not enough revenue coming in, we could lose both." She could see he was beginning to understand her logic. "I do have a plan to help us get a second ship the right way."

Anne noticed Chase smiling approvingly, "You really have a knack for this business, and even though we have insurance to cover most of the pitfalls you're describing, I'd like to hear more of your ideas."

"First," she began. "I think it would be prudent for all of us to take a small pay cut."

"Whoa. Taking a pay cut? How do you plan on convincing the other two? I'm fine with it, but who gets the short straw to tell King and Rio?"

Anne saw his point. Chase lived on board rent free with little or no expenses. He was able to put his money away for the future. She was also frugal, but not so sure about the other two.

"When I tell them it's for paying more off the *Satisfaction*'s note each month, they'll be fine with it," Anne said confidently.

"You mean like paying down a mortgage early?"

"Precisely," she answered while nodding. "Next, we look for other advertisers for the website and sponsors for the cruises. We don't want to be like NASCAR, but revenue from a few more nonalcoholic sponsors would help to pay down the note at a quicker pace. And then-"

Chase interrupted her, "There's more to this plan?"

She popped a strawberry into her mouth and chewed it slowly before answering.

"Yes, and if you'd let me finish, you'd see we can upsell all our advertisers on becoming sponsors on the second ship as well. Instant revenue!"

"Great idea!"

Anne was not finished. "Then, once the *Satisfaction* is paid off and the new ship is in our possession, we would each get a bonus to make up for the pay cut."

Chase laughed as he shook his head, a gesture Anne interpreted as acceptance. "If anyone can sell those guys on this concept, it's you. Do you have any other great ideas?"

"As a matter of fact, I do." Anne was in a groove. "For now, let's enact these changes. I'll work on finding the sponsors and inform the other two about the pay cuts. In a few years, we should have the *Satisfaction* paid off, and The Berth will once again be King's alone. Then and only then, should we consider purchasing a new ship."

"Then, we'll have to buy a marina to accommodate our new fleet," joked Chase.

Anne took a large bite of her sandwich and put a hand under her chin to catch any food trying to escape.

With her mouth full she mumbled, "That's in the *five-year* plan."

A Spanish Shipwreck and Another on the Way

WHEN SUNDAY MORNING came, Chase felt eager to dive. Rio, who nursed a hangover from the night before, would not be joining him. Not wanting to break the *never dive alone* rule, Chase had convinced King to go along with him on an excursion in the upper Keys. There is a series of nine shipwrecks within the Florida Keys National Marine Sanctuary called the Shipwreck Trail. Today they would dive the wreck of the San Pedro.

They left the marina in King's Grady-White at seven a.m. for the two-hour boat ride up to Indian Key. The morning promised a bright, cloudless Keys sort of day, the Grady-White's bow slicing easily through the calm waters. The two passed the time talking about some dives they'd been on, the upcoming hurricane season and debated the pros and cons of Anne's new plan.

Before long, they were upon the shipwreck of the *San Pedro*. The ship, along with twenty-one other Spanish ships, left Havana, Cuba, in July 1733, heading back to Spain. Its hold contained Mexican minted silver coins and Chinese porcelain. A hurricane came upon the Spanish treasure fleet prompting the captain to order a return to Havana. But the order had come too late; the storm intensified and sank most of the fleet off the Florida coast.

The wreck of the *San Pedro* was discovered in the 1960s and heavily salvaged by treasure hunters giving up riches like silver coins dating between 1731 and 1733 recovered from the pile of ballast and cannon marking the place of her sinking. Chase liked to dive the site because of her history, even if the treasures were long gone. *Sometimes history is a treasure all its own.*

Chase entered the water to swim the eighteen feet to the *San Pedro's* resting place. He knew King had a different reason to dive. For a man who liked peace and quiet, the underwater world provided both. King no doubt needed to counteract the hectic bar where people gathered to drink, converse, and sometimes carouse noisily. The irony was not lost on Chase.

The pair swam slowly through the site, witnessing ballast stones and several replica cannons. The originals long gone, taken from the site, and preserved in a museum. They also saw an eighteenth-century anchor, a few coral clusters, and finally a plaque dedicated to the site.

So far, Chase had no visions during the dive. Perhaps it was the early morning, being in a different location, or maybe because he had not been drinking the night before.

In any event, Chase swam next to King with three feet or so between them while keeping his head on a swivel. If he did capture a glimpse of the supernatural today, he did not want to be caught off guard. Apparitions on land seemed a common occurrence but seeing them underwater felt spookier.

It was his first dive since his own encounter with the apparitions. Since then, Chase had done enough research to see no matter how uncommon, they still occurred. He'd found reports from divers seeing equipment disappear before their eyes, unexplained orbs, voices in the depths, and even dead friends standing on the deck of shipwrecks. There even was a paranormal diver investigative unit formed to seek out underwater anomalies.

He hoped his own visions would also remain of the uncommon variety. He kept the sightings to himself, not even telling Anne. The last thing he needed was for his friends to think he had gone mad.

The men stayed below for around forty-five minutes until King motioned to Chase it was time to head back to the boat. The length of time a scuba tank could last underwater depended on variables such as tank volume, depth, and air consumption. They all played a role. King, like Rio, was a cautious diver, but they were only in eighteen feet of water, and though it was possible to stay under a short while longer, they had seen what they wanted. Chase nodded in agreement, and the pair swam back to King's boat.

Still, the thought of staying under longer lingered with Chase. There had to be a workable solution involving better equipment which would not require them to be attached to a hose from a ship. Even the prospect of ghostly appearances below the depths did not outweigh Chases' desire for seeking treasure. He felt it time to do some considerable research on just how workable it would be.

On their way back to the marina, the two men made a pledge to dive the site's eight other trails and convince Rio to join them. That is, if their hectic schedule aboard the *Satisfaction* allowed it.

Later in the afternoon, the four partners sat at the Berth plotting their Gulf excursion ideas. Should the need arise to weigh anchor and leave Key West due to a nasty storm or, God forbid, a full blown hurricane, they wanted to be prepared. They discussed routes, how many crew members to take, what provisions they would need, and how long the trip would take.

"I've researched the Texas licensing requirements, and we should have ours coming soon," advised Anne. She also discussed her marketing plans for attracting passengers and Rio provided a story about pirates in Galveston. "I also contacted some friends from the tourism industry there and it looks as if we'll be welcomed." He grinned, confident he could smooth the way for the *Satisfaction* to make berth and take tourists aboard as long as the right people were compensated.

Chase was leading the discussion on which employees would stay in Key West to manage the enterprises in their absence when he heard the door creak open. He watched Jasper Cobb slide inside the saloon and approach the bar.

"Good afternoon, folks. I wondered if I might have a word with you." When they all remained silent, Jasper continued. "I'll get right to the point. I have a new business proposition to discuss—"

Chase spoke up. "Save your breath, Cobb. I told you; the tour and the *Satisfaction* are not for sale."

"Come, come, everyone has his price. The one you quoted—"

"One hundred million bucks!" Anne interrupted. "It's probably higher now, right?" She looked over at Chase for acknowledgement.

Chase nodded, still focused on Jasper.

"Chase, why are you even listening to this guy?" The exasperation in Rio's voice evident.

King stepped around the bar growling. Chase put his hands up to silence them both.

Jasper spoke again, "As I was saying, the last price you quoted was, shall I say, untenable? So, I relinquish my attempts to buy you out. Instead, I have a different offer. What would you say if we joined in partnership?"

King and Rio started up again, with Anne adding her voice to the mix as all three echoed their protests against such a merger.

Chase spoke directly to his friends in order to calm them down. "Hold on a minute. Let me ask a question."

And then, turning back to Jasper, he asked, "Just out of curiosity, what makes you think we'd have anything to do with you? What could you bring to the table to change our minds?"

Jasper cleared his throat and began, "The second part of your question should answer your first. There is no question you've built a fine business model. I also am aware of your hefty banknote on the *Satisfaction* and you've used this establishment for collateral. Any attempts to grow your business now would be, shall we say, problematic?"

There was no further interruption so Jasper continued, "So, to answer both questions, here's my offer. It's possible to double your reservations and increase your profit margins. This would provide enough money to quickly pay off your outstanding note. However, you would have to allow me to do just one little thing."

Chase eyed Jasper suspiciously. Still, curiosity got the better of him. "And what would this little thing be?"

Jasper smirked before answering, "Buy you another pirate ship."

Chase and his crew sat stunned as Jasper left them alone at the bar to mull over this unexpected offer. Once they were sure Jasper Cobb had vacated the building, Anne broke their silence. "He's so creepy."

"He's like a dead fish come back to life," added Rio.

"Untrustworthy," was King's only comment.

Chase looked at his crew. "No worries, we've already got a plan for a second vessel."

As they nodded in agreement, Chase began fondling his UnReale, pondering the possibility of being a step *behind* Jasper. A position where he would never be comfortable.

The next day, Chase leaned over his desk in the *Satisfaction*'s Captain quarters looking over maps of the *Atocha* debris field with his father. Chase knew Daniel still sought treasure from the Treasure Coast's sands but would not dive himself. His father preferred being above the waves. Still, he knew they shared a healthy interest in shipwrecks and what secrets their ruins held.

Rio entered the room, nodded to Daniel then said, "What's up, Cap'n?"

Rio had recently taken to calling Chase the nickname, even though they all shared in playing the role of Captain during the tours. Rio had told him it just felt right seeing as the whole enterprise had been Chase's idea. Besides, if Rio had to have a nickname, then it made sense Chase had one as well.

"Are we all set for tomorrows run to the island?" Chase asked Rio.

Chase referred to the Dry Tortugas National Park, thirty nautical miles off the coast of Key West. It was discovered by the explorer Ponce de Leon who, upon reaching the island in 1513, noticed sea turtles everywhere, prompting him to name the island *Las Tortugas*, Spanish for *The Turtles*.

Rio saluted before answering, "Yes, Cap'n. Have all supplies loaded, the crew is ready, and we have a full reservation list as usual. Even Pops here is dressing up."

Chase was in awe of his father, well aware Daniel really enjoyed acting the part of a pirate aboard their vessel, studying his distinct roles, and always remaining in character. These traits had prompted Chase to appoint Daniel *First Mate of Training*, a role his father relished and took very seriously. Daniel gave expert advice helping the other crew members with their period dress, dialect, and work routines, taking the whole enterprise to the next level of authenticity.

Chase loved having his father visit Key West and even offered the *Brains and Brawn* for him to live full time, but Daniel had refused with a wave of his hand. "My primary home is in Vero Beach. My *vacation* home is here."

When he did come, Daniel never came alone. He always brought one or two interesting characters with him to play act aboard ship and the lubbers loved each one.

"Once again, I ask you, what are you up to?" Rio, the type of man who preferred answers, would not let go of a question until he got one. Chase knew this yet would try to distract him just to see how long it took before Rio could persuade him to give up the answer, a game they both played well.

"Which story am I telling tomorrow, Rio?" Chase asked, his turn in the rotation to lead the expedition.

"The one where I get to take over the ship?" teased Rio.

Chase noticed the big grin on Rio's face and chuckled at his ruse but not ready to answer the question. "Stede Bonnet, perhaps? That's a good one," Chase prompted.

"Nope. Not sure that fits just yet. How about Blackbeard? Charles Vane or The Woodes Rogers story again?"

Chase structured the stories together in such a way to involve the audience and keep them captivated. It was the hallmark of their tours, and the large numbers of repeat customers proved it. Adding Rio's contributions made it even more of a partnership in theatrics both men found rewarding.

"How about the *Atocha* story? We *are* going to the Dry Tortugas."

"The tourists love that story. A tale of terror, trials, and treasure. So, you gonna tell me what's up, Cap'n? Especially with all the maps?" Rio asked.

Chase hesitated, but then relented. "I have a theory, and it starts with the *Mastery*'s crew looking for the sterncastle in the wrong place. I'm not sure why, but I have a gut feeling it isn't where they think it is. I'm still trying to figure out where it may lie."

Daniel put a finger to his lips and whispered, "Loose lips sink ships."

"I thought storms sank ships?" Chase asked in a mocking tone.

"They do, but metaphorically speaking, so do loose lips. So please, mind yours, young Rio," Daniel said as he pointed to the map. "Too bad there isn't a storm brewing."

"We know … best time to search for treasure," Chase and Rio replied in unison, having heard Daniel use the saying more than once.

Turning back to his map, Chase ran a finger along the long scar of the debris field, lost in thought before Rio broke the spell. "The sterncastle, eh? Boy, would I like to find it. I can only imagine what wealth is hidden in *that* debris field."

Chase wriggled his eyebrows impishly doing his best Groucho Marx impersonation as he pointed at the map on the desk. "Then don't you think we should go look for it?"

"Listen closely, Mates. We're crossing over hallowed sea." The *Satisfaction* ran its Thursday cruise to the Marquesas Keys and Dry Tortugas with Chase telling his tale of terror, trials, and treasure.

"In 1622 a Spanish fleet of ships attempted their return to Spain heavily laden with treasure of gold, silver, and emeralds. A hurricane overwhelmed them near this spot. Two ships, The *Atocha* and *Santa Margarita,* sank taking their treasure and most of the crew down approximately fifty-five feet to the bottom."

Chase bowed his head for a moment of silence before resuming. "Only a few crew members survived by hanging onto the main mast. According to its manifest, the *Atocha* had been loaded with a cargo which included twenty-four tons of silver bullion, over a hundred thousand silver coins, one hundred twenty-five gold bars along with indigo, bales of tobacco, and gold artifacts. The Spaniards attempted to salvage their treasure using an early version of a diving bell. But in October of the same year, another hurricane came through and scattered the wreckage along a wide path. Try as they might, the Spaniards failed to salvage any more of their precious cargo." He paused a moment to let the lubbers think about how vast this treasure was.

"Then, in 1985, a man named Mel Fisher found both the *Santa Margarita* and the *Atocha* to claim their treasures! For sixteen long years, he had searched for those ships. Each day encouraging his team by saying, *Today's the day!*

His day finally came. But at a price. Mel lost his son and daughter-in-law along with another diver in a fire on board one of their salvage ships. He had lawsuits filed against him by both the Spanish and the US governments. Still, Mel prevailed as he and his team pulled up treasure worth an estimated four hundred million dollars." Chase paused again for the crowd to gasp. "Gold, silver, and other artifacts were brought up from the site, most of which can be seen at his museum in Key West." As a side bar, he added, "Please put the museum on your itinerary, you will not be disappointed."

Chase took a deep breath and exhaled slowly, "So, is this the end of the story? Ah, you would be incorrect. What I haven't mentioned is what has *not* been found. Out in the ocean still is the *Atocha's* sterncastle, where the captain's quarters would have been located." Chase pointed back toward the *Satisfaction's* stern to illustrate.

"The captain would secure only the most valuable items in his cabin for safe keeping such as gold escudo coins. Jewelry. Bars of gold and silver. Rare emeralds. So, who knows where this sterncastle may be hiding? For all we know, we're apt to be sailing over it right now as I tell this tale."

Chase paused as lubbers scurried to look over the sides of the ship trying to catch a glimpse of sunken treasure.

Clearing his throat to gain their attention, Chase finished his tale. "One day, if it's found, some lucky salvager will use the famous phrase himself, and whomever it is... will be the richer for it!"

After completing his rendition of the *Atocha* story, Chase looked wistfully over the side of the *Satisfaction* into the clear blue-green waters.

All he saw were emeralds.

A Different Port In Not Just Any Storm

"YOU'RE DOING IT again," Rio informed Chase as they walked to the Berth. "What's got you worried this time, Cap'n?" he asked, pointing at the necklace hanging around Chase's neck.

Rio was still wrong. It was not worry, but concern. And for good reason. A storm approached. A large one. Being a cautious man when it came to the welfare of his clients, he had already canceled the tours for the duration of any inclement weather. To Chase, there would never be a good reason to risk the well-being of a tourist or crew member for an extra buck. He always consulted the National Oceanic Atmospheric Administration (NOAA) and other weather outlets including the weather app on his phone just to make sure there was consensus when a storm approached the Keys.

The *Satisfaction*'s wooden masts could snap, flying objects could puncture the hull or any other malady could occur during the height of a storm with dangerously high winds. The prior storm had not been much of a threat, but after much time spent researching Key West weather patterns, Chase knew with the right conditions any storm could pick up speed and turn into a hurricane.

Those conditions were shaping up to be just right.

Chase shook his head looking over at Rio. "We've got a storm coming which could turn into a Category three or four."

"Really?" Now Rio looked worried. "A Cat three or four? That's one hell of a storm. Can you imagine the damage?"

"Yes. I can."

Hurricanes are determined by the strength of their wind speed to determine their damage at landfall and storm surge. They are categorized using a number system. A Category one, the *lowest*, brings wind speeds of between seventy-four and ninety-five mph with minimal damage. A Cat five brings the *most devastation* with wind speeds of over one hundred and fifty-five mph causing catastrophic landfall damage and a storm surge range of nineteen-plus feet.

The storm heading towards them looked like no ordinary one. It had the potential for a Cat three hurricane or higher with winds pushing upwards of one hundred eleven to one hundred thirty mph so there would be no question about canceling any tours. The bigger issue would be whether to keep the *Satisfaction* in port or activate the contingency plan to head into the Gulf of Mexico.

Chase decided to first check on the storm track before making any decision. If the storm tracked north, then they would head west to Texas. If it followed west by northwest, that piece of information would really give Chase something to ponder. The hurricane would drive right over the Florida coast and into the Gulf of Mexico, which meant sailing west to safety would no longer be an option.

The thought reminded Chase of Jasper's offer, having not spoken to the man since the that day at the Berth. He *had* mulled it over. One pirate ship would pay their salaries. Having a fleet and an additional partner, who could lend solvency to the business, would pay greater dividends.

Seeing the storm clouds gather, Chase felt glad they did not have two ships today for logistical reasons. Multiple ships would mean they could build a dynasty. Dynasties ensure fortunes for all involved including future generations. But it also meant double the exposure during storm season.

The issues with owning a fleet were not insurmountable. He could hire a staff of researchers to find more stories, and the area always offered plenty of available help to build a crew. The theatre majors from local Barry University might assist to act out a few of the lead roles, so Chase would be able to take a less active position on deck. This would free up more time to dive. Lately, he felt the itch to research shipwrecks and try his hand at salvage. And having multiple ships would be the perfect opportunity to do so.

The only issue would be dealing with Jasper. The man was unscrupulous, unethical, and untrustworthy. How did the saying go? *Dance with the devil you know, not the one you don't.*

They certainly all knew the devil by the name of *Jasper Cobb*, having witnessed what happened to Cobb's past dance partners.

Chase wanted to expand to ensure the future of his team and allow him to follow his other dreams, but at what price? No. He decided not to dance with the devil, Jasper Cobb, knowing that dealing with the devilish man would not be worth the risk.

He resolved to stick with the plan Anne had proposed telling Jasper his company would not be doing business with him … not ever. In truth, if Chase were to expand the fleet now, he would need a new partner but not one like Cobb, a shrewd dancer who would eventually step on his toes … or worse.

On August 31st, the storm hovering over the Caribbean strengthened into a hurricane, the Weather Service giving it a name: Bree. Hurricane Bree rapidly intensified to a Category five on September 5th, making landfall in Barbuda, a small island in the eastern Caribbean. It caused considerable damage to the island before striking St. Bart's and the British Virgin Islands the following day. Directly in its path, albeit a few days away, lie Key West.

"It's time to sail," Chase warned, but he did not need to as his partners had already begun preparations to enact their emergency evacuation plan. Just the threat of the hurricane had seen cancellations all over the islands. Tourists were taking no chances of coming to a paradise with the possibility of meeting up with a category three to five hurricane welcoming them. In silence, the four and their handpicked crew made the necessary preparations to set sail in the morning before the mighty storm had a chance to get close enough to stop them.

Daniel arrived unannounced. "I wanted to surprise you," he said, smiling broadly.

"You would have been really surprised had you arrived any *later.*" Chase returned the smile. "We'd have set sail by then."

Rio couldn't resist, "Daniel's a good swimmer, he could've caught up."

King put an arm around Daniel's shoulder. "Good surprise."

Bree was scheduled to hit the Keys on Sunday and head up the Florida coast moving inland where it was expected to weaken to a tropical storm. Chase hoped to return by later the next week and assist with any needed repairs caused by the destruction on the island. Opening the new tourist season in Key West would have to wait, but the Old Towners were a resilient bunch. Chase and his crew traveled around town Wednesday wishing all well and Godspeed.

They left port on Thursday morning, clouds in the distance and a strong wind at their backs pushing the *Satisfaction* under sail towards calmer seas.

"I see the *Satisfaction* left port this morning." Ginger sat on a front porch rocker and sipped her cup of coffee. Jasper had just returned from his morning walk. If the coming storm proved to be as bad as everyone said it would, it might be his last walk for a week. Ginger could tell her father was not having a good morning.

"Cowards leaving a sinking ship," he scowled as he stepped onto the porch. "We ought to get them banned from doing tours here. At the first sign of trouble, they turn tail and run."

"I heard they were planning to take on tourists in Galveston." Ginger offered, taking another sip, and looking beyond Jasper at the approaching storm clouds.

"So, they're going to piss off the Galveston travel industry as well by stealing some of *their* business?"

"Hey, it's America. You have to give them credit. They take their ship out of harm's way and make money at the same time. Gotta hand it to 'em. Those guys are *smart*!" Ginger marveled at the way Chase Porter always seemed to be one step ahead of the competition. Which meant one step ahead of her father, a feat no one else had ever accomplished. And she secretly admitted to herself how Chase was easy on the eyes. An admission causing both pleasure and discomfort at the same time.

Shaking her head, Ginger pushed *that* thought out of her mind. Chase Porter had to remain a competitive enemy. If not, there would be a serious gap noted on the next tax season's ledger sheet for Cobb Enterprises.

Jasper bristled. "Whose side are you on?"

Ginger stopped rocking. The inner calm voice in the back of her head whispered, *Easy girl*. Lately, she had begun listening to this particular soft voice with increasing frequency. She reasoned how everyone had to have their inner voices they listened to. The cautious voice to keep one out of harm's way. Or their positive voice telling them they could do remarkable things if they applied themselves. Still, this voice was different. It spoke to her about what a woman in her position not only could do but what she *should do* to accomplish any goal. It also had an edge.

"Why, your side, Daddy dear, of course. I've been thinking about what you said. Perhaps getting them banned isn't such a bad idea."

Jasper pursed his lips and raised one eyebrow. "What do you have in mind, daughter?"

If only he knew, said that special voice again.

"I haven't thought it all the way through yet. I do have an idea that may need some money and your connections." Ginger resumed her rocking motion as she finished the rest of her coffee. "Why don't you work on the tourism board and see if you can get them banned or revoked for, oh, I don't know, abandonment perhaps? I'll work on my plan a little while longer."

She watched her father smile for the first time.

Before he walked through the door, Jasper patted her on the shoulder. "Perhaps this will turn out to be a good morning after all."

Perhaps it will, whispered her internal voice. Ginger mimicked it. "Perhaps it will."

Safe in Galveston, the *Satisfaction* took on one hundred passengers for a rum cruise. Anne had advertised on the company website and in Galveston, informing potential customers the ship would be coming into town. The advertising worked as Rio's contacts paid off. With the town, the Chamber of Commerce, and the Convention and Visitors Bureau all welcoming the *Satisfaction* into their harbor, the tour was destined to be successful.

Captain Chase took his Texas lubbers out into the Gulf and began his tale. "How many of you have heard of the pirate, *Jean*

Laffite? It's known he had a hideout near here at Barataria Bay where he led a cadre of thieves, vandalizing shipping lanes in the Gulf. They began as privateers, raiding Spanish merchant ships and setting up trade in the city of New Orleans. It's told how during the War of 1812; the British Royal Navy came a-knockin' on his Island door."

The whole crew yelled, "BRITISH ROYAL NAVY?" and spat at the thought, much to the crowd's pleasure.

After the pause, Chase continued. "The English wanted to use Barataria as a naval base off the mainland of Louisiana. So, what do you think our pirate friend, Laffite, did?" The question was met with silence.

Chase answered it. "He addressed the Americans instead, offering his services and asking for clemency for any past indiscretions. He and his followers who served the U.S. during the conflict were granted a full pardon, their reward for military service. Ah, but can a former pirate stay away from the life? What say you?" This time the crowd responded with a resounding "NO!"

"That would be correct. For after a short while, Jean Laffite went back to his pirating ways and created a new pirate stronghold, this time on Galveston Island. Who knows, he still might be there today, because once a pirate, always a pirate!"

After a week of nearly selling out all the rum cruises, where Calico Jack, Anne Bonny, and Blackbeard all made appearances aboard the *Satisfaction,* they felt the coast was clear to begin their return to Key West.

Following the last rum cruise on Thursday afternoon, Chase met with the Galveston Convention and Visitors Bureau as well as the President of the Galveston Chamber of Commerce. Thanking them for their hospitality, he presented them with a generous check from the week's proceeds according to the agreement struck before their arrival. The amount allowed money to be shared with the tour companies who may have lost business due to their presence.

The generosity cemented a relationship ensuring the *Satisfaction* would always be welcomed into the port of Galveston as a partner, not a usurper. Chase had learned a valuable lesson: It is better to spend money to make money, not enemies.

The next day, Chase gave the order for Crunchy to leave the harbor and set sail on a bright, sunny morning. They bid farewell to the port of Galveston, gladdened to know they had a secondary home should it be necessary. No one on board hoped it would come to that.

"She doesn't look the worse for wear," Rio observed as the frigate sailed past Mallory Square on its way into Conch Harbor.

Chase nodded in agreement, but King looked concerned. "We're on the backside of the island, gents. What you want to look at is where the storm made landfall."

The group grew somber as they pulled into harbor and prepared to dock. Once on land, each headed in different directions to survey the damage and see what they could do to help. King hurried to the Berth while Rio and Anne went to their respective homes. Chase walked up Duval Street, wondering if the most famous street in the Keys had survived the onslaught.

What they found was a relief. Water damage from flooding, a few boats thrown up on pilings and seagrass littering the sides of the road. Fortunately, they hoped that was the extent of it. The bridges into Key West from the mainland were still closed, the only way to get to the island was by boat. Each craft carrying supplies and people to help with the cleanup provided a source of comfort.

Around four in the afternoon, Chase and Rio met King at the Berth. "Shit fire. Dodged a bullet."

"Anyone hurt?" asked Rio.

"Nope. Only water damage." King replied, placing a cold beer in front of each of his partners.

"Amen to that," Chase said, lifting his in salute.

The men settled in at the bar discussing their next moves. King poured three shots of rum that he and Rio downed immediately. Chase let his sit on the bar looking like a solitary soldier.

"I spoke with the mayor while on Duval, and we can sign up for clean-up crews," Chase told them. "Mayor said everyone is in good spirits and he anticipated the place will be back in shape in no time."

"Chase, what's the timeline for the hotels? Did he tell you how many are up and running?" Rio asked.

"A few. Most will be open by the weekend. The tourism board is letting everyone know the airport will be clear soon and open for business. They're hoping the snowbirds will start their migration again shortly."

"Yea," joked Rio. "If not, Santa may be short on presents this year."

Chase spun around on his stool in time to see Anne struggle through the door with a complaint, "My house is a mess. A tree crashed through my bedroom window and with all the contractors working elsewhere in the Keys, I can't find anyone to fix it. I may have to find someplace to crash. I guess I could call one of my girlfriends."

"I have a better idea," said Chase, as he grabbed Anne by the waist. "Why don't you move in with me on the *Satisfaction*? I've got plenty of room. It's not like you've never spent the night."

Anne blushed, escaping his grasp, and downed the shot of rum poured for Chase.

"Another, please. If I'm going to cohabitate with this one for a while, I'm gonna need all the rum I can get!"

"Wait a second...?" Chase raised a brow in mock surprise. "Just how long is a while?"

Key West returned to a semblance of normality. Most businesses opened again as tourists returned, filling the hotels, B&B's, and homes for rent. Restaurants and bars were filling seats and the tour businesses began taking reservations again. Considering what might have occurred, it turned out to be more than enough for most of the business owners in Key West.

Ginger's father was not most people. She cringed and put her hands to her ears hearing Jasper yell to her from his office. Why he didn't use the intercom was beyond her.

"Ginger? Ginger! Where the hell are you?"

He was in a foul mood … again. She understood his frustration because she shared it. Owning so many properties in the tourism business, they had the most to gain when all went well but the most to lose when things did not.

"Why are you yelling? What is it?" Ginger stepped into her father's office, brow furrowed and hands on her hips.

"I'm looking at the weekly revenue report … it is ugly!"

The weekly revenue report arrived on Fridays. During the peak tourist season, Friday was usually a good day as receipts were plentiful. In the offseason, they looked at year over year figures and tempered their expectations.

She knew there would be no tempering of expectations today. With the season just beginning and a hurricane ripping through their town, all expectations should have been cast out the window. She tried to explain it all to him. "Well, what do you expect? We just had a Cat three hurricane, and even though we didn't experience the damage they did in Marathon, the only thing tourists are seeing on the news is the devastation in the upper keys. It's giving them the impression all the Keys were adversely affected. The average tourist won't know the difference. C'mon, you know what I'm saying is true!"

The voice in her head warned, *Keep your cool, girl.*

Ginger didn't want to keep her cool, she wanted to rip her father's head off. Instead, she left his head firmly upon his neck, taking a deep breath and listened while Jasper continued to spew his angry vitriol. "I also know I hate red ink. I despise losing money, and I want to hear what you plan to do about it! If we don't get up to speed soon, this will be our worst year on record." He paused before switching gears. "How are we doing with the Porter idea. Since that interloper has spurned my generous offers, he's back in business *and* taking more of my money with him."

Ginger did not hold back. "Why on earth you gave him the idea about buying another boat is beyond me. It's bad enough he's successful with one. Then you go plant the idea of getting another. Really intelligent!" Ginger wanted to scream but kept her voice down not wanting to hear a reprimand from the voice in her head.

Instead, she heard, *you mean stupid ... don't you?*

Ginger silently agreed.

"Daughter," Jasper said, rising slowly from his chair. "It was supposed to be a pathway to get into business with them. He's over-leveraged and can't afford to buy another frigate right now, so I thought it an opportune time to dangle a prize he and his partners would be hard pressed to refuse."

Ginger was not satisfied with the answer and pushed further. "What happened to your idea to complain about them to the tourism bureau?"

"It didn't fly, they hadn't done anything against the law. CMPT is up to code, and unless we have something saying otherwise, the board will NOT take any action. Plus, everyone is in rebuild mode. They have no time for an investigation smelling of a *witch hunt*. Now instead of you criticizing me, you need to come up with a way to first, stop Chase Porter and second, get our business back on track. Now! You said you had an idea. Where is it?"

Ginger stared at her father, the rising anger causing her face to flush. *Temper, temper,* scolded the voice. *There's a time and place. But not here, not today.*

"Father," Ginger began, struggling to hold back her anger by breathing through her teeth. "I'm doing the best I can. Our employees have returned from tending to their own homes, the tourists are only beginning to trickle back, and we're advertising everywhere telling the world we're open for business. What more do you want from me?"

"Blood," said Jasper coldly. "Someone's blood."

She took note of the nasty expression on his face revert at once regretting his words. Her father was not a violent man and asking for blood did not really mean he wanted to hurt anyone physically. Still, once those words left his lips, Ginger's demeanor changed. It went from frustrated to calm and calculating. She sat as if in a daze, pulling together thoughts like the pieces of a puzzle she would turn into a plan.

"Oh, daddy," she said, finding the last mental puzzle piece and securing it gently in place before continuing, "I don't believe it will have to come to that...."

The voice in her head finished her sentence ... *Just yet.*

VOICES CARRY

I T IS SAID the best time to search for treasure is after a storm. Chase's father had drilled the concept into him every time they combed the Treasure Coast's beaches. Hurricane Bree had come through the Keys with a fury not seen by the islands in some time. After the *Satisfaction*'s crew assisted with cleaning up Key West, Chase was ready to dive again.

He and Rio agreed to meet Sunday morning at the dock where the salvage ship *Mastery* lay berthed. Today's dive would further test a portion of his sterncastle theory and see where this information would lead.

Once in the water, the divers followed the same linear pattern as before along the debris arc. But this time, Chase wanted the two to try a different approach. At the specific coordinates he had calculated, they made a break and swam south towards the reef where he had found the Bezoar stone. Chase also brought a new toy with him, a Pulse 8x metal detector. If there were any clues about the sterncastle, this metal detector would help. As he approached the reef, he flipped on the Pulse, careful to avoid the location of the Bezoar stone he had found before.

He heard nothing, which was expected. He saw nothing, which was a relief.

The men continued in a southerly direction until their calculations told them it was time for new tanks. Marking the coordinates of where they ended, Rio and Chase turned back toward the ship. Once in the water again, they followed the same grid but two to three feet to the side of the last path. They practiced that exact grid pattern two more times, covering as much territory as possible before the air in their tanks ran low, forcing another return to the ship.

They were on the last pass through, close to their turnaround time, when the metal detector pinged. Rio stopped swimming as Chase got into position to wave the Pulse over the area once again. Another ping sounded, which prompted Rio to begin to dig for whatever lay beneath the sand. Chase watched as Rio pulled an item from the hole and showed it to Chase. A silver spoon: its surface tarnished a light green color from years of resting on the ocean floor, a crusty substance hiding its ornate markings. Chase passed the Pulse over the hole where they found the artifact, but the Pulse remained silent.

Rio was about to place the spoon into the sack attached to his belt when Chase took it from him and buried it in the sand. Surprise registered in Rio's eyes. Chase ignored his friend and waved at him to continue on. Rio looked at his dive computer and shook his head, giving the thumbs up signal to alert Chase they needed to head for the ship before their oxygen ran out.

Instead of agreeing, Chase shook his head and continued on, knowing by doing so would leave Rio with a choice: follow and take the risk of running out of air or head back to the ship.

Chase continued on his path, the Pulse in the lead. Looking back, he realized Rio had not followed him. But, like a gambler positive his next hand would be a winner, Chase pressed on feeling sure he was on the right track. *Just a few more feet*, he thought, hoping for another ping.

His gauge showed the oxygen levels dipping into the danger zone yet gambled on the premise he could go another ten minutes or so. As he swept along the sand with his Pulse, his eyes trained on the sand in front of him, he felt a sharp tug on his belt, pulling him to a stop.

He swirled around, assuming Rio had returned to convince him to ascend. But there was nothing behind him, only water. *What the hell?* His heartbeat began thumping, forcing him to breathe deeper. *Did I just imagine that?* Looking around to confirm he was alone, he turned to continue his route, chalking it up to nerves. Swimming a few feet along, he noticed his heartbeat returning to normal allowing him to concentrate on the task at hand. He waved the Pulse over the sand as he went, hoping for a ping. Instead, he felt another tug on his weight belt. Again, he spun around, pointing his Pulse in front of him to ward off whatever had just grabbed him. Again, nothing but saltwater.

I didn't imagine that. Did I?

The tugs spooked him to make the decision to return before he got tugged a third time, or worse. As he swam towards the *Mastery*, his head was on a swivel and his thoughts turned towards something other than treasure. *Could that have been the dead boy? If it was him, does he want to warn me? Or worse, keep me down here with him?*

Chase did not stick around long enough to get the answers.

Back on board, Rio came at him like a raging bull shark. "What the hell were you thinking? Were you trying to kill us both?"

"Calm down, Rio. We're onto something. I just wanted another five minutes."

"Yea, we had something," Rio lowered his voice to a whisper, his face inches away from Chase. "Why did you make me drop the spoon! It's a valuable artifact!"

"And how would you explain where you found it?" Chase whispered. "Use your head. We can't let on to what we're doing until we find something substantial. And the spoon? A clue, nothing more. I have the coordinates. We can get it later."

More hurt than angry, Rio replied, "You put us at risk. Didn't you say you'd never let that happen again? You promised. Evidently, your promises aren't any good."

Chase did not like the look on Rio's face as he stormed off. Chase thought of his promise that day in the Berth after Rio tried to tell him the boy's drowning was not his fault. The words coming back to sting him, *I can assure you; I will never let something like that happen again.*

Chase sighed as he got out of his wetsuit and stored his gear in the locker. *It's gonna be a long boat ride back.* The bitter thought ran across his mind before being replaced with a positive one.

But at least we're on the right track.

Jasper was on the phone with Edgar Bell, who had been the family accountant for years. Jasper looked at a balance sheet of all the company assets along with the profit each one made over the last five years on his laptop. The new restaurant venture had its own sheet, projecting profits for the next three.

"Edgar, what valuation would you put on all our assets combined and how it would affect our borrowing power?"

Cobb Enterprises had no debt to service and a healthy revolving credit line should the need ever arise. It seldom did. They replaced old equipment such as boat motors or trolley parts only when necessary and paid their employees a meager, yet legal wage. When a cutback on staffing needed to happen, they approached it with precision-like surgery, three minutes in the office and thanks for your service. If at all possible, to get by without fixing a piece of equipment until the next season, they would take the chance if it meant the difference between red or black ink. The endgame each season for Cobb Enterprises? Write in "black ink" only. The business ran on profits, and they both kept an eye on the bottom line like hawks. Lately, that line sank towards the bottom faster than an anchor. At first, only Jasper and Ginger noticed. Then their accountant and banker spotted it. Now, it seemed everyone with a pair of eyes was aware the business was losing money.

Edgar told Jasper if they put all their assets up for collateral, their borrowing power would be quite substantial. "But," Edgar cautioned, "I highly advise against it. You've had a successful business model for years with a balance sheet most companies would die for. Why risk everything now? What do you want to buy with all the credit, anyway? Half the damned island?"

"Edgar, relax, will you? This is merely speculative at this stage. I'm considering an idea and wanted to have all the information at my disposal first." It was actually Ginger's idea. She laid out the scenario which impressed him. He had taught her well.

"Whew! That's good to hear," answered Edgar. "I wouldn't want to see one of my best customers go belly up on an all-or-nothing bet!"

Jasper hung up the phone and rubbed his hands together. *No, not half the island, just a marina. Then we'll fumigate to rid it of vermin.*

Bill and Mary Hemmings owned the Conch Harbor Marina, one of two prominent marinas on the island. The other, owned by Cobb Enterprises. Bill and Mary had purchased the property along the waterfront in the late sixties and over the years had converted it into a harbor with fuel facilities, a restaurant, and a supply store. The Marina had thirty-five slips to moor boats from small dinghies to one hundred and forty-foot yachts. They had been pleased when Chase approached them about mooring the *Satisfaction* in one of Conch Harbor's slips. Choosing Conch Harbor over Cobb's marina was an easy choice, due to Jasper's questionable business practices.

The CMPT Company proved to be such a good client, Bill had found space on the pier for Chase's operation to build a ticket counter and gift shop.

Chase told Bill he liked the marina's proximity to Duval Street and Mallory Square, within sightlines of all the wharf restaurants and easy access to the major hotels. Frankly, Bill enjoyed doing business with Chase Porter. As a model tenant, Chase paid his slip fees on time, always bought his fuel from the Conch, and supported the restaurant and supply store. He even went so far as to suggest his tour guests try the restaurant for the delicious lobster sandwich, a specialty of Mary's due to her secret sauce, a guarded recipe. It turned out to be the perfect arrangement as Chase and his team had become like family to the Hemmings.

Unfortunately, perfect arrangements could sometimes be tested.

"William?" Jasper inquired as he walked through Bill's office door. "We need to talk."

Bill and Jasper had known each other for years as friendly adversaries. They were in competition with one another, but since both marinas were profitable, they found no reason not to share the wealth. Jasper did not mind a little friendly competition as long as he was able to make a profit. Once he began losing money, his fangs came out. As did plots to create the demise of his rivals.

"Hey, Jasper, what can I do ya for?" Bill said, sitting in his small and sparse office. It had a few nautical pictures hanging on the walls. A single, dusty file cabinet stood sentry near the door. But unlike Jasper's office, there were no chairs for guests to sit down. Bill could be friendly up to a point. Out on the docks he had to talk to people all day long, but his office was his sanctuary; you could enter to discuss something, but you couldn't stay long. He hoped his current visitor would take the hint.

Jasper gazed out the picture window Bill had installed to keep an eye on the docks and said, "I have a problem. I need your help to fix it."

"A problem?" Bill inquired. "What kind of problem?"

Jasper turned his head to look straight out at the *Satisfaction* floating at rest. Without turning around, he stated ominously, "A very large problem."

Since Bill had a direct view of the ship from his desk, he could see the large problem Jasper referenced.

"You ever thought about retiring?" Jasper asked, still keeping his back to Bill. "You and Mary have owned this place for such a long time. You've worked so hard. Isn't it time you sat back and enjoyed your golden years right here in paradise? You might even travel a bit."

Bill smelled a rat. While he tolerated Jasper, the two would never be friends. Jasper had a reputation for being shrewd. He never let friendship get in the way of business, so why all of a sudden did he feel the need to start looking out for Bill and Mary? *What did the sly man have up his sleeve?* Bill decided to find out.

"We enjoy it. Wake up every day, and it's sunny, folks are nice, and we make a good living— "

Jasper cut him off. "It is demanding work, and as one ages, it will get harder. I know, being a marina owner myself." Jasper kept his hands behind his back while talking.

To Bill, it seemed as if he wanted to put those hands elsewhere. Like in Bill's pockets.

"Jasper, you know what they say, If you love what you do, you never work a day in your life. But you didn't come here to make small talk, so get to the point."

Bill got to his feet just as Jasper turned. He noticed Jasper's pensive look, as if calculating the right words to say. The rat smell now more pungent than ever, and Bill guessed what might be coming next but wanted to hear the words directly from the rodent's mouth.

"If you ..." Jasper began, "and Mary ever consider selling this marina...?"

There it is, Bill grinned. He kept listening, without interrupting. Preferring to hear the entire proposition, he sat down at his desk again and folded his arms.

"If you were so inclined," Jasper continued. "Would you consider letting me have first shot at the purchase?"

Bill knew Jasper as a good negotiator. He had run-ins with him over the years and also witnessed some greedy tactics the old man had used against others.

Now moving cautiously, Jasper had released a *trial balloon*; a test sentence to see if Bill had interest in selling the marina. Bill recognized the use of words like *if* and *consider*. Words soft enough to make sure he did not get upset and throw Jasper's ass out the door. Instead of getting angry, Bill felt mildly amused. *What is his end game? Listen some more, and you'll find out*, he told himself, then offered, "You want a cup of coffee so we can discuss this?"

Jasper smiled coyly. "That would be nice. We haven't spent any time together in a long while."

Bill strolled over to the storage closet, pulled out a folding chair and handed it to Jasper, then poured two cups of coffee and sat back in his own chair. He handed one to Jasper now sitting in front of the desk. Bill sipped his coffee and said, "So, Jasper, tell me why on earth would you want to buy my little old marina when you have a big shiny one of your own?"

Bill settled back in his chair with the knowledge he could tolerate the rat smell for a little while longer.

There comes a time in a girl's life when she needs to be independent. Take control of her own destiny. You have to know the time is now, right? Daddy can take care of you just so long before he begins to falter, take a back seat, fade in the background. He's starting to show signs of that now, isn't he? Once he was on top of his game, but lately, things have not been going his way, have they? This Chase Porter business has gotten out of hand, and Daddy let it happen. Now, you have two choices: you can sit back and watch him ruin the business or step up and claim what is rightfully yours. You can fix this problem and build the enterprise to even loftier heights. Key West is the right launching pad but you have bigger plans. Sure, you do. There comes a time in a girl's life and that time is now.

"I know, I know. You're absolutely right." Ginger listened to the voice because it had a harder edge, one driven, prone to take risks—even more, one that sought excitement. She found the ideas exhilarating and hard to resist. Never cautious nor cynical in a way that would stop her from trying some new idea or adventure. Especially now with everything at stake.

Ginger had never experienced failure nor hardship. All she had ever known was success. But now it was all being threatened. The voice of reason, of success, made Ginger want to ... *need to...* listen. No more would she listen to the other weak voice she used to follow that came across uninspired. The perfect word to describe *that* voice would be *Insipid.*

"The time is now," she said aloud to the voice she now referred to as *Proxy.* That voice showed authority and seemed to represent her best interests. The name was also cute.

Ginger needed no further convincing as she pored over the financials. The numbers proved it. Although the marina demonstrated a decent level of profitability, there were always additional ways to cut expenses while raising dock or other fees, throwing more cash to the bottom line. The trolley business would need an overhaul as well. The capital expense of buying new equipment could be put off for a few more years. She felt the B&Bs needed better fiscal management. Closer oversight of the managers could help with expenses. Perhaps firing a few maids would force those managers to actually work by assisting in the daily maid duties?

See? said Proxy. *You have what it takes to turn this ship around. Then you can set your sights on the larger ocean of business that's out there. Why your father doesn't see this is beyond me. Perhaps it's because he's unfocused, playing footsies with the whole Chase Porter business and letting the other pieces of the enterprise take a backseat?*

"Hmmm, an interesting viewpoint. One that needs careful consideration. Our company was built on many moving parts, and when you focus solely on one, the others falter for lack of attention." Ginger walked to the kitchen to pour herself a cup of coffee.

In your father's defense, began the other voice, Insipid. *He is trying to solve the nasty Porter business by himself—*

OH, PLEASE STOP! Proxy interrupted. *Everything that old man has tried has failed and now his latest plan to buy the Conch will fail as well. You ARE aware of this, aren't you?*

It m-might work. He's there making an overture to Hemmings as we speak, Insipid squeaked.

Overture? Who even uses a word like that? We need no more overtures. What is required is action. A bold plan to end the fiasco so we can move on to bigger and better things! Your future is at stake!

"Enough!" Ginger shouted, sick of listening to the two of them squabble. Proxy was right of course; the time had come for Ginger to step up. To stand on her own.

"I have a plan to implement today." Ginger looked out the window over the sink as she put her empty cup there without rinsing it. "It looks like a perfect day to go for a sail."

It may have looked calm outside, but Ginger felt the need to stir up some major waves and with Insipid's voice silenced, Proxy showed elation. *Indeed. Finish the Porter problem, then we'll deal with dear old daddy.*

The sun shone brightly against the clear emerald waters for the *Satisfaction*'s morning run. A southwesterly breeze pushed the craft to six knots, a leisurely pace for Crunchy to teach one of the Garrity brothers the nuances of maneuvering the nine hundred ton vessel. On board, a full complement of lubbers happily sailed along.

Up on the quarterdeck, Captain Rio began his tale of Woodes Rogers: "Have you ever been told of a pirate *paid* to plunder? There's a term for a certain kind of pirate who, under protection from his own government, would be tasked with raiding merchant ships from other countries. They went by the term *Privateers*, yet make no mistake, no matter what name they answered to … they were *all* pirates. Woodes Rogers was such a man."

Rio watched the crowd. He had already caught the eye of a pretty blonde female who looked to be in her late twenties, maybe thirty?

Dressed in a white blouse and a pair of tan pants that showed off her trim figure. A cane sun hat shaded her face while she sported a pair of expensive looking sunglasses, both giving her an air of mystery.

She lifted her glasses above her eyes careful not to push the hat out of position, and winked at him, then returned the sunglasses to the bridge of her nose. Rio noticed. *Is she flirting with me?*

He also noticed something familiar, beautiful, yet familiar. He began to think he knew her … but from where? Maybe if she took off the hat?

The flirting continued throughout the course of his act, too many times to be a coincidence. Rio, accustomed to women flirting with him, picked up the signs easily. He did not readily seek out tourists because one never knew if a husband, boyfriend, or partner would suddenly appear on deck. Today the risk might be worth it because the lady in question intrigued him.

Staying in character, he continued his story. He would get into his *real* character once he finished the show so he could meet the blonde. "During his first term as Governor of the Bahamas, Rogers nearly bankrupted the colonies. Upon his return to England, he was sent to debtor's prison. The British Government gave him a second chance to govern the Bahamas and fared much better until his death in Nassau in 1732 where his motto remained in place until the island gained independence from Britain in 1973. It read: *Piracy Expelled, Commerce Restored.* I hope the irony isn't lost on you that it took a pirate to expel piracy and a debtor to restore commerce." The crowd clapped enthusiastically.

Rio enjoyed playing the captain regaling his captive audience with tales of piracy. His acting improved weekly thanks in part to the coaching he received from Chase and Daniel. He also learned to take practice seriously.

Rio also continued to enjoy the Key West nightlife. Not having to bartend at night coupled with the influx of more cash in his pocket had a surprisingly positive effect on his love life. He no longer dated waitresses and housemaids. It was not as if he no longer enjoyed their company or thought himself above their station in life. As his fortunes grew, so did the caliber of women who now sought *him* out. Women of means who came to Florida to spend the winter where they frequented better restaurants and shops and who lived in better neighborhoods. Female business owners also noticed the successful entrepreneur.

Rio spent less time at the seedier bars and more time at the Chamber of Commerce meetings, the Convention and Visitors bureau, even joining the local Rotary Club. Being an owner had its benefits for the business, but it also played a role in attracting a different caliber of romantic partner. One with looks *and* money.

He walked over to the starboard side of the main deck, where the flirting blonde looked out over the water. Lubbers patted him on the back as he strolled confidently by. As he got closer, a bell in his head tinkled in an attempt to warn him, but he dismissed it.

Sidling up to the female in the hat and sunglasses he commented, "Lovely, isn't it?" The bell tinkled again a little stronger. Once again, he ignored it.

The woman turned to him, her smile dazzling. "It sure is, Rio." Then added, "You did a superb job on the pirate story. How would you like to have dinner with me tonight? Afterward, perhaps you could tell me another?"

The bell in his head no longer tinkled but began to ring like a fire alarm as he realized who the flirting, beautiful blonde female was.

Ginger Cobb.

STORM CLOUDS GATHER

T HE RENTED HOUSE on Olivia Street had begun to close in on Rio. It had suited his purpose when he first arrived on the island, and he felt more at home than cramped sharing the space with the other three tenants. As of late, it felt as if the walls were shrinking. His roommates were now beginning to grate on him.

Rio decided the time to move had arrived. He earned good money. A partner in a successful tour company proved far more lucrative than standing behind the bar schlepping drinks for tips. Flush with cash, he discovered it was not prudent to bring the class of females he now dated back to his little hovel, especially with the roommates. It was akin to telling a prospective girlfriend he still lived with his mother.

One look at the house with the peeling paint and worn steps, any woman worth her salt would turn tail and run. No, the time had arrived for him to invest in a larger home, a place worthy of his success. Perhaps one with a lovely pool in the back for an evening swim.

Rio snapped out of his thoughts. He had a date to get ready for. An invitation to dinner with the beautiful and engaging Ginger

Cobb. On Sunset Key, no less. As he dressed in new jeans, a white shirt, and loafers without socks, he wondered what the others would think about his upcoming date with the competition.

Sure, Ginger was Jasper's daughter, and a competitor, but he and Chase were friends with other competitors, weren't they? Jasper had tried to buy their business and could act a little slimy, but it did not mean Ginger had to be that way, did it? She did not possess a bad reputation as far as he knew. Besides, was there not enough business to go around?

Rio decided, for the time being, it would be best to keep the dinner date between the two of them. He felt happy no one recognized her on the cruise, not that it would have made a difference.

He'd never shared any intimate details of his love life before with any of his partners, it was none of their business. Sure, they had seen him at the Berth with a date and had run into him around town with a few girls on his arm. But Rio was not one to kiss and tell, and he certainly did not plan to start now.

He left the house at 6:30 p.m. and walked from Olivia Street down to Pier B where Ginger would be waiting with her boat to take them to the island for dinner. Which was precisely why he needed better digs. A girl like Ginger, she had her own boat for crying out loud, would never come to spend the night at the simple, crowded Olivia Street house. He made a mental note to look for a realtor in the morning.

As Rio approached Pier B, he spotted the blue and white Sea Ray Sedan Bridge Ginger had described. The name *Ginger Snap* stenciled in cursive letters on the stern proved it was hers.

He saw her waving from the helm, her blonde hair tied in a braided ponytail draped over her right shoulder. And as he approached, Rio realized *Ginger Snap* was no boat, but a yacht. Top of the line. He would definitely be calling a realtor in the a.m.

"Nice boat," he said with a bit of sarcasm, as he boarded.

She motioned for him to come up to the helm as a deckhand on the dock untied the ropes from the yacht's cleats, setting it free.

"Ginger Snap?" he asked with a suspicious eyebrow raised. "As in the cookie? Or, how you treat your men?"

She laughed it off with a casual, "You'll find out."

Rio watched her push down slowly on the throttle, paying close attention while taking the Sea Ray from its berth. Once free from the pier he said, "So, you're a woman of many talents. You run a company, take tours, invite guys to dinner, and even pilot your own yacht. Amazing."

"There is no end to the things you may learn about me," Ginger said, as she steered the Sea Ray into open water. "Let's start with a little trip around Sunset Key and Wisteria, shall we?"

Rio appreciated her confidence but paused. The bell was back, still sending out alarms, albeit not as loud. Plus, he began to see with all her beauty, talents and wealth, the woman might be out of his league. Way out.

"Ready?" she asked, flipping her ponytail to the other shoulder.

He shook his head and swept away those negative thoughts. Sailing across the water on a pleasant, cloudless evening with a beautiful woman who invited him to spend the evening with her … what's not to enjoy? *Besides, we're only having dinner.*

Sunset Key lay approximately five hundred yards off the coast of Key West. The island had both private residential and commercial resort property accessible only by boat. They tied up and walked down the dock, their fingers touching every so often as if not ready to commit to clasp together. He noticed she had arranged a candlelit dinner on the beach at a cottage her family owned and rented to a higher-paying clientele than the local B&Bs.

They sat across from each other at a white linen-covered table while they dined on salmon. "I'm so glad you said yes to dinner, Rio." Ginger sipped the wine she had brought over from her collection. "Isn't this nice?"

Rio wasn't sure if she meant sitting out by the beach or the wine. No way in hell he would be able to tell the difference between a Riesling or a Chardonnay but at this moment, he couldn't care less. Even though they spent only a little over an hour together, he had enjoyed himself more than he had in a long time.

Despite the warnings, he decided to ignore the bell ringing. The warning bell had served him well in the past during his wild bachelor days. It warned him of *Clingers, Gold Diggers*, and *Crazies*. Females he should avoid.

But this girl … woman, was different. She was perfect. Perhaps *too* perfect. *Maybe that's what bell's trying to tell you, dummy.* The bell ringing returned, a soft tinkle, then dissipated once more as Ginger urged Rio back from his thoughts. "Rio? Are you ok? I asked you a question, and you zoned out on me."

"Oh, yea, this is great. Sorry, I got caught up in the moment. A beautiful evening with a beautiful woman. Thank you so much for inviting me out here."

"It's my pleasure," purred Ginger as she put her warm hand on his thigh. She pointed to Rio's glass. "That's a 2008 Littorai Thieriot Vineyard Chardonnay from the Sonoma Valley. Have you ever been to California Wine country?" Rio tipped his glass, finishing the last drops.

"No. But I would love to go there. Are you making an offer?"

Ginger looked out at the ocean. "Wine country will have to wait." Storm clouds loomed on the horizon. "We should go inside where it's a little cozier before we get drenched."

As if to acknowledge her claim, a flash of lightning in the distance showed itself and they both looked at its direction. They were rewarded with a thunderclap, and as Ginger flinched, Rio pointed to the Chardonnay. "Let's go, I'm guessing you have another one of these bottles inside?"

"I've got more than that," she said with a telling wink.

It began sprinkling as they ran through the sand to the cottage. Once inside, they listened to the thunder inching its way closer. Rio leaned in and kissed Ginger, and she returned his kiss, but then hesitated.

"Rio, we might be moving a bit too quickly," she said pulling away, but not far enough for him to release her.

"Oh, we're moving at just the right speed," he countered, pulling her towards him and kissing her again, the bell no longer audible.

Ginger returned his kiss, her mouth pressing even harder against his. They stumbled into the bedroom, stripping away their clothes. As they fell onto the bed, the lightning illuminated the room with increasing frequency. Rain hammered the thatched cottage roof until the sound was drowned out by a thunderclap. As the storm passed, one last flash of light shone in the distance followed by a long thunderous exclamation point announcing its departure.

"He did *what?*" Chase asked from behind the desk in his captain's quarters. Bill Hemmings sat across from him, relaying the details of how Jasper Cobb had offered to buy the Conch Harbor Marina.

"And you turned him down, right?" Anne asked nervously.

"Well, he did make a fair offer," Bill teased.

She shook her head, not taking the bait. "Mary would have your hide if you ever sold to that snake oil salesman."

"Yea, when he left, I had to go into the bathroom and wash my hands. Twice!"

Chase took it all in. "Did he say *why* he wanted the Conch? He already has a marina."

Bill nodded. "Said he wanted to add it to his portfolio of assets. He and his kind are just a portfolio of asses if you ask me."

"So, what did you tell him? I mean, did you give him an answer?" Chase looked eager to figure this out, thinking how Jasper as a landlord would turn out to be nothing but trouble.

"Nope. Told him to come up with a better number, and we'd talk more. I want to find out what that rascal is up to. I also told him I had to talk with Mary, our attorney, my family priest. Hell, there's a list of people I should talk with just to stall him for months till we do find out."

"Save your breath," King said, stepping into the captain's quarters. Everyone turned to look at the large, bearded man. "He means to kick us out."

"And how do you know that?" asked Anne.

"In bars, people talk." King explained. "A lot."

"If the rat thinks he'll get my marina now, he's got another thing coming," Bill said, his agitation rising.

Chase listened closely as King explained his theory on Jasper's motives. King found out about Jasper's first marina purchase and what he had done to a few tour operators by listening to disgruntled tenants who frequented the Berth. Raising the price of slip fees and lack of room at closer marinas effectively eliminated competition. It made sense … if he bought the Conch Harbor Marina, he could use the same ploy to oust Chase and company. They would have nowhere else to go because Jasper would then own the only two marinas in town big enough to accommodate a ship the size of the *Satisfaction*.

Anne spoke up to calm the still agitated Bill. "The best way to defeat a man like Jasper, is to beat him at his own game and I have an idea how to do it."

Chase looked at his girlfriend with pride as Anne shared the details of her plan.

The CMPT company would lease the property from Bill and Mary. The slip and rental fees they now paid would be eliminated and added to the lease payment. They would use the rest of the profits to pay off the bank note of the *Satisfaction*. The company was close to retiring the boats previous owner's debt, freeing up more money. Once the banknote was retired, they would use the ship as collateral and borrow the needed funds to pay for the marina buyout.

"As the Company moved to better financial footing, we'll double up the bank loan payments and retire the debt earlier than the agreed-upon-terms. Bill and Mary would live on the marina property rent-free for as long as they desired, ensuring them a secure and well deserved retirement."

She shared how her plan even offered Bill the chance to work on the docks or on board at the prevailing rate if he chose. Once the marina was paid off, they could think about a second ship.

King responded in admiration with his customary "Shit fire!"

They all knew the plan was sound, and once Jasper found out, *when* he found out, which one of them would *not* want to be a fly with a front-row seat on Jasper's wall?

So, this happened to be Anne's five-year plan, thought Chase.

"The two parties need to get their respective attorneys to draw up the paperwork later in the week, but we still need to discuss one more item to protect the property from Jasper. Because Bill and Mary have no children," Anne explained. "We need you to amend your will to include the CMPT as the marina's sole beneficiary should anything befall Bill during the lease period." The buyers would not want the marina to be passed on to the state of Florida.

Anne added, "It would be prudent if the CMPT inherited the marina while protecting Mary from those estate taxes by having the company cover them."

Anne finished laying out the plan. "Bill, the first thing you need to do tomorrow morning is to see your attorney and amend your will. Are you sure Mary will be okay with the plan?"

"She will. You kids are like family to us. As long as you promise to take care of her if something happens to me, everything will go as planned. What's next?"

"Here comes the hard part. You have to go tell Jasper you'll never sell to him. Ever!" Anne stood waiting for his answer.

"Hard part?" Bill exclaimed with a wide grin. "That'll be the highlight of my year!"

They watched as a whistling Bill Hemmings walked down the plank on his way home, the air fresh from its cleansing by the recent storm. He had a bounce in his step they had not seen in years marveling at his exuberance.

"Man, I cannot tell what he's happier about; the marina plan or the upcoming conversation with Jasper Cobb?" Chase mused aloud.

"Both," stated King. "Both."

Bill Hemmings got Jasper's voicemail but hung up before leaving a message. Although late, he had hoped to reach Jasper before he retired for the night. Bill wanted to give Cobb something to lose sleep over. He knew he should follow Anne's advice on changing the will before telling the bad news to the rat, but he could not help himself. He felt too giddy to sleep. He just wanted to hear the vermin's voice after telling him he would never get his marina. Unfortunately, Jasper did not answer. Probably for the best.

While Bill wanted to tell him the whole plan, he did not want to break his word to Anne. Besides, tomorrow he could walk in and tell Jasper face to face and watch as he squirmed. Bill planned to come out of his attorney's office and head straight to Francis Street, where he would walk right into Jasper's office, and sit down.

"Maybe, I'll even ask for a drink first," Bill said aloud, giggling like a small child surrounded by presents at Christmastime.

If anyone deserved a bit of karma, it sure was Jasper. The man had weaseled, connived, and downright hoodwinked his way through the last thirty years, leaving a path of broken livelihoods in his wake.

Mary called down to her husband. "Bill? You coming to bed?"

"Yes, dear. On my way." Bill headed for the stairs to the apartment over the office, where they had lived for most of their married life. It would now be their home forever thanks to Chase and Anne. He felt it high time Jasper Cobb got a little taste of his own medicine and Bill had just what the doctor ordered. *I get to deliver a small dose of poison to my favorite rat tomorrow,* smiling as he ascended the stairs to bed. He'd finally had enough of the stench.

BEST LAID PLANS

"**Y**OU DID *WHAT*?" asked Chase incredulously, staring at his best friend.

"I had dinner with Ginger Cobb the other night."

Chase had asked Rio to stop by the *Satisfaction* early before the morning run to bring him up to speed on the marina lease-to-buy plan. Rio's news was the last thing Chase expected.

"She's smart, sophisticated, and charming… and did I say gorgeous?" Rio said as he tried to defend his actions.

"I don't believe it!" Chase buried his head in his hands. He had been sitting at his desk going over the numbers on the marina's acquisition for the lawyers but was now so distracted he did not think he could finish.

"Chase, I've been around a lot of women, but this is different. She makes me feel special, important, loved."

Chase looked up. "After only one date? Let me try to help you describe it. How about foolish, manipulated and used. Any of them fit? If not, get ready because I guarantee that's what you'll be feeling sooner or later. She's bad news!"

"You're wrong, Chase. She *is* different. I'm seeing her again tonight. And any other night or day I choose. You'll see I'm right."

"Rio, listen to me," Chase pleaded. "You've heard the saying; *The apple doesn't fall far from the tree?*"

"Yea, everyone has. But I bit into said apple, and I like the way the fruit tastes."

"Jeez, tell me you didn't sleep with her?" Chase knew the kind of woman Cobb's daughter was and it was not her way to treat men as if they were special or important unless she wanted something special and important *from* them. Once Ginger got her hooks into Rio, she would do everything possible to take him for a ride. Far, far away, drop him off, then leave him without a way back. And then Chase and company would be stuck dealing with the aftermath.

"Well, duh!" Rio said with a defiant tone.

Chase reached for his UnReale. "Ok, then at least do me a favor. When she starts asking about our business, because she will show a lot of interest in it, please clam up. If she's insistent or gets angry because you won't give her information, then it's a big red flag she's only using you. Got it?"

If Rio was going into the cage with a lion named Ginger, Chase wanted his friend and partner to be forearmed and forewarned with a whip and chair… or a bazooka. "And please, my friend, do not sign anything without talking to me first, OK? This isn't a fairy tale."

"Sure, it is, just like in the movies, happy ending and all," Rio said, always the optimist.

"Rio, this is *not* a fairy tale." Anne interrupted their conversation as she walked into the captain's quarters. "There will be no happy ending, believe me." Anne stood with hands on hips, a frown deepening. "This is a bad idea. A really bad idea."

"And why can't I have my happy ending?" Rio asked, scratching his chin.

Anne, never one to mince words, replied, "Because you're sleeping with the enemy."

"I don't believe it," said Jasper, feeling like he just got punched.

"It's true. I took him to the cottage on Sunset Key, and we had a nice dinner. I'm biding my time before I try to get some intel out of him. Fear not, I have my ways of getting what I want. And I *always* get what I want."

Sitting at his desk, Cobb fidgeted. He didn't doubt Ginger knew how to get what she wanted. His daughter was getting bolder by the day … and more calculating. "Does your plan include sleeping with the pony-tailed playboy?" Rio had a reputation in town, and Jasper did not like this development one bit. Jasper may have been unscrupulous in business, but when it came to sexual mores, he leaned conservatively to the right. Especially when it came to his only daughter.

"Already did."

"You already did …what?"

"Father, relax, will you? I'm not a teenager. It's all part of the plan. If I can get intel, it's a plus. If I can get him to marry me, I can control his part of the company. Then take it away from him and dump his ass. Brilliant, eh?"

"*Marry him?* I don't like this plan at all, in fact, I forbid you to go forward with this," Jasper said. He was now shaking.

Ginger walked over to her father, her eyes softening. She clasped his hands in hers before answering. "Look, I can take care of myself. If your plan to buy the Conch Harbor falls through, we're going to need a backup plan. This is mine. So, you focus on buying the marina, I'll focus on getting my man, and together we'll get what we want. We're a team, right?" When Jasper held back a response, she added, "Teammates don't use the word *forbid*, do they?"

Jasper cringed hearing her use the phrase *my man*. He missed his daughter of years past, now no longer the sunny little girl who would run into his office and show him a high grade always trying so hard to impress him.

"You couldn't have aimed for Porter instead? He's the brains of the operation."

"I could have, but he's stronger than Rio. I can't manipulate Porter. Rio has no entanglements to dispose of. Chase does, and Anne Braun is one tough cookie I want no part of." She ran her fingers through her hair before explaining. "My strategy is to divide and conquer. The divide part occurred the other night."

Jasper cringed again at the reference. Even though he did not care for her methods, she exhibited a firm commitment to both him and their business. He made a mental note to listen to her ideas more carefully and to take stock in the fact she was not just his daughter, but his business partner as well.

The old saying, one should not mix business with family popped into his head, but he dismissed it. It might be sage advice to others, but Jasper thought it best to have Ginger in his corner and not as an adversary. He would just have to trust her with this new Rio development.

"All right, I may not like the means, but it might justify the end result. Be careful, will you?"

"Yes, Dad ... I mean, *partner*." Ginger kissed her father on the cheek before heading out of his office. She did not get far when Jasper heard her greeting Bill Hemmings at the front door.

"Is Jasper in? Got something to tell him and thought it best to do it in person."

Jasper leaned back in his chair as Ginger led Bill into his office. Bill sat in front of Jasper's desk. Ginger leaned against the back wall.

"I'll get right to the point. Just want to tell you man-to-man under no circumstance will you ever get your hooks into the Conch Harbor Marina."

Jasper stared at Hemmings in disbelief. He was sure they could have come to a mutually beneficial agreement. He placed both hands on the desk to steady himself, unused to receiving so much bad news at one time. *First Ginger and now Hemmings?*

"Let's be reasonable," Jasper began, the tension causing a slight twinge in his left temple.

"Too late," Bill gloated. "The lawyers are drawing up the agreement as we speak. It's a done deal."

"A done deal?" Jasper slumped back in his chair. "Won't you reconsider, Bill? I can make it well worth your while. *My* deal would allow you a very pleasant retirement." He hated pleading with Hemmings. It was beneath him.

"No need. This plan will be more than worth my while and ...."

Jasper frowned at the news and tuned out Bill's voice, letting him drone on about lease payments, getting to live there and a succession plan. Jasper surmised the line for succession went through Chase Porter and Company. Soon they would be competing on two fronts, which Jasper found intolerable. He looked over at Ginger and saw her listening intently to Bill's rambling, his smugness filling the room like a dirty smoke from a burning house and choking the life out of anyone left inside.

Ginger didn't appear to be fazed one bit. Instead, she looked happy.

She must be thinking the same thing about Chase and company being Hemmings succession plan and if that's the case... Jasper contemplated the idea, getting ready to kick the horse's ass, Hemmings out of his office... *maybe her plan just might work.*

"I'm starting to get a bit concerned about Rio," Chase said, tracing the cross on his UnReale.

"Starting?" Anne commented, a look of exasperation crossing her face. "Starting? It's like saying I'm starting to think we have to sail tomorrow. Of course, you should be concerned. He's dating the enemy!"

Chase shook his head. "If Ginger believes she can weasel her way into our business, she's sadly mistaken." Even though Chase made it clear to Rio not to engage in any business conversations with her, he knew when a man fell in love, all common sense flew out the window.

"Have you seen them in public? They're like two high-school teenagers in love for the first time." Exasperation turned to disgust as Anne stood up from her chair and headed to the desk where Chase sat. "It's sickening to watch. We're all aware of what she's doing except Rio. I just hope he comes to his senses soon before he does something we may all regret."

Chase shifted his attention away from Anne and towards his desk, poring over maps around the Dry Tortugas while wondering about the missing sterncastle. "Where are you?" he asked softly as he fondled the UnReale.

"I'm right here talking to you, but you aren't doing any listening."

"I'm sorry. Sometimes I focus on a topic a little too laser-like and shut off everything else around me. Bad habit. My apologies." Chase put an arm around Anne's waist and pulled her to him until she plopped onto his lap.

"What's with these maps?" she said, pointing to the desk.

"Nothing to worry about. Just looking to see where to find more treasure near the debris field site. Finding something substantial would take a little pressure off our financial picture with the marina purchase."

"Instead of those maps, how about giving *me* some laser-like focus, my captain?" One corner of her mouth upturned as her exasperation began melting away.

"Sure, but I don't want to be accused of being sickening like Rio and Ginger."

"Not a chance, we're not out in public, so sicken away!"

Chase pushed the maps away from his desk scattering them across the floor. Anne showed her wicked little smile, the one he absolutely adored which told him they were both on the same page.

"Focus away," she whispered, laying back on the desk, taking him into her arms.

"Gather round, ye lubbers, so I can share a tale about one of the greatest pirates you may have never heard about." Captain Rio greeted the lubbers who had assembled to hear a new tale.

"If you were a betting lubber, would you wager your gold on which pirate captured more ships in his lifetime? Would you guess Blackbeard? Charles Vane? Captain Kidd? If you wagered on any of those three, you'd have lost your treasure. The answer lies with only one pirate known as... Black Bart."

Chase noticed Rio showing off to his blonde girlfriend as he told the story. Rio had invited Ginger to come along as his guest, and unfortunately, she agreed. A decision no one in the inner circle was happy about. To keep peace, Chase had urged the team to stay friendly and keep their mouths shut. "Eyes, on the other hand," he pointed to his own, "should remain wide open."

Rio went on, "Bartholomew Roberts, a Welsh pirate who raided shipping lanes off the Americas and West Africa between 1719 and 1722, was arguably the most successful pirate of the Golden Age, capturing far more ships than any of the best-known pirates of his era. An estimated four hundred and seventy ships were taken by Black Bart."

As the story continued, King came up from below and motioned to Chase with a look of concern on his face. "We've got a problem." He shook his head. "Water coming in."

Not wanting to alarm the lubbers, Chase casually went below deck to check out the problem. "Shit fire!" King said as he bumped his head at the base of the stairs.

Chase ducked to avoid a similar fate then followed King to the port side hull. He noticed a stream of water squirting through the planks. "It doesn't look too bad now, but it could break and then we'd be in real trouble. Do we have anything to patch it?" King shrugged.

"Shit fire." Chase said softly, mimicking his partners catch phrase.

"What's the plan, Cap'n?" asked King.

Chase scratched his stubble, unsure of how much time they had. The last thing they needed was for the small leak to burst into a gusher. They needed to act quickly. "I know someone who might have an idea." Chase spun around, careful not to bang his head, and went up the ladder. On deck, he casually walked over to the ship's helm to discuss the situation with Crunchy. "We have a slight problem down below and need a solution," whispered Chase. "Any suggestions?"

Crunchy looked dour as he explained. "The sails are half full, and we're cruising at eight knots. No need for the diesel engine to be running now. But if saltwater gets into the engine housing, we'll be dead in the water trying to bring her into berth."

"Can you get us home quickly?" Chase asked. "I'll reach out to the Coast Guard and let them know of our situation."

"I'll turn the ship around and head her back to port. I believe I can bank her on her starboard side to slow the rush of water over the opening. In the meantime, do we have any wooden planks aboard?"

"Don't know, but I'll look. Why?"

"If you can find something to cover the leak, it could give us enough time to get back to port and unload. And you might want to get something soft to slide against the leak before you cover it with the plank. It'll act as a seal."

"Like what?" asked Chase.

"Man, you're the captain, you figure it out. I've got my hands full turning this ship!"

Chase smirked as he headed below deck to get started on the repairs using Crunchy's idea, sending King in search of any items to plug the leak. He then headed to his quarters to alert the Coast Guard.

As Rio neared the end of his talk, Chase joined him on the quarterdeck and announced, "Mateys, you're in for a real treat! Our Sailing Master, Crunchy, will show us how to pick up speed and avoid capture from hostile forces like the British Royal Navy." He waited for all to turn and spit before continuing, "Grab the railing or anything you can and hold on tight!"

He signaled Crunchy to turn the ship. The Garrity brothers waited for instructions and Crunchy delivered quickly. "Unfurl the main sails!" he shouted, and the boys clamored above the decks. The sails began snapping outward as they filled with wind, forcing the *Satisfaction* to list to her starboard side.

Lubbers screamed in either delight or fear as the mighty ship came about and headed back towards Key West.

King poked his head out of the entrance and nodded to Chase who made his way over. "Leak is covered. Hope it holds."

They sailed until the island came into view. A Coast Guard Cutter appeared, escorting them just in case. Crunchy gave the orders to pull up sails and start the diesel engine in order to bring the ship back into the harbor.

Upon hearing the engine come to life, King poked his head out again giving Chase and Crunchy the OK sign signifying the crisis had been averted.

"What did you use to cover the leak?" asked Crunchy.

"We stuffed it with a raincoat we found in your bunk," offered Chase, a sheepish grin on his face. "You told me to figure it out. Consider it figured." Crunchy only frowned and looked away to concentrate on the task at hand.

Chase looked out at the sea behind them, then down the deck filled with lubbers, wanting to make sure they were all safe and they were buying the story. Some lubbers continued to hold onto railings to steady themselves, even as the ship righted itself. One person, in particular, still held onto Rio.

In all the excitement, Chase had forgotten about Ginger being on board. She stared straight at him, ignoring Rio's ramblings. A smug expression frozen to her face. After a few moments of intense eye contact, she lifted her right hand and waved. Her fingers moving up and down as if playing the keys on a piano. *She's up to something,* Chase sensed. *Does she know what's going on?* Chase shuddered at the thought looking back at Ginger still waving ... and still smug.

NEWS TRAVELS FAST, BAD NEWS FASTER STILL

THE *SATISFACTION* SAT in dry dock ready for the hull to be copper plated in order to seal leaks from the outside. The process would also allow the ship to go faster by killing marine organisms which worked to attach themselves to the hull. CMPT gave the public the last part as the reason why the company had to cancel upcoming reservations for the repairs.

The interior of the hull was treated with a thick rubber coating to act as a secondary defense against leaks. "We cannot have any more leaks on board." Chase warned.

"Or off board, either." King chimed in and Chase shook his head to agree.

They crafted the cover story and sold it to the press and on their website. The crew hoped their customers would understand this as an unavoidable business interruption and reschedule the next time in town. Having to explain a leak in the ship was something none of them wanted. So, having the vessel out of commission for a brief period proved to be a much better option than having it in the water with no customers. The work would be financed in part by business interruption insurance, something Anne had the foresight to purchase, but the amount was not enough to cover the whole job. The company had to use what savings they had to pay for the repairs upfront, which left their finances in a tenuous position.

"What's left in the account?" Chase asked Anne, not sure he wanted to hear.

"Not much. Still, I'm expecting a sponsorship check shortly, and sales from the store are still brisk. By the way, your father called me."

"Is he okay?" Chase asked quickly, concern in his voice.

"Yes, he's okay. Daniel asked if he could help. We brainstormed and came up with a plan. He's coming down to do tours of the ship. Says he's done a lot of research and has some great tales to share. It won't bring in a lot of money, but it's something to keep customer enthusiasm and we'll take prepaid reservations."

"Why didn't Dad call me?"

"Because," she explained, "I have better ideas. Would you have come up with this one?"

Chase shook his head while he stifled a little laugh, knowing his girlfriend was right.

"And don't worry about the finances. Got 'em under control," she said confidently.

"We'll get some money back when the insurance company sends us the check. We'll make the rest up once we're seaworthy again."

She is so on top of stuff, Chase marveled. *How would I ever get along without her?*

He hoped he would never have to.

Ginger waited patiently for her father to end his call, the white light on her office phone indicated his preoccupation. Excited to show him her plan, she tapped her finger on her desk in nervous anticipation. When the light went off, she grabbed the laptop off her desk and walked the short distance down the hall to his office.

At his desk, Jasper sat with his left hand cradling his forehead while he wrote some notes with his right. He lifted his head as she entered the room. "I hope you have good news. I could use some right now."

Ginger sidled up to her father's desk. "Loose lips sink ships," she said, as she sat atop the corner of his desk. She placed the laptop on the desk and opened it.

"Ginger, please. I'm swamped, I don't have time for idle conversation. Please either tell me what's on your mind or let me get back to work."

"You'll never guess where I came from?" she said, ignoring her father's snarky remark.

"I hope it's not from that ne'er do well's house. The last thing I need to hear about is your sordid love life."

Just tell him. He'll change his tune, egged on Proxy.

"I was with Rio but also doing research. My plans are now returning results. Don't you want to hear about them?" she asked, clearly relishing her success where her father had failed.

"Ginger," Jasper began, his voice starting to show more than just agitation. "Please, for the love of God …. SPIT IT OUT!"

Proxy sniped, *What an ass. He should show a little more respect.*

Ginger ignored her to tell her father, "The *Satisfaction* is out of commission now, right?"

"Yeah, they gotta make sure nothing sticks to the hull. Old News. Get to the point."

Nothing is more important than this. Go ahead, assert your authority, and tell him.

"How about some fresh news? There was another reason."

"Another reason?" he murmured while continuing to focus on his work.

Ginger slammed a palm onto his desk, and Jasper jerked his head up as if someone had pulled him by the hair.

"Another reason. Yes, they're plating the bottom of the ship, but not the reason it's in dry dock. The real reason might have sunk the last tour as well as the company."

"What?"

Now she had his full attention.

"It seems there was a little incident on board," Ginger started. "I was on the last tour and noticed King and Chase having a quiet conversation. I did some snooping and found out there was a leak in the hull."

Jasper just stared at her as she continued. "The interesting part was none of the tourists seemed to think it out of the ordinary. Chase and his crew did a masterful job of hiding the trouble. Had the leak been any larger or uncontainable, the life rafts would've been deployed."

Jasper, now fully engaged, asked, "So, they're deceiving everyone?"

When Ginger nodded, he put his hand up to scratch under his ear in thought. "Hmmm. Very interesting. The question is, how do we use this information to our advantage? I could leak it to the papers or other news outlets."

"My dear father," said Ginger, shaking her head. "The best way to get the news out isn't with the old media. You want the news *to go viral.*"

"You mean like a sickness?"

"Worse. A plague." She turned the laptop around and tapped a few keys, bringing up the CMPT website. "Let's go to the comments section and…start reading here." She pointed to the most recent comment.

Jasper read it aloud. "Something strange happened on the tour I recently took. It was going as planned when all of a sudden, the ship turned around and headed back to port. The operators announced the turnaround as a way to show how pirates avoided capture. Most everyone bought the story, but I saw the looks of concern on the crews' faces. Then, as we got closer to port, a coast guard cutter escorted us in. I suspect something happened on board they did not want us to know. And now, the ship is under repairs. Not sure I like being misled. Anyone else have the same idea?"

Jasper looked up at his daughter. "This was you?" She nodded and pointed to the screen. Jasper read more comments. Terms like *misled* turned into *lies* and finally *dangerous* spread throughout the thread. "You did all this?"

"Not all. I used a couple of different names for the first few on the thread and then let people come to their own conclusions. Like this comment." She pointed to the screen again. "I suggested by the way the ship turned, listed starboard, and sped back to harbor one might suspect a leak. I merely started the dialogue and let it spread like—"

"A plague," Jasper interrupted, and Ginger nodded in approval. "And the repercussions?"

Ginger chided her father. "Patience, Daddy. These things take time, but I foresee a drop in their reservations coming real soon."

"Can these comments be traced back to your laptop?" He asked, pointing to the device.

She shook her head. "Nope. Not mine."

Jasper got her message. "The tourists will have to go somewhere. How do we get them to come back to us?"

"I'm on it. I have our new website ready to go once we do one more thing. The headline will read, "The safest crafts on the ocean. No one cares more about your safety than we do."

"I'd like to see the faces of those bastards when this comes crashing down on them," Jasper said, studying the screen a bit longer. "Wait, what's the one more thing you mentioned?"

"We need to alert the authorities one of our competitors ships may be unsafe and ask for an inspection."

"Good. You do that. Now, I have to get back to work, but tell me how it goes." Looking up and seeing her still standing there he added, "Go on, shoo. I have a lot of work to do."

Ginger left her father's office feeling let down. Stress made him a little edgier than normal, but he could have at least acknowledged her smart tactics. Proxy added her two cents. *You'd think he could loosen those lips and congratulate you on a job well done? The ingrate.*

"Oh, he will soon enough," replied Ginger. She had other things to occupy her time, "Loose lips are not the only things to sink that ship."

Oh, do tell, urged Proxy. *Do tell.*

Chase and Anne had taken up housekeeping once again on *Brains and Brawn* while their ship underwent repairs. After breakfast, Anne had her laptop open and a look of concern came over her face. Chase noticed. "Anne, what's bothering you?"

"Chase, have you seen our website today?"

"No. You look like someone shot your dog."

"Some online complaints about our repair issues." Anne showed Chase the comment section. It wasn't pretty and getting uglier by the minute. "And we've already gotten some cancellations because of it. People are saying we deceived them."

"How the hell did this get out? I thought we contained it." Chase shook his head as he read the comments.

"Someone on board got suspicious. It didn't help we had the Coast Guard escort us into port. Maybe someone has a connection with them?"

"Could be. Right now, we need to get ahead of this. Got any ideas?"

"Yes, I do. We're going to need a little help. Get Rio and King to come over."

Chase appreciated the way Anne took over in a crisis. Most people caved when presented with a difficult situation. Anne was not most people. Her ability to identify a problem and get to work on it endeared her even more to him. Her bluntness could be misconstrued as aggressive or even bitchy by the uninformed, but Chase believed it to be a strength, not a character flaw.

"What are you waiting for? Call the guys," she commanded.

Chase reached for his cell phone. *I'm sure glad she's on my team.* He speed-dialed King who answered on the second ring.

"Yea," King said, in his typical gruff tone.

"We need you to meet us at the marina. Seems someone started a leak of their own online, and we have to strategize *damage control.*" Chase began to draft some notes while he spoke. "And bring Rio."

"Can't."

"Why not? Where is he?"

"Day off and he's with Ginger."

Ginger. Could she have something to do with this? She was on board, and that look she gave made me nervous, Chase ended the conversation with King and started a new one with his girlfriend. "Hey Anne, do you think you could pull some info for me?"

Anne looked at him. "Sure, like what?"

"The ship's tour list for the day we had the leak. I have a suspicion."

"Already on it. I'm printing it up as we speak. There are almost one hundred and fifty names. And you want to know if we can match any of those to the comments on our website?"

"Yeah. How did you know?'

"Because I knew of one person aboard before you asked me the question."

"Ginger Cobb," they said in unison.

Rio Grande was officially off the dating market. He was now seeing Ginger exclusively. No more staying out late looking for his next conquest. The conqueror had finally been conquered.

He had called a realtor, and they discussed what style of home he wanted. Because he wanted it to be a surprise, he had not mentioned it to Ginger. Other than the search for a house and their respective jobs, the two had become inseparable. She told him her history and showed him a side of the island held exclusively for the wealthy. He told her of his aspirations but had not shown her the seedier side of the island.

At first, she seemed interested in what he wanted to do with his life. He had never met someone so completely tuned in, which encouraged him. But then the questions began, innocently enough at first. "Where do you see yourself in five years?" or "Do you plan on staying on the island your whole life?" Eventually, the discussions drifted towards his workplace. A simple query about his workday would lead into questions about CMPT's expansion plans.

Rio took the advice Chase gave him and deflected as much as possible, using his trademark sense of humor to lighten the mood. "Let's not muck this up by mixing business with pleasure," he replied with a sly wink. "And speaking of mucking...."

The last time he'd tried this diversion, they'd had dinner at her place, and it worked as she lovingly slid her fingers down Rio's chin and purred. "Let's have less speaking, more mucking." Then she'd taken him by the hand and led him into her bedroom. He followed willingly, deciding he would have to find other smart quips to keep the diversion from business to the bedroom going.

Then he began to notice slight changes… and not for the better. After several weeks of dating, he started to see cracks in Ginger's sweet facade. At first, she made innocent suggestions. She took him clothes shopping saying, "We need to clean you up a bit." Which led to, "Why don't you cut your ponytail? You would look so good with a short haircut."

Over time the passive-aggressive behavior became less passive and more aggressive. Her suggestion about buying a marina and expanding his enterprise seemed blatant and pushy. He recognized the fishing for information ploy and deflected it with a joke. "Nah, I don't want to go *underwater* with that type of business."

This joke backfired, prompting their first real quarrel. "But you're already in the marina business, aren't you?" She cornered him with his lie.

He tried to explain, but she did not give him a chance. Clearly frustrated, she countered with a sneer and the comment, "You can't be a pirate your whole life, you know. You have to grow up sometime."

This was the first time she had shown her mean streak, the words cutting Rio deeply. Her questions about his business became more direct, and their lovemaking and her friendly nature grew scarce. Because he no longer wished to live the playboy life and believing he had found his soulmate, Rio wanted to settle down. At first, he passed her actions off as growing pains present in any healthy relationship.

This morning, for reasons he didn't understand, the growing was not feeling painful at all. That's odd, thought Rio as he and Ginger enjoyed breakfast on board the *Ginger Snap*. *She hasn't made one mention about business yet.*

The conversation aboard her yacht felt light and breezy, and she showed more affection than she had in a long time. They had made love the night before, and a second time in the shower before breakfast.

Her demeanor became playful and fun, and she seemed to reroute the conversation concerning business as if she knew the topic was off limits, not wanting to push him at all.

"What would you like to do today?" Ginger asked before she took a bite of her toast.

Rio tilted his head. "We could take a cruise. You know, get out of town for the day and head up north."

Ginger kissed his cheek. "Whatever your heart desires, my love." Rio took her hand in his. "It's my day off, and all I want is to spend it with you."

They decided to take the *Ginger Snap* out to sea where they did not have to deal with traffic and, as Ginger seductively said to Rio, "So, we can have … ahem, some privacy."

Rio smiled at the thought. Ginger had been so sexually aggressive of late. Rio just hoped he could keep up.

The reservation cancellations continued to pile up. Chase and Anne wracked their brains on how to triage. The head count on their future tours declined from sold out at full capacity to half. There were still customers who wanted to experience what the *Satisfaction* had to offer, but the word got out: *she wasn't a safe craft.*

"Damn, we need some good press. This is killing us!" Chase said, frustrated.

"Social media is rough these days. Anyone can start a lie and people eat it up as the truth and tag on even more," Anne replied.

"So, how do we stop the negative press and get it turned around in our favor?"

"We have to create our own dialogue to show we're safe operators."

King walked in, and immediately offered his advice. "Find the leak first. Then counteract it." He pulled out a business card and gave it to Anne. "Call him. Friend of mine."

Chase and Anne looked at King with curiosity. "What's he do?" Anne asked.

"Web stuff. Can find the source."

Anne put the base of her palm against her forehead and bumped twice. "And then discredit it. King, inside that rough exterior, you're pretty smart."

"Am I the only one who does not know what you're talking about?" Chase liked to think himself as one of the smartest guys in the room but didn't feel it now.

Anne explained. "Every computer has what's known as an IP address. When an email or file is sent, it can be traced back to the sending computer. Not all internet communication is anonymous."

"So, we can get the original comments and find the person who sent them?" Chase said, a hint of hope in his voice.

"We can't." King tapped the card in front of Anne. "He can."

"Is it legal?" Chase asked.

King shrugged his shoulders. "Legal? Who cares?"

"Is it expensive?" asked Anne, always concerned about the bottom line.

King shook his head. "Not for us," he explained. "Owes me a sizable bar tab."

"So," Anne surmised out loud, "We find the source, we can get them to stop and then change the narrative?"

Beginning to catch on, Chase nodded.

With the legality of the operation still in question and the price in their comfort range, Anne dialed the number hoping to choke off the negative press and stop the flow of red ink.

LOOSE LIPS

"THOUGHT I'D BRING you more good news. It's Friday and you know what that means?" Ginger said as she bounded into Jasper's office.

"Time for the bloodletting to commence?" Jasper asked cryptically.

"No, silly, not today." Ginger asked her father to open the email attachment of the weekly financial report sent just before walking to his office. Her wide smile and sparkling eyes gave away her excellent mood. Still, she decided to sit in the visitor chair rather than jumping up to sit on the corner of the desk.

Don't want to poke the bear, eh? commented Proxy.

"This *is* good news!" Jasper exclaimed enthusiastically. The trend in reservations continued to rise since Ginger's social media attack became viral. "If this keeps up, we'll return to last year's levels by midseason."

"Well, it took brains and a damaging storyline." Ginger fished for a pat on the back. She was the mastermind behind the plan and wanted him to acknowledge her, especially after Jasper's failed attempts. *She* brought the company back into the black, not him.

"In any event, we're back on track," Jasper said, not taking the bait. "Time's a wasting. Let's get back to work."

Ginger sat stunned.

Go ahead, ask him directly now. I told you he wouldn't give you any kudos, Proxy hissed.

When Ginger did not move, Proxy prodded. *C'mon. He's not going to offer up any congratulations. If anything, he'll probably step up to take the credit.*

Ginger would have none of it. Anger set in as the blood rushed to her face. She tried to control it by counting to ten and hoping in those seconds her father would not do anything stupid. She could live without the praise, having done so all of her life. But if he took credit for her best plan ever? She shuddered at the thought of what she might do.

"What is it, Ginger? You look like you're about to rip someone's head off."

Taking a deep breath, she got out of the chair, and turned towards the door.

He called out to her, "Hey! Excellent job, by the way."

Her anger vanished as quickly as it appeared. Ginger beamed again, feeling like the little girl so many years ago. She stopped hoping to revel in his praise a few minutes longer.

Jasper looked up and added, "On the spreadsheet."

Ginger's anger returned with a vengeance. She grabbed the back of the chair and pushed it to the ground, the loud bang echoing throughout his office.

"What the hell?" Jasper jumped up.

She did not answer as she stormed out of his office, slamming the door behind her.

Sad, so sad. Proxy sounded almost sympathetic.

Ginger's anger abated as she limped back to her office. Feelings of defeat slumped her shoulders and released a flood of sorry-for-herself tears she could no longer hold back.

The next few days were filled with activity from the *Satisfaction's* crew. Video of lubbers enjoying themselves onboard, an apology on the company website, and a local TV story airing on stations throughout the state all helped stem the tide of customer defections, causing the reservations to rise once again. The kicker had been an idea from Chase. He had hired a videographer to produce a short, but effective, clip from the boat inspector announcing the *Satisfaction* had passed all seaworthy tests.

The ship, thanks to the copper plating on the hull, could now fly faster across the water than before the leak. The crew did not have to use as many sails, and the diesel engine remained silent save for windless days or when they entered or exited port. Each new trip went according to plan with no fresh incidents to report.

Videotaping the captain's stories and the interaction of the lubbers became a new revenue stream as the videos were uploaded to thumb drives and sold at the retail store. This further enhanced the positive safety reputation as lubbers would take the video home to share with their friends and neighbors or post on social media.

The negative comments began to subside, replaced by positive ones from delighted customers. When negative feedback appeared, Anne responded with a quick message asking the commenter to call the office so they could rectify the problem. No complaint calls came her way.

As the reservations grew, so did the CMPT's coffers. They had weathered the storm and come out on the other end in much better shape. To celebrate, Chase booked a Sunday evening party at the Berth for his entire crew.

Chase and Anne wanted to have the celebration in honor of the people who made the company successful. The *employees only party* quickly filled to capacity. One bonus of restricting their party to employees only kept Rio's girlfriend out of the bar.

The restriction almost resulted in Rio's absence, but in the end, he showed up solo.

Chase climbed up on the bar and raised his hands to speak. "Folks, can I have your attention please?" As the noise subsided, he cleared his throat and continued. "I'd like to thank each and every one of you for your hard work these past two seasons aboard the *Satisfaction*. Without our fine crew members, we would not have a successful business." Lifting his glass, he yelled, "Can I get a *huzzah* to the crew?"

They all toasted in unison and gave a long and hearty *Huzzah* … everyone but King. He stood alone in the doorway between the bar and the backroom.

Amidst the celebration, Chase jumped off the bar and approached him. "What's the matter with you? You look as if they just took away your liquor license, hombre." When King did not react, Chase dropped the joviality. "What's wrong?"

King handed over a piece of paper to read. The letterhead showing the name on the card King had given to Anne.

Chase's eyes rolled quickly over the words. When he looked up, he found Anne observing him a few feet away. He attempted a weak smile but failed. She walked over, frowning in confusion. Chase handed over the letter. Looking up, she turned to the two men already scanning the crowd, posing the question on all of their minds. *Who's going to tell Rio?*

At the same moment, Rio popped out of the crowd and yelled across the room, "Hey Chase! Over here!"

Chase looked forlornly at Anne and King. Sighing, he mouthed, *Wish me luck.*

He wormed his way through the crowd until he stood next to his dear friend. The noise level rose to a high decibel range; too loud to conduct a delicate conversation. "Hey Bud," Chase yelled. "Need to talk. Outside for a sec?" He began to walk toward the door, and Rio followed. Once outside, Chase stalled. "How's it going?"

"Great! Excellent party."

It was apparent Rio could have fun with no sign of animosity given Ginger's exclusion. Chase squirmed. Even though the party would soon close down, he knew his friend's good time would come to a screeching halt.

"Look, there's something I need to tell you."

"Spit it out, partner. It can't be so bad on a night like tonight...." Rio's face dropped as his sentence trailed away. Seeing the pained expression on Chase, he asked, "What is it?"

"I'm just gonna tell you straight. We hired a guy to find out where the negative comments originated."

"Smart. Where?" Rio asked.

Chase looked down before continuing. "Yea, about that. The guy found an IP address and followed the trail of the first and then different comments to a single computer."

"So, what you're saying is all the negative comments came from the same person?"

"Yes and no, The first one, yes. Then there are other negative comments from different names coming from the same IP address as if the person tried to make it look as if there were even more customer-complaint comments. One person started it and then kept fanning the flames with many more comments under different names until it went viral."

"Great, so how do we catch the perp?"

"We know who it is," Chase said softly, lowering his head.

"Man, you are dragging this out. Tell me, who's the *bastard* trying to wreck our company?"

Chase spoke slowly so it would sink in. "No one thinks you're a bastard."

"Then let's get on th...Wait, what?" Rio looked flabbergasted.

"Rio, the comments came... from your laptop."

"No way!" he protested. "You don't think I'm responsible, do you? I would never do anything to hurt our company. Are you sure?"

"The guy we used is a pro. He ran a number of the negative comments, and several point back to your laptop."

"I *never* post comments. I don't even like social media. That's Anne's responsibility, not mine." Rio dropped his head as he spoke.

Chase observed his friend trying to think through the ramification of what he had just learned. Certainly, Chase did not want to tell Rio his suspicions. He didn't have to.

"Wait a second," Rio raised his head to look Chase in the eye. "You aren't blaming me. You think it's someone else using my laptop, don't you?"

Chase nodded slowly, not wanting to set off Rio with damaging accusations.

"Do the others have the same suspicion?" His deep voice asked through clenched teeth. Chase looked at him sadly without answering.

Rio got the message and glared at his friend. "You're all nuts," he stammered. "She may be the competition, but Ginger would never do that to us or to me!" Like a spooked horse, Rio reared up and stormed off.

"Wait!" Chase called after him. Rio's last response to Chase came in the form of an extended middle finger as he power-walked into the dark Florida night.

Ginger was in a foul mood, agitated about not being invited to the CMPT party going on right now down at the Berth. As

Rio's better half, or as Proxy might say two-thirds, Ginger had every right to be there. Even though the party was thrown for employees only. Rio should have stood up to his partners and insisted she be invited. Ginger did not appreciate snubs, especially from the likes of those Key West carpet baggers. Who did they think they were?

Another reason to be upset? While her plan first worked like a charm, now it was failing. Her competitors seemed to have come back from the dead and were now thriving, which angered her. What did she have to do to get rid of these people?

The question went unanswered as her cell phone rang. Rio. She wrestled with the decision to answer, in no mood to speak with anyone, especially him after he abandoned her.

Yeah … Let it go to voicemail, insisted Proxy. *He'll figure it out when you don't pick up for a day or two. Guys are so dumb.*

Ginger contemplated it all as she let Rio go to VM.

He'll try your office line next, predicted Proxy.

"Yea, but he won't get me there either," Ginger said aloud, smirking as she sat on the deck aboard the *Ginger Snap* moored on the other side of Wisteria Island. Rio, so predictable it wasn't even funny. And malleable. She could bat her eyelashes and lie right to his face, and he believed her. What a sucker.

But you like that sucker, don't you?

"Oh, please do shut up. I don't have time. Not when there is mayhem to conduct."

Ooh, not a denial.

"It is what it is," she countered.

Deflection is not denial either, pressed Proxy.

"Well, I've got to speak with him sometime." Ginger scowled, changing the subject. She knew Proxy had the right idea about stringing him along. Let him dangle awhile so he sees how much he hurt her. She had the urge to hurt someone herself. If she felt pain, why not spread it around so everyone would be miserable. She opened Rio's laptop and searched the CMPT website. "Time to leave another comment." She loved to hear the sound of her voice while being evil. "Spew more dissent."

Good girl, acknowledged Proxy. *Spew away.*

As Ginger typed, her cell phone rang again. She ignored it.

The day after the party, Ginger reluctantly met Rio for coffee. Aware he was scheduled to work the morning tour, Rio told her he had taken the day off. She sensed he was troubled about something and assumed it had to do with going to the party by himself.

Proxy could not stay silent. *Let's see how he likes being shunned, eh?*

"Morning babe." Rio greeted Ginger, bending down to kiss her on the lips. She only turned her cheek to him. "What's the matter?" he inquired.

"Nothing. I don't want to fight with you."

"About what? I didn't even see you yesterday. I called a few times, but you didn't call me back until this morning."

The waiter came to the table and took their order, briefly interrupting their conversation. Rio broke the cold silence. "Babe, there's something we need to discuss."

"Yes. There *is*," she barely whispered.

"No. I'm serious. We haven't spoken much about business recently, and we've been getting along so well. Something's come up, and I need to ask you a question."

Ginger gazed intently at Rio, hoping he would finally reveal insider details about his business. Evidently, he had another agenda.

"We've had some negative comments on our website. Comments meant to drive business away from our company."

Uh oh, warned Proxy. *Tread carefully.*

"What does that have to do with me?" she snapped back. "You and I aren't supposed to discuss business, REMEMBER?" She screeched out the last word.

Good. Stay on the offensive.

"Anyways, I um. I wanted to know…." He finally just blurted it out. "Have you seen my laptop? It's gone missing. I've looked everywhere for it." Rio winced as he finished the last sentence.

Time to divert. Deflect, deflect!

Ginger looked hard at Rio as she waited for the right way to start her defense. Proxy did it for her and gave her the words. *This is what you wanted to talk to me about? A stupid laptop?*

"A stupid laptop? This is what you wanted to talk to me about? When we have more important topics to discuss?"

Rio sat back and stared at her but said nothing as he nervously toyed with his ponytail.

Ginger spotted the surprise on his face. It spoke volumes.

It's working, keep going, Proxy prodded. *He doesn't know where you're gonna go next.*

Ginger did. "You get invited to a party and leave me all alone! Do you know how much you hurt me?"

"Honey, I explained already. No one brought their significant others."

"Anne got to go, didn't she?"

"C' mon, you know she's a partner."

"STILL! Chase got to have his girlfriend there, and you didn't. Doesn't it make you mad?" The anger in her voice continued to rise.

"No. I mean, yes. No one else brought a date. It was employees only."

Don't stop now, you're doing fine.

"Surely you could have made an exception?"

"We surely could not have fit half of Key West into the Berth, could we?" Rio's feeble attempt at a joke backfiring.

"Oh, you mean if girlfriends were allowed, you'd have half the island there as your guests? Those *whores!*" she hissed. To further emphasize her point, she looked away in disgust.

"Whoa! Hold on. No one said anything about past girlfriends. I went by myself!"

"Why are you lying? I know for a fact there were at least two former girlfriends there, maybe three." Ginger lied convincingly. She had no idea who attended the party but felt it a sure bet with all the females Rio had dated, a few had to be in CMPT's employ. A small island with a limited work force ensured the odds stood in her favor. Odds she suddenly did not like. A strange emotion came over her. Was this jealousy? No. It couldn't be.

Yes, it could, but get your head back in the game.

Ginger brushed aside the thought.

"Baby, listen to me. You're getting yourself all worked up over nothing," Rio pleaded. "Let me take you out for a nice dinner tonight, your choice of restaurant, K?"

Hit him once more. Go for the kill shot.

"Don't you love me anymore?" Her doe eyes lowered, glistening with crocodile tears. And that was all it took. Rio was hers.

"Aww baby, of course, I do." He took her by the hand to stand up so he could hug her as tears streamed down her cheeks.

Nice touch, whispered Proxy.

"It doesn't feel like it. Do you really?"

"I love you, baby, you're the only thing I care about, and I'm going to prove it to you," Rio encouraged as he held her tighter. Ginger smirked against his shoulder.

Girl, you are so good, Proxy said, admiring her performance. *So good!*

"Let's sit back down and have a nice breakfast together," Rio suggested as the waiter came back with their food. When he left, they ate in silence. Every so often, Ginger would lift her face to him, eyelashes still wet from her manufactured tears. Rio, in turn, offered a reassuring smile.

She kept up the act until she was certain he was past asking for answers about the laptop.

A Different Hurricane Makes Landfall

GINGER, FOCUSING HARD on the work at her desk, snapped her head back in surprise when her office phone rang. She ignored it. She did not want to waste time with this much at stake. Plus, she had a bug to squash before it continued to suck the lifeblood out of their business. *Her* business.

Her cell phone rang next. Rio.

Hmm, wonder what lover boy wants now? asked Proxy.

Despite her better judgement, she answered.

"Ginger, glad I caught you. I called your office but got your voicemail."

"Sorry, speaking with my father," she lied. "What's up? You miss me?"

"Of course. What are you doing tonight? I have a little surprise for you."

Surprise? Proxy inquired. *Could it be? Well, that didn't take long.*

Ginger dismissed the comment. "I may have a late meeting at the new restaurant with the contractor."

Good, play hard to get.

"Uh, it's…" stammered Rio. "It's kind of a big thing. When will you know for sure?"

"Let me make a call, and I'll get back to you." She ended the call, sat at her desk looking at her phone and waited. She had no one to call, her lies continued to grow like weeds in a neglected garden.

So, you think he's going to pop the question? This is rather unexpected, Proxy announced, pushing Gingers buttons.

"It can't be that. It's way too early."

Early for you. But what if it's not too early for him? There's only one way to find out now, isn't there?

Agitated, Ginger processed how an engagement would get her what she wanted; a piece of the CMPT Company. Hadn't this been her plan all along? Then why so apprehensive?

Because you like him. Admit it. Proxy taunted like a schoolmate on the playground.

What's next, passing notes in class?

"That's enough outta you." Ginger felt enough time had elapsed, so she picked up the phone and called Rio.

"Hey, baby," she cooed. "Seems I'm free now. I told the contractor to put off the meeting until tomorrow. So, what's the plan?"

"I'll meet you at your office around six. I'll tell you more once I get there. Then we can stop for dinner."

Ginger contemplated what to say next before blurting out, "Do you want to see my dad while you're here?"

Oh dear, no, cautioned Proxy.

Rio paused before answering. "Umm, no. He hates me."

Proxy started up again, but Ginger shut her down. "Shut up!"

"I'm sorry, did I say something wrong?" Rio asked.

Recovering quickly, she lied, "No. I meant 'shut up, he doesn't hate you.'"

"Oh, Ok, then I'll see you around six."

She ended the call, feeling confused. Is it not customary for the fiancé to ask the father for his daughter's hand in marriage?

Girl, That's so old school. No one does that anymore.

"No?" asked Ginger, looking disappointed. "You better get prepared, because if he's popping the question, I'm going to say yes." She was trying to sound certain. In the divide-and-conquer plan, apparently the conquer part of the program was upon them.

Not satisfied, Proxy asked, *I'm prepared for the surprise tonight. Are you sure you are?* Ginger couldn't give the voice in her head a straight answer, because, despite all her planning, she wasn't.

Rio found a house he liked on Catherine Street. A quaint historic Cigar Maker cottage with two bedrooms, one and a half bath, a pleasant front porch, and a spa pool in the back. It even had a small guest house for visitors. The property was a bit out of his price range, but real estate values were always rising in Key West, so he felt justified his investment would pay off in the future.

He planned on taking Ginger to see it, hoping she would love living in a quaint, modest home so close to everything. If she could love him, and he thought she did, then she could come to love the little house where together they would make it their home.

When he arrived at her office, she acted all loving and sweet, pestering him playfully about the little surprise awaiting her. Much to his relief, there was no more talk about meeting up with her father.

Excited, he asked her to drive up Catherine Street, anxious to show her where they could build a future together. "Park over there." He pointed at a parking space in front of the cottage.

"This is the little surprise I wanted to show you."

She gave him a look of uncertainty as they walked up the path and onto the porch. Rio opened the realtors lock box, produced a key, and opened the door. Ginger pursed her lips and narrowed her eyes.

Rio felt a cause for concern. The bell in his head began to sound off. Why did she not look excited? Did she or didn't she like his surprise? He honestly could not tell.

"After you," he said, waving her inside. As she entered, he reached into his pocket grasping a small box. The second surprise he planned for the evening.

Ginger still had not said a single word. She looked around the room as if inspecting a crime scene, sliding her hands inside her slack pockets, giving Rio the impression she did not want to touch anything. The bell increased in volume.

"I want to buy this for us," he said, hoping to push her to say something. Anything. "Surprise," he managed to say weakly. Rio considered the possibility she might want to make some changes, even to expand. He never expected what she said next.

She turned on him and shrilled, "Are you kidding me? I wouldn't live here if you paid me. I already have a great condo on the golf course and have access to all sorts of property! Did you forget our dinner at Sunset Key our first night together? Why would I want to live in a little shithole like this? And here I thought you had higher ambitions?"

Ginger continued her diatribe, shocking him with her vile words, amazing him on how quickly she could turn from sweet to caustic. Who was this person hiding inside Ginger? Why had he not seen her in this light before? The bell in his head returned, sounding as if there was a five alarm fire blazing nearby.

The realization hit him like a baseball bat to the head. Ginger Cobb did not want an equal relationship between partners. No.

Ginger Cobb wanted to be in control of everything, even though she could not control her own emotions. The irony was not lost on Rio.

The soft and loving female she had showed herself to be of late just disappeared, replaced by an angry, foul-mouthed creature. He saw himself as an actor playing a part in a movie and she, the director, telling him what role he should play and who he should become. She made it clear she found Rio attractive, not the person, but for what she wanted him to become. *Who* she wanted him to become.

"It's time to grow up, Rio," she spat. "And it doesn't mean playing house with the white picket fence and three kids in this… dump!" Ginger's anger rose with the tone of her voice. "Time to put on your big boy pants, get a haircut and stop acting like a child playing PIRATE games!"

Unbeknownst to her, Ginger had just overplayed her hand.

She failed to realize Rick Grande loved playing the role of Rio Grande; A character he had created who was a personality around town. He loved the friends she tried to make him avoid. Loved being a part of the company she attempted so often to horn in on. He especially loved his turn on the best stage in Key West and in no way would he ever give up the *Pirate Life.*

Rio knew her feelings on the issue and on his hairstyle. She had miscalculated the affection he had for his ponytail. Did she not get the concept of his style being a part of his identity? He would not cut off his ponytail for love nor money. Not for Ginger, not for anyone.

Love really is blind.

Rio heard the old saying repeat in his head as sadness flooded over him. Seeing her true personality caused him to realize he had been stumbling around in the dark for some time now.

After this outburst, Rio finally concluded the relationship was not going to change whether they got married or not. He slid the small box deeper into his pocket.

Although he wished he was anywhere else, they continued on to dinner at a local high-end restaurant. She continued her diatribe about the house and what *she* wanted … what she deserved. He let it go on until he felt it his turn to talk.

Rio did not hide his disappointment or frustration at the turn of events as they got into a big row over Rio's perception. Ginger had shown him another side of her. Perhaps her true side. He didn't care for it one bit. Curt, bossy … and mean.

Of course, she disagreed with his assessment. All narcissists are under the mistaken premise it's always someone else who's at fault.

"What happened to the girl I fell in love with?" he asked, shaking his head.

"Nothing happened. You can't deal with a strong woman, can you?" she countered.

"No, I don't have a problem with strong women. I've been around strong women all my life. I have a problem with the *wrong* woman!"

"Oh, so I'm the wrong woman now? I'm the best thing to ever happen to you. I've pulled you out of the gutter and made something of you."

Rio shook his head. "How could I have been so blind?"

"Go on back to your lowlife friends and shitty company. Good luck with that. I got the ball rolling, and there won't be anything left when I'm through," she hissed.

"What did you say?" Rio asked in disbelief. "Got the ball rolling?" He blinked as it finally dawned on him. "Oh my God, it's true. You were behind those web comments!"

Rio saw fear in her eyes with the realization of what she had just done.

"I, uh, I have no idea what you're talking about. I don't even know where your laptop is!"

"Who said anything about my laptop? Jeez, I feel so dumb. They told me they suspected you, but I wouldn't believe you could do such a thing!"

"Rio, baby, c'mon. Sit down, and we'll discuss this," she cooed, trying to calm him.

Rio no longer bought into her act. "There's nothing more to discuss. We're through." He threw money down for the check and walked out, leaving her alone at the table. The bell ringing in his head stopped as soon as he passed through the restaurant door.

Walking home, he called his realtor and told her he wanted to put an offer in on the Caroline Street house. Ginger had been right about one thing. He needed to grow up. No more love blindness. It was time to take back control of his life. And despite not sharing this house with Ginger, it was still a sound investment.

Ending the call and about to shut off his phone, he noticed Ginger had left a voice message and text.

They both went unanswered.

The door to Jasper's office flew open, and Ginger blew in like a tropical storm.

"How dare he!" she fumed. "Does he not know who I am? Who *we* are?"

Ginger's nostrils flared like a bull ready to charge. Her face reddened, eyes wild, chest heaving as she stomped over to her father's desk. She looked as if she had not slept all night.

Jasper closed the folder with the notes he was reading and gestured to her to relax. "Calm down, let me fix you a drink." He got up and poured a snifter of brandy and handed it to his still shaking daughter before he returned to his seat. His watch read only nine a.m. And while he did not condone morning alcohol, by the looks of things, his daughter needed something stronger than coffee. "Now, tell Dad all about it."

Ginger shared the details from her evening with Rio, visibly upset about the breakup. This confused Jasper. Her plan all along had been to seduce the lothario and manipulate him into turning over his portion of the business to her. Evidently, her plan had run aground. He resisted the urge to tell her, *I told you so.* Instead, he tried empathy. "Have you tried to reconcile with the lad?" The sentence tasted like ash in his mouth. To say he didn't care for Rio Grande was a huge understatement.

"I've been calling and calling. I even went to his house. He won't see me. He said… he said…" Ginger's anger drained as she tried to finish the sentence. Her shoulders slumped and her hair, usually coiffed to the latest style, now fell about her face looking like a bird's nest.

Jasper's unflappable daughter was falling apart before his eyes. She began to cry.

"There, there," he patted her on the arm in an awkward attempt at comfort. "This too shall pass."

In between sobs and her hitching shoulders, he swore he heard her say she did not want it to pass. *Could it be she had fallen in love with the cretin? Was it remotely possible?*

When his phone rang, Jasper put Ginger into a chair and urged her to empty her glass.

"Drink up, it'll help. I have to take this call. Then, we'll figure out what to do about … *him.*"

Jasper talked on the phone while Ginger slumped in the chair, occasionally sipping the brandy, her hitches becoming less frequent. When he ended the call, Jasper turned his attention to his daughter and as she lifted her head, noticed she was no longer crying.

"That was the lawyer on the phone," he told her. "The marina deal between Porter and the Hemmings' is complete."

Ginger, peering through red eyes and pieces of matted hair, looked at her father with an expression so evil it startled him. She wore the look of a woman scorned. A look Jasper knew all too well. He had seen it on Ginger's mother's face many years ago. Nothing good had come from his ex-wife after witnessing the same expression on her face. Her actions afterward had resulted in a one-way ticket to the mental hospital. He knew this recent look on Ginger spelled trouble.

"No one treats Ginger Cobb like this and gets away with it," she growled. "You wanted blood; you'll get your blood."

Jasper knew then what lengths his hurt daughter could go to get revenge and it frightened him. This was no longer about business. This was personal. Deeply personal.

The marina plan came together without a hitch, the lawyers working out the details amenable to both parties. Chase and Bill shook hands and consummated the deal over a bottle of champagne. King, Anne, and Mary were ecstatic. Rio seemed less than enthusiastic. He had not said much to his friends since the party. Chase did not like Rio distancing himself from the group. He walked over and sat next to him. The tension in the room felt palpable but Chase mustered the determination to make amends. He had never seen his friend so down.

"Hey buddy," he whispered. "About the other night at the party-"

Rio put a hand up. "Stop, I know you were just trying to help. And you were right."

"What?" Chase had not expected this reaction.

Rio raised his voice to include the others in the room. "I'm not upset with you guys; I'm upset with myself. Last night I broke it off with Ginger."

"WHAT?" shouted Anne as she jumped into the conversation. "Why?"

"You guys were right about her. She tried every which way to get information from me about the business. I kept deflecting her questions, thinking at first it was just pillow talk. She was relentless. Then she got worse by pulling a Jekyll and Hyde move. She was so sweet and loving I thought we had turned a corner in our relationship. Then last night I finally got smart and saw Ginger Cobb for who she really is. I showed her the house I wanted to buy for us, and she ripped me to shreds. Damn, she was brutal." Rio looked around sheepishly. "Plus, you were right on another front. Ginger all but admitted she was the person leaving those nasty comments on the website. That was the last straw. So, I told her we were through."

"How'd she handle it?" asked Anne.

"Don't know. I walked outta the restaurant. She's been calling, but I don't want anything to do with her. I'm so sorry, guys, I'm an idiot for not listening to you. Feel like such a fool."

"Laptop?" inquired King.

"Can't find it. Looked all over. It's *gone.* My take is she stole it. God knows where it'll end up." As an attempt at humor he added, "I see no one wants to correct me on the *idiot* or *fool* comments." This did not elicit the intended laughter, only silence. "I know, you want to tell me *I told you so.* You were right from the start."

Anne looked over at Chase before they both turned to Rio, who now shook his head sadly. The hurt on his face from being played was quite evident. Neither Chase, nor Anne, would make judgments about their wounded friend.

Mary came over and put her hand on Rio's shoulder as King handed him a glass of champagne. "You're among friends now. We all care about you. You'll find someone down the road. For now, be happy with who you are, not who she is."

"Oh, I know who she is," he nodded, showing his trademark humor through the pain.

"She's Hurricane Ginger. Is there such a thing as a category ten?"

Everyone, including the lawyers, chuckled at the comment.

"There is truth in humor," Rio continued. "We need to be wary of the truth *in this* humor."

With Hurricane Ginger storming through Key West, this truth could prove downright dangerous.

The next day, as Jasper finished his morning walk around the block, he studied the pineapple cutouts along his fence. He was decidedly not in the mood to extend the welcome mat for anyone these days.

He had been under siege by Chase Porter, siphoning off his client base and more recently, by the haunting specter of his ex-wife and the effect her genes were now having on his daughter.

The signs had never manifested before. Jasper believed it was because up until now Ginger had lived an easy life. No struggles to speak of until this Porter business. The possibility of financial strain and a failed relationship may have triggered his daughter. Having her heart broken by the long-haired pirate wanna-be pushed Ginger closer to the edge. If Jasper wanted to save his daughter, he needed to get her help before it became too late. The thought of her sinking into the same hole as her mother was untenable.

He walked up to the front door and entered the house to an eerie silence. Usually at this time of the morning, Ginger would be at her desk chatting away on the phone, working on a new idea, or going over the books. Perhaps she was still asleep?

Walking to his office, he saw his door slightly ajar. He distinctly remembered closing it before he left for his walk. He also remembered leaving the light on as well. Pushing the door wider, the light from the hallway spilled into his office and across his desk.

"Good morning, father," Ginger's voice called out to him from the mostly dark office. He could see her outline sitting behind his desk. She reached out and switched on the desk lamp, her expression unnerving him. Head bent slightly downward with one eyebrow raised. Limp pieces of unwashed hair hung down around her face, her mouth half-open in a crooked grin.

Jasper's worst fears were being realized. If he hadn't known this was his daughter, he would have sworn the woman sitting behind his desk was someone from another time. Someone he had not seen for a long while and for good reason.

"Come in." She motioned to the visitor chair in front of the desk. "We need to talk."

"So, talk." Jasper eased into the chair without a challenge. Assessing the extent of his daughter's condition, he proceeded with caution. "What's on your mind?"

"I need to go speak with the franchisors in Miami," she explained. "We need to make sure this restaurant starts making money from day one."

"I couldn't agree more," Jasper said, his concern about his daughter's mental state increasing. He knew better than to rile her and kept playing along to see where the conversation would take them. "Would you like me to go with?"

"No!" barked Ginger, with an intensity that shook him.

Her crooked grin returned and her tone softened. "You have important work here."

"Fine, but wouldn't it be prudent to clean up a bit? You look, err, disheveled. And we don't want anything to take away from your meeting, do we?"

Jasper Cobb knew if she took his advice, cleaned herself up, it would be a good sign. Otherwise, he would be forced to call in a specialist.

"Agreed. I'll need to look presentable," she said in a monotone. Her face brightened. "Perhaps I can get my nails done before I go as well."

Jasper relaxed a bit at this change in expression. "It will do you good to get off the island for a few days. Get back into the swing of things. A change of scenery will do you good."

"Yes, Papa," she said in a flat monotone, again unnerving him. "Whatever you say."

"Do you want me to make your flight arrangements?" he offered.

"No. I'm taking the *Ginger Snap*. Want to stop along the way. I have a package to drop off." Getting up, she walked around the desk toward the door. As she passed by, Jasper caught an unpleasant whiff causing him to wrinkle his nose and turn his head away.

"Do me good," she said in a sing-song manner as she headed for the shower, humming a little song, and nodding her head in agreement.

A Bold Path

CHASE SAT STRAIGHT up in bed. He had been sleeping soundly but now felt fully alert because of the dream. This was not the usual nightmare version of the drowning boy, but disconcerting just the same. He shook his head to regain clarity as he got up and put on a pot of coffee.

While it brewed, he sat at his desk and began to dissect the dream. In it, he saw a shipwreck with a lone survivor ... a sailor sitting on one of the masts like one would straddle a horse. The waves kept splashing rhythmically against him. His body drenched, his clothing tattered, fear plastered across his face. Like the dead boy, he too reached for a helpful hand that would not be reaching back.

As the mast and its survivor kept drifting further away, the sailor morphed into the dead diver, his wetsuit glistening like a baby seal. Instead of arms outstretched for help, the dead boy signaled Chase to follow, a slow finger beckoning ... *this way*. Chase read his gesture as a clue, one with a specific meaning, but what could it be? The last thing he wanted was for the boy to beckon him to the deep to stay, but the dream felt otherwise.

As if the boy wanted to show him something. Chase glanced at his phone. Five a.m. He turned his attention to the maps strewn across the desk.

In 1622, two hurricanes blew through the Keys in succession. One in September and a second in October. The Spaniards knew the location of the *Atocha* after the first storm but lost the ship during the second. What if the sterncastle had broken from the ship after the second hurricane? Perhaps if that had happened, it might have floated some distance away from the other portion of the vessel, dropping some of those items like the Bezoar Stone Chase had found during previous dives. Could there also be a different debris arc formed as the second hurricane shifted the sterncastle's trajectory in another direction? Starting with the coral reef?

He and Rio had been looking south of the debris field, but what if the sterncastle went further? Did the dead boy on the mast want him to follow a more southern path?

His phrase, *This way*, stuck firmly in Chase's head, poking him relentlessly. He felt sure the-message-in-dream could be the missing piece to his theory on the sterncastle. The idea prompted him to research hurricanes from the National Oceanic and Atmospheric Association (NOAA) website.

The sterncastle could have drifted in the opposite direction of the rest of the ship after the second hurricane. If this was the case, no wonder they could not find it. They *were* looking in the wrong place!

He drained his first cup of coffee, then after pouring a second, returned to his desk and punched NOAA into the search engine on his computer. Chase tried to find information on both 1622 hurricanes from the NOAA website, but there were no statistics from the time period as the U.S. weather service was not established until 1870, and Congress did not create the weather bureau until 1890, under the jurisdiction of the Department of Agriculture.

His research showed how hurricane patterns across the Keys could vary. In 1935, the Labor Day Hurricane ran across the Keys into the Gulf of Mexico, running along the western coast of Florida and then upwards into the Atlantic Coast States, listed as a category five.

In 1960, Hurricane Donna came up from the Bahamas passing through the Keys as a category four. It crossed the mainland of Florida and circled back out to the Atlantic until it made landfall again in North Carolina.

Then Hurricane Andrew in 1992, Katrina *and* Rita in 2005, all swept westward through the Keys on their way into the Gulf of Mexico to damage Gulf coastal cities.

When hurricane patterns changed, they also changed what happened beneath the water as sand shifted revealing an object of value which had stayed buried for hundreds of years.

Hurricane Bree had recently come through the area, and Chase once again remembered what his father taught him years before: the best time to go treasure hunting was right after a storm.

The theory Chase proposed relied on from which direction he thought the 1622 hurricanes *might* have come. If both storms had gone across the Bahamas and Puerto Rico, then the sterncastle should be in the line of the debris field arching from south to northwest where most of the original treasure was found. But if his assumptions were correct, well, that would be a different story altogether.

Jasper was traveling to Tallahassee for a business meeting of his own. He called to check in with Ginger, whose disposition improved immensely. She stayed animated during the phone call and debriefed Jasper about the franchisor meeting and assured him everything with the new restaurant was on track. There was also no mention of her previous entanglement with that slug, Rio. These were all positive signs, relieving Jasper. They discussed fresh marketing ideas, price increases on those businesses proven able to handle it and expense cuts where business softened. Their conversation was calm, cheerful. Gone were any signs of distress.

But just to be sure she'd been completely honest with him, Jasper planned to follow up with the franchisors from his hotel room later in the afternoon. He hated to snoop behind her back, however business was business, especially when your CFO daughter showed signs of a mental breakdown.

Jasper sighed in relief. "Now we can get back to rebuilding our water business by handling this Porter problem." Ginger agreed enthusiastically. He felt relieved she was back in tune with him. Perhaps a doctor call was unnecessary. Having a premature discussion of this sensitive nature would undoubtedly result in a consultation which could lead to overnight observation, a course of action he did not want to put his daughter through for no reason.

"On the Porter front, something drastic might have to be done," Ginger announced.

The word *drastic* gave him pause. Up until then, their conversation had been cordial and positive. He decided to push her. "What do you mean by *drastic?*"

"Oh, Daddy, don't you worry. I have some ideas of my own. I can handle this. Besides, I want to surprise you."

After discussing her homeward travel plans and saying their goodbyes, Jasper ended the call. Five minutes earlier, he had been confident Ginger was on her way back to normal. Now, he second guessed himself. *Drastic, Ideas of my own,* and *I can handle this,* expressed individually could be construed as innocent enough.

But stringing them all into a few sentences could spell disaster. And another thing, he didn't want any more of her surprises.

He'd had enough of those.

To take Rio's mind off his failed relationship, Chase took him back out to the *Mastery* for another dive during the middle of the week. He planned for the two of them to have the day off, confident King and Anne could handle the day's tours.

"The serenity will do you good," he told his friend.

"I need a little serenity after dealing with Hurricane Ginger," Rio joked. Then added with a serious tone, "You're not going to leave me again, are you?"

"No. I'm not," Chase shook his head. "Never again, I promise."

"Good, now I won't have to kill you." Rio laughed half-heartedly at his own joke.

At least he's retained his sense of humor. Chase knew how Rio, being accustomed to his role as the heartbreaker, did not appreciate being on the other end as the broken-hearted. While Chase was glad the horror of Rio's love affair was over, he did wonder what the lasting effect would be on his friend. Chase could only hope humor would prove to be a great place to start the healing.

Chase drove King's Grady-White out to the *Mastery*, their equipment filling up the back of the boat. On the way out, Rio's voice yelled above the roaring engines, "Any luck on the theory of yours?"

Chase nodded, knowing Rio would be on board with the plan. On the way out to the dive site, Chase shared the crux of the theory with Rio, who nodded in agreement. They approached the salvage vessel and the two men tethered their boat to the larger ship.

Chase's theory conflicted with the Captain and his crew, but the only one privy to this information happened to be Rio, and he followed Chase wherever he led ... to a point.

"You ready?" Chase asked as they approached the dive platform.

"Born ready. What's the sense of having a theory if you can't test it?"

The two splashed into the surf and headed down to their grid. Once there, they headed in the northeasterly pathway expected of them. Within five minutes of swimming along the path, Chase motioned to Rio, and the two changed course, heading south, away from the arc. They swam until their calculations told them it was time to get back to the ship for new tanks.

They marked their coordinates and turned back. As they'd done on their previous dive, they practiced the grid pattern three more times covering as much territory south as possible before the air in their tanks went below 500psi, or their 'reserve,' forcing another return to the ship. There would be no pings coming from the Pulse this day, not unusual for treasure seekers.

On the way back to shore aboard the Grady-White, Chase throttled down the engines so they could have a normal discussion without having to yell to each other.

"We covered some good ground today even if we didn't find anything," Rio, said, but did not hide his disappointment at returning empty-handed.

Chase, on the other hand, felt confident. "I'm convinced we're on the right path. We have to keep going farther south from the ship." Although Chase did not show disappointment about their lack of artifacts, he surprised himself with regret no ghostly visions had appeared that day.

Even though it had frightened him at first, Chase had become intrigued by the dream and the dead boy's insistence he come *this way*, meaning south, wanting him to follow the ghosts' direction to see where it led.

"That's not gonna happen with the equipment we have," Rio said, breaking Chase's train of thought. "Those tanks will only take us just so far. I wish there was another way to stay down under water longer."

"There is," Chase stated.

Rio eyed Chase, a puzzled look on his face. "Ok, how many steps are you ahead of me this time?"

"Several," Chase responded as he pushed the throttle forward, waking up the mercury engines. He yelled it again over the roar of the engine noise. "SEVERAL!"

Lubbers boarded the *Satisfaction* for the second tour of the day while deckhands prepared for their roles. Anne dressed in the captain's quarters as King went below deck to practice the swordplay routine, eager to do it justice. Crunchy barked orders to his crew, then, when no one was looking, shifted his eye patch.

King came topside and surveyed the noisy lubbers still boarding the vessel. *We have a rowdy crowd today.* He inspected a few young lubber's stumble on board. *Already into the sauce, I see.*

There were couples, families with children, retirees, a bachelor party, and students on break from school. The regular touristy types who signed on for the late afternoon cruise. King wrinkled his nose at one passenger in particular, noticing the man come aboard alone. It was uncommon for a land lubber to come by himself. The tours usually consisted of groups or at least couples. King felt this man was out of place.

King noticed the man walk about the ship, focusing on the side rails, the main deck and, it seemed, he also took an interest in the rigging. King could not stop watching the guy because something just did not feel right. His instincts had proven trustworthy over the years, so when the hairs on the back of his neck stood up, King took notice.

When all the lubbers were onboard, Crunchy yelled to pull in the gang plank and cast off the ropes, as he steered the craft out of the marina under low diesel power. King took his place on the foredeck and brushed away thoughts of the lone man as he prepared to address the lubbers while the *Satisfaction* sailed into the bay.

"Rio is right," Anne said unexpectedly.

"Right about what?" Chase asked as the two swung slowly in a hammock hanging between the main and mizzen masts on the quarterdeck. It had been a long day, and the couple took some down time to relax and unwind. They had just made love down in the Captain's quarters, and Anne suggested they move up to the hammock for some star gazing during the late evening.

"He says you play with the fake coin around your neck whenever you get worried. What does he call it? An UnReale?"

"Yea, he's funny like that. I'm not worried and I keep trying to tell him the same. I am trying to work through something, and this UnReale helps me focus."

To say business was good would be an understatement. Chase was pleased the company continued to see reservations grow. They had a solid marina lease with Bill and the *Satisfaction* would be theirs, free and clear, sooner than planned thanks to Anne's repayment plan.

Still, Chase Porter had a nagging feeling their troubles were not over.

"So, what are you trying to work through? Must you make me dig for everything?"

Chase also felt pleased for Anne's love. Not many couples had their type of relationship, and to have her in his life was a blessing. He admired her patience. Most women would find his quirks frustrating: his restless need for adventure, the way he focused on a concept until he understood it, and his penchant for stroking the coin hanging around his neck.

Still, Anne Braun was not patient with the way Chase failed to answer her questions with a direct answer. He made a mental note to rectify the issue … starting now.

"Alright, alright. I think it's time for a trip," Chase fessed up.

"So, Jasper's idea struck a nerve, did it?"

Chase looked at Anne, his right arm tucked under his head, his left firmly holding her close to him. This time he went directly to the answer so she would not have to fight him for it.

"No. Not to *buy* another ship. We've got to stick to your plan about the marina first. It's the smart play. I meant a trip … a vacation … just you and me."

Living on the *Satisfaction* had its perks. No mortgage and after selling the truck, no auto expense. His slip fees and cell phone were paid by the company; he had no other expenses but food. The only thing Chase did with his money was save, invest, and repeat the process. Over the last few years, he had done very well doing both. He had a financial advisor over on Flagler Street who helped him invest in a pretty aggressive portfolio and it prospered. A man of little needs and even less extravagance, Chase took little out of the business for his own personal use, save for investing in the Loyalty Program and of course diving equipment. Until now.

"You sure know how to sweep a girl off her feet, sailor." Anne snuggled closer into the crook of his arm. "I do need some time off. Can't tell you the last time I had a real vacation."

"Then how would you like to take an adventure down through the Caribbean. We'll take the *Brains and Brawn* and sail from island to island, swim naked in the morning, check out each little dive bar along the way. Dine at a different cafe every evening. We could gaze at every sunrise, enjoy each sunset, and look up at the stars every evening before the real fun begins."

"You're full of romantic ideas, aren't you, darlin'?" She climbed on top of Chase showing sparkles in her eyes. Bending down, Anne stole an unending kiss for the second time that evening. They could always look at the stars later.

A lone, hooded figure crept silently along the docks toward the *Satisfaction*, its towering masts overshadowing the other ships in the harbor.

The timing was perfect for the task at hand. The time of night between closing bars and early waking hours for fishermen. A time no one should be on the streets of Key West save for those up to no good. A time best fit for performing mayhem.

The hooded figure lay flush against the dock and reached beneath it. After groping around with a gloved hand, he found and brought his prize dockside. It was a box containing two small canisters, each no bigger than a beer can with no discernible markings. Then, pulling a pen from the pouch of his hoodie, poked a hole in each of the canister's screw caps. Next, he unscrewed the cap on each, pulling a small wick through the cannister holes, making sure they were thoroughly drenched from the liquid within before screwing the caps back on tightly. He held the canisters at arm's length for fear of spilling the flammable liquid on himself. He didn't care about the gloves. They would be disposed of shortly, tools of the trade designed to leave no trace.

This task was routine for the hooded figure. Just another day on the job, wherever his services were needed. Tonight, they were needed in the Conch Harbor Marina.

Standing in the shadow of the large craft, he produced a lighter. Within seconds the wicks came alive with fire. He threw the canisters onto the *Satisfaction*'s main deck; a flash of light illuminated the beautiful wooden deck as the incendiary devices did their job. He took off his gloves and placed them in the box which he slipped into the pouch of his hoodie.

His job finished, the hooded man disappeared into the dark night, leaving only flames behind.

LIGHTNING
STRIKES TWICE

*T*HE WARM SUN *shone brightly against the hull as the sailboat cut through the calm waters. The captain's right hand rested on the column, the wind blowing through his hair as he watched Anne sunbathe in a yellow bikini, her tanned body contrasting with the white bow.*

He called out to her and when she did not turn, he called again, expecting a smiling response. Who would not smile on such a glorious day with the wind at their back and a full week of sailing ahead?

Anne turned slowly toward him, resting an elbow on the deck for support. It reminded him of a pose from a model in a swimsuit magazine. Her pale green eyes the color of the back of a leaf turned to accept an incoming rain shower. Chase smiled broadly, lucky enough to be out on the water with the woman he loved.

Gratitude shifted to puzzlement as Chase realized Anne did not return his smile. Instead, she gazed at him with a look of angst. Was it something he had said or done to make the woman show any other emotion than bliss on a day such as today? It seemed as if she was trying to tell him something. He leaned closer, but that proved to be futile. Her agitation was noted yet he could not make out her words. Then, something terrified her which in turn gave Chase added cause for alarm. Her look of horror turned into a scream.

His confusion at what she was trying to convey added to the mayhem of that gawd awful scream. He wanted her to stop but knew she wouldn't. And then, his mouth filled with the unmistakable, acrid burning taste of smoke. Heat that should have been from the sun above him came from his right. Instinctively, he knew it meant fire. But he did not see any flames … the daylight so bright, blinding him.

Anne screamed louder and louder for him to finally hear.
"WAKE UP!"

The words dissipated the dream into grey wisps of smoke. The sailboat, blue sky and bikini all evaporating into darkness. Orange flames replaced the sunlight of his dream as he opened his eyes to see Anne, standing next to the hammock, shaking him.

"Fire! Get up, Chase!"

Chase fell out of the hammock and clumsily landed on the deck. He stumbled his way to the port side emergency box where they kept life jackets and fire extinguishers. Anne raced to the starboard box. The main deck now engulfed in fire, flames licking at the rigging. It would be catastrophic to the rest of the masts if the flames kept climbing, jumping from one to another, bringing them all down into piles of ashes.

Fully awake now he ordered, "You start with the deck!" Anne nodded, pulling the pin on the fire extinguisher. "I'll get the rigging under control!" Chase barked. It took several fire extinguishers each to try and quench the flames, but to no avail. The ship's rigging was coated with a pitch-like substance to withstand the salt from the ocean.

The pitch also made it extremely flammable. The fire shot across the railings and onto the foredeck. Try as they might, Chase and Anne could not extinguish the flames as they began to engulf the ship.

"Anne!" Chase yelled as he realized the situation would only get worse if they continued their attempts to put out the fire. They were now on either side of the quarterdeck. He pointed to the poop deck where they could get to a higher position, the heat pushing them farther away from the main deck. "We need to get off!"

Anne's face looked defiant as she shook her head and kept using the remaining fire extinguisher. While there were other extinguishers on the foredeck, access to them was now impossible. As the flames crept closer towards them, Chase made a quick decision. Running the few steps across the poop deck, he grabbed Anne by the waist and dove off the side of the ship into the harbor, barely missing a sizeable wooden pylon attached to the dock.

Chase broke the surface and searched frantically for Anne, spinning his head around in all directions. He prepared to dive under in search of her, when she bounced up through the surface to his right, spitting out water and obscenities. They swam to a nearby boat, climbed its stern ladder and crossed through to the dock, running back towards *Satisfaction*, the orange glow from the fire lighting their way. The intense heat stopped them.

"Anne, move. NOW!" Chase screamed, grabbing her arm, and pulling her. As the ship burned in its berth, Chase realized the other boats moored near *Satisfaction* were also in danger.

All the boats in the area to include the *Satisfaction* had one item aboard he wanted no part of when fire danced along the dock … Fuel.

The two ran towards the marina's entrance as the Key West Fire department arrived. A fire department boat, already sidling near the *Satisfaction*, aimed its powerful water hose, drenching her. Firefighters ran up the dock with their hoses as well, and together they extinguished the fire in short order. As a precaution, paramedics attended to the couple. "You okay?" Chase asked Anne, touching her arm.

Yeah," she responded. "Just a little bruised and slight headache. You?"

"Have that *same headache* with a slight ringing in my ears. Otherwise, I'm okay." Chase brushed away the thoughts of what might have happened, thankful Anne woke him.

The fire inspector came to the scene to assess the situation but would not discuss anything with the two until he'd completed his investigation. Upon hearing the sirens, King and Rio showed up, as did most of the crew to find the *Satisfaction* flames extinguished. News traveled fast on the island and friends gathered to support their own.

"Good thing you were on deck when it started. Did you hear or see anything?" Rio asked.

"No. We were sleeping. Anne woke me up, then we tried to put out the fire." With tears forming in his eyes, Chase broke down. "How could this have happened?"

Anne rested her head on his shoulder, but he would not be consoled. "Our company is sunk. We have nothing left. Just look at her. We're ruined!"

They all turned their gaze to the ship once the centerpiece of their operation. It now looked like a burnt skeleton, their grand vessel reduced to a shell filled with charred timber and ash ... just like their dreams.

Later that morning, Anne began canceling reservations and updating the website while Chase sat at the police station answering questions before heading over to his insurance carrier. Rio busied himself by seeking a carpenter to assess the damage and begin repairs as soon as the fire inspector report came back.

It did not take long. By the middle of the afternoon, the inspector claimed his team had found pieces of a partial canister on the *Satisfaction*'s deck, and traces of accelerant onboard, clues pointing to arson. Everyone wondered who in their right mind would want to burn down such a glorious ship. Chase had an idea and agreed anyone attempting a heinous act such as this was clearly *not* in their right mind.

At the police station, Chase tried to control his rage. "Chief, you have to look at Jasper Cobb."

Chief Robert Deakin sat at his desk across from Chase. "We're looking at everyone. Our job isn't to point fingers but gather evidence to find a suspect and make an arrest based on the evidence."

"He's tried everything to get his hands on this business, and once he realized he couldn't do it, Cobb decided to kill it once and for all. He burnt down my damn ship!"

"Whoa, hold on. You can't just throw accusations around. Let us do our job." The chief got up from his chair, a clear signal their meeting was over. "I'll get back to you if I hear anything. In the meantime, stay close to Key West."

"Wait, am I a suspect?" Chase made a face, incredulous at the thought.

"As I said before, we're looking at everyone," the chief said again as he closed the door behind the stunned ship owner.

Chase grew increasingly agitated as he left the police station. He kept asking himself how could Chief Deakin suspect him? He'd built the business into a success, overcome significant challenges and even fought to put out the fire that nearly destroyed his ship. He worried about additional problems which could arise as he walked down Roosevelt Boulevard and towards his insurance agent's office on Leon Street.

After arriving, he sat in the waiting room, hand firmly attached to his UnReale, until his agent, Carl Lampley came out to greet him. Chase stood and shook Carl's hand. "Carl, I need to get repairs started right away. A lengthy hiatus is gonna kill us. When can you get an adjuster over there?"

"Chase, first let me say how sorry I am for this tragedy. Secondly, I cannot send an adjuster until the investigation concludes. If we're talking possible arson, then we have specific rules about that type of fire damage."

"How long will it take?"

"Depends on how quickly the investigation wraps up."

Still shaken from the night's events, Chase knew being labeled a suspect in a crime he didn't commit only made things worse. Now he needed to figure out how to get the funds to rebuild … if possible. "What would stop you from paying out the claim?" he asked Carl.

"If it's found you or someone you employ intentionally set the fire or you paid someone to do so."

"What if someone else did it?"

Carl paused before answering. "That's a bit tricky. With the commitment of a crime, the carrier would want proof you weren't involved, and then you'd have a case, falling under the vandalism clause in your policy."

"But it's still no guarantee? C'mon Carl, you know me. I would never do something like this."

"Sorry, Chase, but that's how the policy is written. Until the investigation is over, my hands are tied."

Chase left the building panic-stricken. He was a suspect in an arson investigation, their business in shambles, and now no guarantee he'd ever see a dime of insurance money. What the hell had he done to deserve this? And what should he do next? As he walked down the street, one thought came to mind. He stopped, got his bearings, and started walking again. He knew exactly what to do. Head to the Berth.

King knew a lot of people on the island. People who heard things. His job would entail talking to as many of those people as possible to find out what they might have heard, what rumors were floating around. Any clues to help him answer the most pressing question: *Who set the Satisfaction on fire?*

He understood the police were investigating as well. It was law enforcement's job to find out what had happened and arrest the perpetrators, but King also knew the police did not possess the same contacts he had. No one on the island did. Running a bar in Key West had its benefits. Especially a bar with its share of regulars and a barkeep with open ears.

Folks confided in King. They sat at his bar and told him things they wouldn't tell their spouses, bosses, or family members. In a way, the bar acted like a confessional and King, not a mere priest, played the role as the bishop, the Berth his parish.

People came, they drank, they confessed. He listened and then absolved them. And now he would listen for a specific piece of information. The process would take time, and he wouldn't push. Detectives took their time, listening and waiting. They gathered facts. This task would test his abilities like no other, but King needed to exercise patience.

He knew eventually someone would break their silence. And when someone did, he would be ready. For the confessor, he would grant absolution. For the perpetrator of this heinous crime, he would not. The act was a cardinal and *unforgivable* sin.

One thing he did not have to wait for was Chase's arrival. King could sense the distress his friend brought with him as he walked through the door and headed directly to the bar.

"Give me a shot of rum with a beer chaser," Chase asked King, pulling out a twenty from his wallet.

"Chase, is this a good idea?"

"King, is this a bar?"

"Yup," replied the big man.

"Is it open?"

"Yup."

"Is my money good?"

King thought about the question before answering, "Nope. It's on me."

In troubled times, patrons came into the King's bar to forget about their problems using the warmth and relaxation of alcohol. Chase had an unusually large amount of trouble staring him in the face and a lot to forget. As King poured the first shot, the bar owner hoped he had enough alcohol to help Chase relax and forget. Just in case, he left the bottle on the bar.

Two hours later, King saw the door open and Anne slid her way inside. "King, why can't you get a door that isn't so hard to- ", she began. A frown on her face, hands on her hips, she glared at Chase as he sat at the bar with his head slung low.

"Chase?"

King monitored Chase as he slowly turned his head, eyes half closed, sporting a silly grin.

"There's my darlin'," Chase slurred. "Come join me fer a drink." When he reached for the bottle, it slipped through his fingers. King reached out and grabbed it before it could crash to the floor.

"Gimme a kiss." Chase reached for Anne, but she stepped back.

"Chase, what are you doing?"

"I'm having a drink. A… A lie-bay-shunnnn." Chase nearly fell off the stool before he caught himself. He took another shot of rum, then wiped his mouth with his forearm.

"Is this how you're going to act every time you have a setback? Drink yourself into a stupor? Is this what you call moderation?"

"Lessee, I don't have a boat … burnt up." He put his fists on either side of his head and made the familiar explosion gesture accompanied by a whooshing sound. "And," he continued, "no asur-ance money. Nope. None." He put his head down momentarily before adding, "An I'm pretty sure I'm goin to jail. So. So, I'm havin' a drink with my fren here." He wiggled his finger, pointing at King, who only turned to Anne and shrugged.

"I can't do this," began Anne, the anger in her voice apparent. "You're not the only one who lost everything! We're all affected by this, but you don't see me sitting at the bar drinking myself stupid. Are you going to be a quitter and drown your sorrows or are you going to stand up to face your problems like a responsible human being?"

Chase had trouble pronouncing *responsible* before giving up. "You all," he said, moving his finger in a circular motion. "You all got jobs, this bar, things you can do. Me? I got nuthin'." To make his drunken point, Chase tried to say it louder spewing spit in all directions, just missing Anne. "NUTHIN!" He looked at Anne, then at the bottle on the bar before making his decision. "Escept this…" He reached for the bottle, but King grabbed it first, placing it back behind the bar. Undaunted, he asked anyway, "Could you pour me another, my good man?"

"We're done, Chase," Anne stared at him, her eyes glistening with tears. She strode towards the door and pulled hard. "Dammit!" she swore in frustration as she struggled to leave.

Both men watched her exit, then Chase turned to King. "Oops. And now … looks like I do not have a girlfren. How's my day lookin' so far?"

"Shit fire." King responded. He now felt guilty for letting this situation play out in front of Anne. She did not deserve it. No one did. It was not the time to let off steam, but the time to figure out what they had to do next. He went into the kitchen and returned with a cup of coffee, placing it in front of Chase.

"Whass this?" he asked, looking at the cup.

"Redemption," King told him. "You've had enough alcohol for one day."

ONCE INNOCENT, TWICE GUILTY

"KING, THANKS FOR letting me sleep it off on your couch last night." Chase sat at the bar drinking coffee. His hangover a foggy reminder of the previous day's activities. He rubbed his UnReale as he thought about what to do next. Only one thing came to mind.

"Do me a favor, eh King?"

The big man poured Chase another cup of coffee and grunted in the affirmative.

"Do not, under any circumstances let me drink like that EVER AGAIN. You gotta cut me off. These days I don't know where the line is."

King nodded as he washed glasses from the night before. "Especially if I'm buying." His lame attempt at humor sounded uncharacteristic.

"So, now you wanna be funny? Please, Don't make me laugh. My head hurts enough. As soon as I can get off this barstool, I need to find Anne and apologize."

When the bar phone rang, King answered and spoke in monosyllables finishing with a "K" before hanging up. Chase rubbed his temples, trying to rid his head of the nasty ache. The smell of stale beer and cigarette ash didn't help.

"Get up," King commanded. "Time to go."

"Yeah, you're right. Where do you think I can find Anne? God, I hope she accepts my apology."

"Can't. Police called. Want you at the station."

"That'll have to wait. I need to find Anne first."

"Not a request," King stated, shaking his head.

Chase got up from the barstool, clutching the UnReale and headed towards the door, his head still pounding. Two uniformed police officers met him on the street, ready to escort him to see Chief Deakin.

"Shit fire!" he whispered, as the officers put him into the police cruiser for transport to the station.

It took a short five minutes and once there, a Sergeant Willis escorted him into a sparse room. Three windowless cement walls and a mirror on the fourth. A small table in the middle of the room with two chairs told him everything he needed to know. The interrogation room.

"Sarge, I already told you guys everything." Chase was tired and wanted to find Anne.

The sergeant just stood by the door.

Chase tried to engage him again. "Am I still a suspect? Cause we were on the deck and fought the fire. I'm telling you we did not start it."

The officer remained silent but turned to open the door for Chief Deakin who entered and sat across the table from Chase. He opened a laptop, spun it around, and Chase studied a grainy video of the Conch Harbor Marina. The chief pointed to the screen, asking. "Can you identify anyone?"

Deakin pointed to people heading to or from boats around dusk. If Chase did recognize a face, he said so. Most he did not. Every so often, he would catch sight of the *Satisfaction*, her masts standing straight and tall, her lines majestic. Unburnt. He grimaced at each glimpse.

When they were done with the first video, the chief showed him a second video of a hooded figure. Chase winced at the flash of light as the figure tossed the lit canisters onto the *Satisfaction*'s deck, igniting it. The video continued for another few minutes as the flames grew.

What looked like white smoke appeared to come in bursts from the deck. Fire extinguishers. The video also captured the splash next to the ship. Then Chase and Anne climbing up onto the boat, then the dock.

They now had visual proof of arson. Whoever this hooded figure was, he/she knew what they were doing. The person knew about the cameras and how to avoid showing anything to implicate him/her except the intention. It was as if the perpetrator wanted the police to see the act itself. Chase shook his head trying to rid himself of the dark images and the pain they caused.

"Am I no longer a suspect?" he asked the chief.

"No longer," replied the chief. "Visual evidence puts the blame solely on the hooded person of interest."

Person of interest. To Chase, it sounded like looking for a forgetful grandparent who took a walk and got lost. "I told you they burnt my...." Chase stopped himself from swearing in front of the chief again. "…. my ship. Now, what are we going to do about it?"

Deakin replied, "First of all, WE are not going to do anything. Let *us* handle the investigation going forward. We don't need any vigilantes running around."

"And second?" Chase asked.

"Tell me more about your suspicions concerning Jasper Cobb."

Chase gave the chief a blow-by-blow synopsis of the attempts Jasper had made to assert control of the CMPT, Deakin making plenty of notes. After the discussion, Chase left the police station grateful to no longer be a suspect, yet angry the chief did not believe they had enough evidence to arrest Jasper. Deakin told Chase he would call Jasper in for questioning as part of the investigation but could promise no more than that.

Chase strode back to the Berth, hoping King and Rio were there. He also hoped Anne would be there so he could apologize. He realized how much he needed her now. When he got there, King and Rio were deep in conversation, but no Anne.

"Well, if it's not the jailbird," Rio joked, happy to see his friend. "Who posted bail?"

Chase was in no mood for humor. "Not remotely funny. Guys, the good news is I'm no longer a suspect. The bad news is the chief says there's no evidence yet to incriminate Jasper."

"What about all the crap they've tried to pull?" Rio asked. "The Cobbs are the only suspects. They have the most to gain!"

"There's no crime in trying to buy a business," Chase replied.

"What about the negative reviews?" King chimed in from behind the bar.

"And my laptop?" added Rio.

"I asked the chief about that. Not a crime to make negative comments online. If that were the case, half the world would be indicted. And as far as your laptop, have you found it yet?"

Rio shook his head.

"We need evidence. Not circumstantial, but TANGIBLE evidence. King, you press your contacts and keep your ears open. Somebody has to know something. Rio, how we doing finding a carpenter?"

"On it Cap'n. Got a few names. Waiting on a call back. What are you gonna do?"

"First, I have to find Anne and apologize. Then I need to figure out how to raise money. We have a ship to rebuild."

"Atta boy!" King called out to Chase.

"I think I can help with the second task," Anne interrupted, making her presence known as she walked towards the bar. She tossed the box she carried to Chase. "Thought you might need this." Then added sarcastically, "Boss."

He struggled with the catch but secured the box before it hit the ground. A new cell phone. "Thanks," he said, smiling meekly. She in turn frowned, then looked down at her own phone and typed something before turning it towards the group.

"What're we looking at?" Rio asked, too far away to see the screen.

"A GoFundMe Page. Someone started a fund to restore the *Satisfaction*. It's already up to ten thousand dollars."

It took a moment to register before King broke the silence. "Not enough."

"But it is enough to start. I have to go back to beg for the insurance money now that I'm no longer a suspect."

He turned to Anne, "Baby, I want to apolog—"

Before he could finish, she cut him off. "Save your breath. Going forward, we are business partners only. My focus is getting the *Satisfaction* seaworthy again." She stormed towards the door, pulled it open with little struggle and slid out.

"Man, she is angreee! What did you do to her?" Rio asked.

"Shit fire." King muttered already knowing the answer.

Chase didn't respond as he surveyed the door wondering how he would fix the riff with Anne. *If* he could fix it.

The *Satisfaction*'s restoration began in earnest. People from all over the world had seen news of the damaged vessel. Thanks to social media, the donations were pouring in. The ship and her crew had fans everywhere. By the next day, thirty thousand dollars had been raised.

Daniel Porter arrived to help anyway he could by working at the store, assisting King at the bar, and even getting a license to do a walking tour of the wharf.

Because Chase had been cleared as a suspect or accomplice, a check would be coming from Carl's office completing the financing for the restoration. They hired a contractor and hoped to restore her as quickly as possible.

Fortunately for the company, the *Satisfaction*'s previous owner had used a flame retardant while building her. There was damage to be sure, but most limited only to the rigging, a few sails and both side rails. Surprisingly, the decks only needed resurfacing.

Rio shared this good news with Chase. "The contractor tells me he can have her back in action in a few weeks. Boy was the builder smart. We should send him a gift."

"That's a good idea. I'll get Anne on it." Chase looked for any chance to speak with her. He should have been ecstatic their business had risen from the ashes like a phoenix. Previously, the future looked bleak. Instead, his joy was dampened by the fact Anne remained angry with him. Volcano eruption angry. Chase tried several times to talk to her, but each time she put a hand in the air to shut him down.

Her refrain was, "If it does not have to do with the business, I'm not interested." Many men might have given up, but Chase stayed determined and persistent. He would never consider giving up on Anne. It was not in the cards. He only needed to be dealt a better hand. Or be a better player with the one he was dealt.

"Rio, I need to run an errand. I'll be back this afternoon. Call my cell if you need me."

"Where ya goin'?" Rio asked. "What's so important you have to take off?"

Chase walked down the dock and yelled over his shoulder. "I need to stack the deck."

Several hours later, Chase's Hunter sailboat pulled into Conch Harbor Marina and slid into its slip, in plain sight of the *Satisfaction*. Rio, King, and Anne stood on the dock overseeing ship repairs and watched as Chase stepped off his craft and began to tie it down. Bill walked over to help and together they secured the sailboat.

"What the hell?" a perplexed Rio asked, as Chase and Bill met them at the *Satisfaction*.

"What do you think?" Chase asked feeling proud of himself. Rio looked puzzled while King silently scratched his beard.

Anne broke the silence. "Chase, what are you doing?" Even though her words showed a hint of anger, Chase thought her voice sounded wonderful.

"I promised you a trip to the Bahamas, and I plan on delivering."

"I'm still not talking to you." She put her hands on her hips as if to accentuate the point.

"Sounds like she is," Rio whispered to King from the corner of his mouth, prompting a nod from the big man.

"Anne, look. I'm sorry for the way I behaved. You have to believe that."

"You hurt me. Twice. I don't think I can go through life with a partner who'll fall apart every time he runs into a rough patch."

"I'm not that guy."

"You said you had nothing left. I'm calling bullshit. Take a look around at the friends you have, they're everywhere." She pointed to Bill, King, and Rio. "You have more than most peo-ple. Great friends, the admiration of people across the country. Hell, they're donating money, for goodness sake. So, don't tell me you've lost everything. And if you'd step up and be the man we all know you can be…" She paused before lowering her voice. "You'd also have me."

Chastised, Chase pleaded with her. "I know. I screwed up. Give me one more chance to show I can be that guy. Look, I've got a surprise for you." He pointed to the sailboat.

Anne looked at the boat, then back at Chase. "I don't want a trip. I just want my boyfriend back. The one I can trust."

"I want the same thing. I promise you. I *will* be a better man because I'll have you by my side. No more wallowing in self-pity, no more blaming others for my mistakes. And no more heavy drinking."

Rio and King looked at each other when the word *heavy* was mentioned. "A loophole, methinks," King whispered to Rio who nodded in agreement.

"Look, I own my faults and now want to correct them. But I can't do it without you." Chase noticed the usually resolute Anne Braun soften. He grabbed her hand and led her to the boat. "Come on, let me show you."

On the stern, the name now read *Brains and Braun*. Anne laughed at her last name and jokingly asked why she got double billing.

"That's easy. In a battle of wits with you, I'm only half armed," he teased.

She frowned. "Isn't it bad luck to change the name of a boat?"

"I didn't change it, I altered it. Corrected, so to speak," he argued. "Interesting what one letter change can do, eh?"

"Oh, great, so not only is it bad luck to change a boat's name, but you'll also have the bad luck of a woman aboard. Jeesh, whatever could go wrong?"

Chase took her sarcasm as a good sign. "Nothing, as long as you're my partner." He then instructed her to open the galley doors, and colorful balloons drifted into the bright blue sky making her laugh like a schoolgirl. She then turned to him; her mouth scrunched up in suspicion.

"Wait a second, mister. You think a name change and a few balloons are going to fix our problems?"

"No." Chase answered seriously. "I am." Noticing a hint of a smile, Chase added, "If you don't want to go on the trip, I can always cancel it."

"Let's not get crazy. When are we leaving?"

"So, I'm forgiven?" he whispered softly.

"Maybe, but I won't forget. if you ever do that to me again, I'll kill you in your sleep," she whispered back.

Chase didn't doubt *that* promise for a second.

It didn't take Jasper long to learn the identity of the mastermind behind the *Satisfaction* arson attempt. His daughter had just told him she was the culprit behind the fire.

"Are you out of your mind, Ginger!?!?" Jasper raised his voice, upset and rightly so. "Arson is a felony and this one's under investigation! If this comes back on me, so help me God!" Jasper had recently returned from a trip to Tallahassee, Ginger from Miami where they'd heard of the *Satisfaction* fire. It seemed as if both had alibis, one unintentional, the other, not so much.

"This was the surprise you had for me?"

"Father, relax, will you?" They were in Jasper's office with the door closed, though it needn't have been, for they were alone in the house. Ginger walked to the bar by the bookcase and poured herself a scotch, plunking a few ice cubes into the glass. "The ship is out of commission. And let me assure you, I took great pains to make sure this cannot blow back on us. I hired a professional from out-of-state. Well, let's say, *through* an intermediary. He doesn't know who I am so there is no way anyone can trace this back to us."

She returned to Jasper's desk and sat on the corner before making her next point. "We had no idea Chase would be sleeping on the deck when the fire started. I mean really, he should have been in his quarters. It's too bad Rio was not onboard when it lit up," she said, swishing the ice around in her glass. "Shame."

Ginger seemed nonchalant about the latest attempt to stop the Captain Morgan Piracy Tour juggernaut, and that scared Jasper. He didn't mind getting his hands dirty when it came to business, but arson? This business took dirty tricks to a whole new level. One he did not think his little girl could ever conceive of let alone pull off. And where had she gotten the money to pay this fool? He made a mental note to start digging into the books to find out.

"Supposing we are free and clear. You do know they're rebuilding the ship, don't you? It may take time, but they will be back in business within the month!"

"Yes, Daddy, I'm aware," Ginger sipped her scotch. She always prided herself on her looks, how she carried herself. But now Jasper saw her in shambles; her hair looked like she hadn't washed it in days, her outfit appeared as if she'd slept in it. Jasper thought the breakup with Rio would have been old news by now and Ginger would be back to her old self. Evidently, her new self-torched wooden sailing ships.

"Maybe you need to get out of town, take a long vacation," Jasper said. "It'll do you good. Why not go somewhere in the Caribbean? No, Europe, you love Paris!"

"Daddy," Ginger said slowly, her head bent, eyes looking down at him malevolently. "I can't leave now. I just returned from Miami, and there's so much work to be done. Besides, it's time to execute the next plan." She finished her scotch, placing the glass on the bar before heading towards the door. "I will be taking another trip to Miami soon."

"Wait," Jasper said, taken aback. "There's a next plan?"

"Of course, silly!" she answered, stopping at the door. "There is always a next plan. Weren't you the one who said you wanted someone's blood?"

This time, it was not the tone of her voice that gave her father chills. Although it did make the hair on the back of his neck stand up. What gave Jasper chills was the evil expression she sported when she spoke about *someone's blood*. It was *telling*. Ginger meant to deliver on what her father had asked for.

Literally.

In Plain Sightlines

WHILE THE *SATISFACTION* underwent her restoration, Chase and Anne left the harbor towards the Caribbean on their newly named sloop, *Brains and Braun*. They slipped free of Key West on a Sunday morning to head south with a soft breeze filling the sails. Any other power to guide them would be unnecessary. Their first port of call would be in the Abacos Islands. After that, they would run down the eastern edge of the islands, stopping at Harbour Island, Cat Island, or whatever port they desired before heading back north again to Conch Harbor.

Chase had taken down the Bimini cover, letting the warm sunshine fall upon his face while the craft maneuvered smoothly to his every touch. His first mate in a pretty yellow bikini sat to his left, her hair tied in a ponytail swinging every time she moved her head. They had been looking forward to their trip without remorse during the rebuild of the ship. They both had feelings of guilt for leaving port, but reasoned they were wasted emotions. Anne's good sense reminded him it would be more constructive to accomplish something good during an unpleasant situation, rather than sit home with nothing to do.

"Two rules while we're out to sea," Chase said, the salty breeze blowing against his face.

"And what would those two rules be, my captain?" Anne asked, a hand raised in salute.

"No shop talk."

"Fine by me. What's number two?"

"It's quite obvious." The captain reached out and took Miss Anne by the hand, kissing her fingers. "Have fun!"

Anne gripped his hand, stood up and snuggled into Chase's lap, kissing him on the nose and whispering, "Let the fun begin."

They sailed blissfully southward until late afternoon, when Chase brought the *Brains and Braun* into a cove off of Spanish Cay in the Abacos Islands and dropped the anchor. While he tended to the sails and set up for the night, Anne jumped into the water for a quick swim. As he worked, Chase gazed at her effortless glide through the crystal clear water. Again, he felt glad they decided to get away. *God knows, for all we've been through, we earned this short trip.*

With the boat moored, he sat down at the helm, never taking his eyes off her as she swam back to the stern and climbed the ladder. He had a beach towel ready to dry the saltwater dripping off her tanned body.

"You know something I've noticed?" Anne looked over at him while drying her hair.

"What? That I get better looking every day?"

Anne giggled. "No. I haven't seen you stroke your UnReale since we left."

Smiling lecherously, his voice lowered and his eyes brightened. "I've been thinking of other things to stroke."

Her hand pushed against his arm softly using her *be serious* gesture. "Really, having you out here, all to myself, seems to be great for your stress level. You've been relaxed, funny-"

"A great lover," he interjected. She snapped her towel playfully at him.

"I mean it. We should slow down and let others do the acting parts. You and I can manage the business going forward. It will take some of the pressure off you."

"Working with you every day? That'll add tons of stress!" he joked, but knew she had a point. Their trip away from Key West had been a great stress reliever. It had not occurred to him he had neglected his UnReale. What did occur to him was the last few nights before their departure, he had slept like a baby. No nightmares. No dead boys. Chase hoped the trend would continue.

"I know you want to dive more. This will give you the opportunity. Just try to consider the option. In the meantime, I'm going below to shower the salt off," Anne said as she headed into the cabin. Chase jumped out of his chair and stepped down the stairs behind her.

"I'm feeling a little salty myself," he called after her, shedding his T-shirt and swim trunks.

While absent-mindedly wiping down the bar, King brooded. He felt unhappy his usually sound intelligence system was not producing results. Even though people spoke about the arson, most of it remained speculation and hearsay. Nothing concrete to rely on, no fingers pointing to a specific person or persons. Like the father and daughter Cobb.

Whoever set the fire proved adept at this type of work. Get in, light the target up, and get out. Leave no trace. The idea of no clues frustrated King. Someone had to *know* something, *see* something, *hear* something … anything? Even a small clue like…

like someone standing out in a sea of strangers for no particular reason.

Questions swirled around King's brain. How had this guy gotten in and out of the marina undetected except by one camera? How had he gotten on and off the island without anyone noticing, and so quickly?

Still, the biggest question was WHY? Who was behind it all?

Experts in the pyro technic field did not work for free. If they did not find the person who attacked the *Satisfaction*; they would need to find the person or persons who ordered the hateful deed. Both were daunting tasks. King hoped the chief could find evidence against the main suspect, Jasper Cobb and make it stick.

King was still deep in thought wiping down the bar when Rio walked in and took his customary seat and asked for a beer.

King stopped wiping to grab the bottle of beer and slide it along to Rio.

"Have you heard anything from our wayward partners lately?" Rio asked.

"Nope! And don't expect to ... *vacation*."

"It's great for them to get away. The Cap'n has had too much on his plate lately, and he needed some free time. We should be halfway done with the repairs by the time they return. Can't wait to finish so we can take her out on a test run to get the bugs out."

King nodded.

"Any luck yet, hearing anything about... the perp?"

King shook his head and started wiping down the bar again. His mind continued to stew about Jasper. He and Ginger were not in Key West at the time of the fire. Having an alibi did not erase fingerprints on a crime. One could always hire someone to do the deed if you were miles away. How convenient! King thought, as he began to restock the beer bottles into the coolers under the bar.

Hearing about the fire, the Cobbs expressed their condolences along with their condemnation of the attack. "Wasn't it an assault on all the tour operators? Myself included?" Jasper claimed, showing a feint attempt at indignation. Their actions seemed coordinated, rehearsed and most of all, fake.

King could smell a phony a mile away, and the stench from the Cobbs lingered. If he could only find the person responsible, King would be able to make him divulge who had hired him. King needed to double his efforts in order to find the perp soon, or the trail would grow so cold they would never find the truth.

The perp King sought after was a guy by the name of Barry Stallings. He had learned how to live off the streets at an early age. Raised by a drunk and abusive father along with a weak and enabling mother, they gave little incentive for a kid like Barry to want to go straight home at night. He felt safer out on the dark streets until the old man passed out cold. Barry chose whatever the darkness held in store for him versus the bruises he received any day of the week.

Older streetwise kids showed him how to make money by shoplifting, breaking into homes or hustling drugs. But Barry's penchant for burning things caught the attention of those who required that specific type of service. His first time was burning down an old building frequented by drug addicts. Once he lit the fire and gaped as the flames took hold, Stallings was hooked.

Barry found he had a knack for getting into a target and lighting it up in such a way by the time anyone got there, it would be a total loss. For insurance claims, he scoped the place at night until he figured what would make sense; an electrical fire or an errant cigarette were usually his best options. For destruction jobs like the *Satisfaction*, where the client did not need an insurance claim, he liked to use an accelerant, placing it in the right positions to do the most damage in the quickest amount of time.

After taking a cruise aboard the *Satisfaction*, he felt the right cocktail would ignite both the deck and the rigging. Pity though, Barry enjoyed the crew's energy. It was obvious the show they put on was meticulously rehearsed. Stallings really liked their research and he learned a few things. Plus, the rum punch tasted delicious. Even when it was time to take the obligatory picture as he boarded, he didn't mind. A raised left hand across his face would make certain he couldn't be identified. For him, the tour fee was worth every penny for the entertainment value he received.

Still, he had a job to do, and when Barry Stallings did a job, he never got emotionally attached. Emotion meant carelessness and mistakes. He could not afford to be careless or prone to errors in this line of work if he wanted to continue to roam freely outside of the penal system.

He had asked and received confirmation concerning occupants. No one would be on board that night. Barry Stallings, an arsonist? Yes. A murderer? Absolutely not. Unfortunately, his recent employer had not been as informed as they had led him to believe, or they had been lying. Either way, there had not been just one soul, but two aboard the ship. Fortunately for Barry, they both made it out alive and unhurt.

The only thing to do now was to sit tight at the Coconut Garden and wait until the cruise ship came into port, spending each day relaxing by the pool and enjoying a beer or two. A few older couples and one young honeymooning couple paid him no attention, precisely what he wanted. He blended right into the scenery.

Once the cruise ship heading to the Caribbean arrived, he, with his disguise and new identity as Mr. Donald Sharpe, an insurance agent from Illinois, would be more than ready. Only then could he relax to do as he pleased without suspicion. When the cruise ended, he would disappear, and neither Barry nor Donald would ever come back to this island again. Barry hated close calls. Staying near the scene of his crime may have been a good tactical idea but provided a call way too close for comfort.

Jasper fidgeted at his desk unable to work, the look of worry etched across his face. His thoughts turned to his wife Janet. When they first met, she had been charming, beautiful, and hailed from a good family. He also liked the way she did not play by the rules and made up her own as she went along. He initially found her strength and independence appealing.

Unfortunately, it turned out not to be the case. Janet Cobb was a strong woman, but the illness overpowered any strength she tried to muster. Janet suffered from a disease diagnosed as Antisocial Personality Disorder.

When sick, she became manipulative, had little or no empathy and was prone to be mean by finding the weaknesses in people and exploiting them for her own gain. When treatment failed, Janet's anxiety levels spiked, and her suicide attempts increased. Jasper had no choice but to place her into an institution. Keeping her secluded and away from Ginger was for everyone's benefit. At least that was how Jasper rationalized the situation. Trying to recall the last time he paid her a visit, the man felt ashamed for not being able to remember.

As much as Jasper would like to deny it, Ginger began to display some of the same symptoms. She had been quite irritable and impatient lately. She became especially hot tempered concerning that Rio Grande fellow. Her mood swings—one moment confident and robust, the next, disheveled, and angry. Sullen, scary moods followed where Ginger refused to take any responsibility for her behavior. She blamed him for not being able to solve the Porter issue as their business continued to lose money. And now the violence.

Jasper ran a weary hand down his face. His daughter had hired an arsonist to torch the *Satisfaction* and had absolutely no remorse about doing so, even after realizing people could have been hurt, or worse, killed because of her actions. He had to act now. Had to get her the help she needed so she could live an almost normal life before she hurt anyone else or herself. And if he acted now, it was possible to avoid doing the same thing to Ginger as he had to do for her mother. Just the thought of having to institutionalize his beautiful daughter pained him.

He would call his physician who would recommend a specialist. Right now, he needed to do some research before she returned from Miami and whatever the hell she was now up to. Hopefully, nothing as drastic as the last action she had taken.

Jasper sat down at his desk, turned on his computer and punched in the search field: "Treatments for Antisocial Personality Disorder."

A week after they began their journey, *Brains and Braun* sailed into the bay on its return from the Caribbean. Chase and Anne wore deep tans and looked relaxed. They were both anxious to return to Key West and the possibility the arsonist had been apprehended.

Slicing through the turquoise water, they passed Mallory Square and saw the *Satisfaction*'s tall masts standing like sentries guarding the marina. Smiling at each other, they were happy to be returning home to their friends and their business. They enjoyed their getaway, sailing through emerald waters to visit islands filled with food and drink. They made new friends along the way, enjoying the beautiful sunrises and sunsets together. Both decided they would someday return to recreate their Caribbean adventure, but for now it was back to reality.

After tethering their craft in its slip, they walked up the dock to the *Satisfaction* where Rio met them. "Well, if it isn't the two lovebirds back from their adventures on the high seas!" Pointing a thumb at Chase, he asked Anne. "Are you sick of him yet?"

"On the contrary." She smiled demurely. "I had a hard time keeping my hands off his cutlass!"

Rio let out a loud guffaw. "Why, you old dog," Rio grabbed Chase's hand and shook it furiously. "We missed you guys. Not much fun with just King and I."

"Any news on the arson front?" Chase looked hopeful.

"No. They've searched everywhere. It's as if the guy was a ghost who did his dirty work and disappeared into thin air. King has his ear to the ground, still nothing. On the flip side, the work onboard is progressing well. The old girl should be ready to sail before you can say, *bottoms up!*"

Chase looked up at the men working on the *Satisfaction* with awe. Unlike Rio, who had no problem having multiple women in his life, Chase only had three. Anne first, the *Brains and Braun*, and of course, the *Satisfaction*. With the repairs almost complete, Chase hoped he could make sure to safeguard all of them from any further harm.

"What are we waiting for, let's go!" Anne sped up the gangway followed by Rio as Chase took up the rear. For the first time since leaving Key West, Chase unconsciously rubbed his UnReale as he went aboard.

ONE STEP AHEAD

GINGER COBB ACTED like a happy gal having just returned from her latest business trip to Miami for meetings that had gone well. Extremely well. She cruised in the *Ginger Snap* under the guise of speaking with the franchisor concerning their new restaurant. She took that meeting to mask her real agenda for going north. The actual meeting took place with friends of a friend who had told her they could provide the specialized services she sought for the right price.

These friends would send a team down to the Keys in order to accomplish the job quietly, quickly, and efficiently, then disappear before anyone became the wiser. Ginger knew Jasper would be concerned with the cloak-and-dagger techniques. She would have to assure him they were well insulated with no trace back to them. She felt the cost should be seen as an investment into their future earnings once the reputation of the *Satisfaction* and its crew sank. Much like Rio's laptop dumped into the Florida Strait.

In discussions with her father, she laid out the plan designed to create an incident to cause tourists to question the sense of a tour aboard the *Satisfaction*. "Tourists flock to Key West in order to relax and have fun, not worry about terrorists stealing their belongings… or worse, their own safety," she told Jasper.

Proxy reiterated, *Or much worse.*

Ginger told him how she believed the *Satisfaction*'s crew would be woefully unprepared for that type of an attack. The negative publicity would ruin the reputation of the high and mighty Chase Porter and Co. allowing Cobb Enterprises to lead the way in enforcing stricter safety measures for tour operators. Measures which included engaging the Coast Guard for more patrols and allowing her to sweep up the frightened tourists onto their well-guarded boats.

Ginger thought the plan foolproof. As predicted, Jasper was still not convinced. "Nothing is foolproof. I hope you know what you're doing. My concern is with getting caught. But I can see how this plan makes sense. Discredit the competition and come to the rescue as heroes." He thought for a moment before adding, "It would be nice to win again."

Yes, Yes it would, said Proxy. *For a change.*

Jasper added one more caveat. "Assure me no one will get hurt and no property damaged?"

"Father dear," Ginger began, well aware her father hated the way she said it. She often did so just to see him wince every time she addressed him as such. "I have this under control. I've planned to make sure nothing goes wrong. They come in just as the *Satisfaction* is headed for the sunset at Mallory Square, scare the shit out of everyone on board, then slip out. We, on the other hand, will be seen at the Fantasy Fest Parade in town, so our alibi is intact. No one would suspect the great Jasper Cobb would dare be involved in such a diabolical plan. Even if they did, they couldn't prove it. Trust me, we have all bases covered."

"That's what I'm worried about … Steinbeck."

"What do you mean by that?"

"The best laid plans…" Jasper trailed off wanting to take his mind off *Of Mice and Men.*

Ginger left her father and walked back to her office. She had important work awaiting her. Duties that included the transfer of Cobb Enterprise funds to a secret offshore account. Then transferring *those* funds to the account of the intermediary who had arranged for the next installment of her *Let's get rid of Chase Porter* campaign.

Embezzlement again, is it? Proxy asked, reveling in the new plan.

"I prefer the term *'funneled'*; if you don't mind. *Embezzlement* has such a negative ring to it. Don't you think?" Ginger said, rationalizing with the voice in her head.

I'm not judging, dear heart. Funneling funds is fun.

"With no paper trail!" Ginger giggled as she played along.

You should have gone into banking, Proxy told her. *We'd have made a bundle in Switzerland instead of screwing around with this other shit.*

Ginger ignored the last comment as she finished the transaction. She had built a simple plan to siphon off a small amount of cash from each of the business units then deposit them into the offshore account. Her role as the company's CFO made it easy. Her father had relinquished the purse strings to her, and as long as she showed a profit on the books, he never questioned her. It was an ideal arrangement for both parties. She funneled, he remained blissfully unaware.

In the beginning, her rationale had been purely for self-interest.

A girl had to think about her future, Proxy commented, justifying Ginger's actions. If necessary, the lost revenue would be made up once she took over her father's position as CEO. For now, the untraceable war chest proved invaluable to her. Ginger sat back in her chair and contemplated life without Chase Porter.

It's good being the queen, isn't it? Proxy asked.

"Yes, yes, it is," responded Queen Ginger. "And now, it's time to celebrate. Let's go have us a drink."

Proxy answered reverently, *Yes, your highness*!

The day after they returned from the Caribbean, Chase woke up and rolled out of bed, careful not to wake Anne. He started a pot of coffee and went to his desk where he studied the maps and plotted just how far he may need to swim away from the *Mastery*. He needed better equipment and believed he had found what he was looking for. He studied the picture he'd enlarged on his open laptop.

The device, called a Rebreather, absorbed the carbon dioxide a diver exhaled by scrubbing it with a canister filled with soda lime. The apparatus then recycled the unused oxygen of each exhaled breath rather than expelling it into the water as did open circuit systems. Oxygen needed to be added either manually or electronically to make sure the diver always had enough air to breathe. The end result allowed the diver the ability to stay underwater far longer than conventional scuba equipment. The process was efficient and practical.

Chase studied the photo of the best rebreather on the market, then added it to the manufacturer's online basket. He stared at the submit button for only a second before he pushed it, then he printed the receipt. YOUR PRODUCT WILL BE SHIPPED SHORTLY, read the message. "Thank God for online shopping," he whispered.

Getting up, he poured a cup of coffee. Seeing Anne still asleep, he sat back at his desk to look over the maps again, recalling the dream of the boy sitting on the mast beckoning for Chase to follow. *This way!*

He got up from the desk and looked out at the dock housing the *Satisfaction.* The site still excited him, although the rebuilding work had not yet started for the day. His eyes drifted to a bird at the end of the pier. Every so often it darted under the wood out of sight. Before long it would emerge back into the open.

"Wait a second," Chase said quietly, a faint idea forming. One that had angered him at first … but as he wrapped his mind around it, his anger shifted to excitement. "What if?" he asked aloud, talking to himself. "What if…it was time to take a walk?"

He quickly dressed, slipping out of the *Brains and Braun,* and walked up and down the dock as if inspecting its worthiness. He strode past the *Satisfaction* in the same direction the exiting perp would have taken. Coming to a stop a short distance from the bow, he got down on his knees and looked underneath the dock. A knowing smile formed as he looked beneath the planks.

The bird had given him a clue that everyone else had missed. A new theory seen from a different angle. When he stood up, Chase began walking out of the marina and headed for the police station. And if the chief was not in yet, he planned to wait.

Chase did not have to wait long. He had just settled in on a bench in the waiting area when Chief Deakin walked inside. With a surprised look, the chief asked, "Did we get in some trouble last night, Chase?"

"Nope. But I do have a theory I wanted to run by you. Do you have a moment?"

"Sure. Coffee?"

"Yes please, I only had time for one cup this morning. Could use a bit more caffeine."

As the two entered the chief's office, the senior of the two poured the coffee while Chase asked, "Something occurred to me concerning the video. Can we see it again?"

Deakin nodded, went to the desk, and opened his laptop careful not to spill his coffee. The screen crackled to life, and the footage rolled again showing the same hooded figure attempting the destruction of the *Satisfaction*.

With the deed finished, the perp disappears from the camera. Chase said, "Stop it there, please." The chief complied. Chase pointed to the spot where the hooded man was last seen on camera. "If he's coming from land to the docks, he would've had to come by some form of transportation."

Deakin nodded. "Car, motorcycle, cab, Uber … we're checking on all the ride shares and so far, nothing."

"Right," began Chase. "But he would also have been picked up on another camera, right? Roll the video further and tell me what you *don't* see."

The chief clicked on the reverse button and studied closely as the hooded figure disappeared after the ship ignited. Looking over at Chase, he nodded. "We didn't see him enter the dock or see him leave either. We already know this. What's your point?"

"So," Chase continued, "there are a few logical conclusions …."

Deakin finished the sentence, "He left the dock by sea."

Chase cocked his head and pursed his lips in the *maybe* gesture. "That's one possibility, but what about another option? What if he left not by sea, but by a different route?"

"Then we'd have captured it on video. As you can plainly see, he disappears."

It was Chase's turn to interrupt. "Yup, just like Houdini." He then proceeded to explain what he had discovered.

Deakin looked at Chase admiringly. "If this tourism thing doesn't work out, would you consider a career in law enforcement?"

With repairs complete, the refurbished *Satisfaction* left port for its initial test run. Chase also wanted to do a dress rehearsal before they reopened for business. On board, were the four principal owners: Chase, Rio, Anne, and King along with Daniel, and twenty-four crewmembers. They usually needed a handful to sail, but Chase thought it would be prudent to have the entire crew tighten up the old acts and practice new ones.

A security firm had installed a state-of-the-art system and Chase wanted to make sure all the principals knew how to operate it. In addition to some new pirate tales, he had also hatched a special project needing additional practice. This first run proved to be the perfect time to do so while out of sight of non-employee eyes.

Like his mother, Chase hated the saying, *practice makes perfect*. Her preference was, "Practice does not make perfect, nothing does. It will, however, make better!" He never forgot the old-fashioned saying and made everyone practice each role they played over and over again, bringing those stories to life. Chase always had a slew of innovative ideas spring from the practice sessions which continually improved the show.

Having all the crew members aboard meant they would all be ready to execute the new plan should the need arise. Chase hoped it would not come to that and yet, after what had already happened to the *Satisfaction*, he was not taking any chances. The same person or persons might attempt to cause trouble while the ship took their passengers out to sea.

Chase ran the special exercise over and over again, substituting crewmembers and asking for ways to improve until all were exhausted. People could say a lot of things about the crew of the *Satisfaction* ... being unprepared for another attack surely would not be one of them. Chase marveled at his crew's loyalty and work ethic.

Always try and stay one step ahead, ran through Chase's head as they sailed back to the harbor and docked her for the evening.

Afterward, they all met at the Berth for a drink, the crew relaxed for the first time since the fire. With the new security system in place and the police on guard, Chase felt reasonably sure the *Satisfaction* would be safe in its slip at Conch Harbor. Bill Hemmings joined in by patrolling the docks late at night so no other ships would suffer as the *Satisfaction* had on his watch. Everyone understood the threat was not over until the perpetrators of the arson were apprehended and locked up.

The discussion arose about possible new threats to the ongoing investigation. Questions hung in the air like stale cigarette smoke. A few had been answered, but the big ones still floated around and they all smelled like sewer gas.

Anne spoke up first, "Do they have any suspects yet?" Then added, "As if we don't already have our own."

"Not that I know of. I'm no longer sure Jasper would stoop so low as to commit a felony like arson. We have to let the police do their job." Chase didn't mention his latest visit to the chief, or his new theory on how the perp escaped without being seen.

King had not heard any whispers from his sources at the Berth or around town, a cause for concern. "My usual contacts are all strangely quiet."

"Saves you their free beer," Rio tossed out.

Chase was aware whoever pulled off the arson had done so with an efficiency of a military operation. The absence of chatter about the event told him there were only a few people involved. The old saying, *It takes two people to keep a secret if one of them is dead*, did not apply here. There were no dead bodies to be found in their case, leaving Chase understandably confused. Sometimes, even without loose lips, the ship could still sink.

One Attack, One Repel

"**E**ither your thumb and index finger are gonna fall off, or you'll wear a hole in that UnReale, Chase. You really need to relax," Rio said as Chase kept a keen eye on the passengers coming aboard the *Satisfaction* about to launch her first official voyage since the fire.

"We've gotten all the repairs done, the ship looks better than it did before the fire, and we've got a full deck of lubbers today. There is nothing to worry about."

"You're right. The ship never looked better." Chase let go of his UnReale.

While repairs were being completed on the main deck, the crew did a complete cleansing of the ship, scrubbing everything from fore to aft, bowsprit to mizzen mast. "Relax," Rio said again. "This is gonna be fun. We've been in port too long. Time to dazzle our guests again. It's showtime!"

As the last lubber came aboard, Rio called muster. Their ritual, mandatory for boat tour operators, instructed each passenger what to do in case of an emergency, showed where the life jackets were stored and where the lubbers were to assemble in an emergency.

Once the program ended, Rio blew his bosun's whistle, and the great ship began to retreat from its mooring.

Captain Chase stepped forward to greet his new shipmates. "Welcome, aboard the *Satisfaction*, lubbers," he began with his usual greeting. "This craft is a frigate, one of the fastest ships of its time and can outrun any ship on the high seas. My name is Captain Porter, and we're in for a full day of adventure out on those high seas! Can I get a Huzzah?"

The tourists were treated to a sunny, cloudless day with a southwesterly breeze on their journey to The Dry Tortugas. They enjoyed their rum punch or beer as they toured the ship's decks to see what living conditions were like as a pirate during the 17th and 18th centuries.

Synchronized like clockwork, each of eight crewmembers took a group of lubbers and went systematically around the ship and due to almost full capacity on this cruise, the crew had to repeat the exercise.

Rio waited in the bunking quarters and storage areas while King stayed down in the battery to talk about how they operated the cannons during battle. The Garrity boys climbed the rigging and sat in the crow's nests showing a few brave souls the art of their scary, yet useful trade. Crunchy held court near the mizzenmast discussing the merits of tacking into the wind or charting navigation by the stars. Chase welcomed groups into his Captain's quarters. Anne had the day off.

After a day of swimming, touring the fort and snorkeling, the lubbers all clambered aboard the *Satisfaction* for the sail home to Key West. The crew scrambled to their stations while the southerly wind filled the sails as Crunchy steered the great ship northward. The lubbers were content to sit back and relax.

Vessels of all types cruised the waters off Key West. It would not be uncommon to see other vessels in the distance. Yachts cruising by, fishing charters looking for the next wave of catch, or the occasional cruise ship heading in or out of the Keys. Each watercraft would show courtesy by keeping a safer distance from the *Satisfaction* with its tall masts filled with the salty wind.

But not this day. Both Garrity brothers yelled from the crow's nests, warning of an approaching boat disregarding a safe distance and speeding towards them. Chase looked up to John Garrity and made the sign of the cross, the signal to stay on your toes for any trouble.

John relayed it to his brother, Tom. They both whistled, capturing the attention of other pirate crew members on board, and passing the signal on to them.

Chase passed the signal to King who then relayed it to Rio on the quarterdeck before heading down to his position inside the battery. Rio went to the helm and whispered to Crunchy, who nodded in recognition. Rio stepped up to the poop deck. Each member of the crew now communicating by sign language. Within minutes, all were in place and at the ready. As practiced, the pirate crew kept smiles on their faces so as not to alarm the unsuspecting lubbers.

Chase signaled John Garrity for an update. *Five hundred meters and closing fast,* Garrity signed back.

Markings?

None. White as a ghost.

This was a bad development. By law, each craft must have serial numbers marking it, much like the tags on an automobile or the numbers on the tail of an aircraft. The approaching boat had no such markings, indicating they did not want anyone to know who owned the boat, where it came from or where it headed. None of which could be taken as friendly.

Chase and the others had trained for any such assault on their pirate ship. "Practice makes better," Chase whispered. Hopefully, better would be enough.

"Lubbers, can I have your attention, please?" Chase began, setting the plan into motion. "As captain of this vessel, it is my duty to make sure we are well armed in the event we find a target to raid or an enemy who wishes to attack us. So, let me show you the armaments we have at our disposal."

Chase looked up as Tom Garrity pointed toward the port side, the information then relayed down to King in the battery. Chase continued. "If you glance over the port side of the ship, you'll see the hatches below begin to open." Right on cue, King opened them exposing the barrels of the cannon.

From the crow's nest came the signal, *300 meters, and closing.*

"This is where we house our cannons. We do not want to sink a ship, only to disable it for it might have valuable treasure and goods aboard to capture. We also reserve the pirate right to commandeer the ship and add it to our fleet. Do we have anyone out there brave enough to captain our next vessel?" Nervous laughter came from the crowd, yet no one raised a hand.

Approaching port side, signaled Tom Garrity to Captain Porter.

Chase gave Crunchy the signal to slow the ship, and the white boat sidled up, bobbing up and down in the waves, a few hundred meters to the side of the ship. It was a trawler with six masked figures holding weapons. The boat's pilot, also masked, slowed his craft, coming close enough for one of the masked gunmen holding a bullhorn to address the *Satisfaction*'s crew.

"This is a raid. We've come to seize your vessel."

Chase swallowed the anxiety creeping up his throat and, as if it were part of the entertainment, announced loud enough for the attackers to hear, "Avast ye! A boarding party is attempting to take over our ship! All hands to battle stations! Prepare to repel the scallywags! And give no quarter!"

Turning to the crowd, he continued, "Folks, we have swivel guns strategically placed on the upper decks to ward off any attackers who get too close to the ship out of range of our heavy cannon armed with chain shot. That's two cannon balls tied together with a chain. Imagine the carnage those weapons could inflict?"

The lubbers looked a little confused at first, but after listening to Chase and seeing the confident air about him, they began to see the adventure as part of the show. Like visitors to the zoo, the lubbers congregated against the port side curious to see what would happen next. They were not disappointed.

Upon hearing Chase speak, the pilot of the attacking boat dropped his engine into reverse, slowly backing up, but was quickly shoved by the man with the bullhorn and forced to put the gear back into neutral.

Mr. Bullhorn lifted it and announced, "Resistance is futile. If you allow us to board, no one will get hurt."

"Under what authority?" Chase responded coolly, his leg resting on the railing, hands on his knee. "I see no colors flying."

Mr. Bullhorn raised his weapon in a threatening manner, about to speak again but was shut down by Chase who addressed his shipmates. "What say you? Shall we let these bilge rats aboard?"

A resounding "NO!" rang out from all on deck. Pirates and lubbers alike jeered and howled at the attackers, everyone wanting to play a role in the pirate drama.

"Arrgh, you heard 'em! You'll have to do better than those pea shooters, mate!" yelled the captain. "Aimed in your direction are fifteen cannon ready to fire should you attempt any chicanery. And if you think you'll get any closer, you'll be met with these swivel guns sending you to Davey Jones Locker before you can get within ten feet of the hull!"

Rio and a few crewmates operated the swivel guns from up on the poop deck and fore deck. Rio taunted the intruders with a wave.

Mr. Bullhorn lowered his arm as he took a moment to ponder the situation. The six men aboard the trawler looked at each other in confusion. Chase sneered at them; now confident he had control of the situation. Other crew members and lubbers followed suit, backing their captain with taunts of their own.

Mr. Bullhorn slowly raised it again and spoke. "Don't be foolish. We've been told you don't arm this ship. You just use gunpowder for effect. Now if you—"

Mr. Bullhorn never finished his sentence. King fired off a cannon sending the chain shot spinning over the top of the attacker's craft, causing its occupants to duck. The pilot, still crouching, slammed his shifter into reverse, aligning his boat perpendicular to the *Satisfaction*. His bow pointed directly at the large ship, offering King a smaller target should he decide to fire again.

"You were saying?" Chase shouted; his sneer replaced with a huge grin. Cheers erupted from the *Satisfaction*'s deck, the lubbers enjoying the unfolding events.

"Whoa! Take it easy!" shouted Mr. Bullhorn, both arms raised.

Although his intention may have been to signal a parlay, the shotgun in his raised hand must have appeared menacing to King who, interpreting it as a hostile act, fired another cannon shot. This time a thirty-two-pound ball landed to the port side of the attacker's boat sending a wave over the side, almost swamping the trawler.

Chase nodded to his swivel gunners, who took a few shots with smaller four-pound balls, landing them close enough to show the pilot they meant business. The balls may have been smaller than the larger cannon shot, but they still had the intended effect. The pilot slammed his craft into reverse until the vessel slipped out of range, then he forced it into forward and sped off toward the mainland leaving everyone onboard the *Satisfaction* cheering wildly.

Lubbers and pirates alike clapped each other on their backs. Hugs and handshakes made their way around and finally a loud round of *Huzzahs!* filled the air aimed at the man who had held his ground. Captain Chase wiped the sweat off his forehead and signaled to Crunchy to get them back to port. Crunchy did not need to be told twice.

Once back at the dock, news traveled quickly. Lubbers lauded the trip all over social media, explaining how the tour company had taken the experience to the next level of adventure.

The crew members were sworn to secrecy and instructed to go along with the narrative as to how the day's events had been a planned part of the cruise. Had the hijack been successful, it would have been a public relations disaster and who knew how much damage it would have done to their business. Chase had once again saved the day by having his crew prepared for any encounter on land or sea. Not perfect, but it was enough ... one step ahead.

It now seemed there was another problem. The reservations would continue to pour in, but going forward, the new lubbers would be expecting a naval battle. Chase summoned the principals to meet in the captain's quarters to discuss the situation. Even though she had the day off, Chase felt the need to call Anne to come join them. She was not happy.

"What could be so important to call me in?" she complained, stepping into the room.

Chase apologized first to calm her, "Sorry, but we had an incident at sea." He explained what had happened and how the crew had done its job admirably.

"I'm glad no one got hurt," she said, no longer angry.

"What fun! I could've sunk 'em." A wide grin shined through King's beard.

"I know, King, you showed great restraint. We don't need the coast guard poking around looking for survivors on a boat we just sank. Would *not* have looked good."

"I personally do not look good in stripes," Rio said, "especially prison ones."

"Not to mention sinking our business along with the trawler," added Anne.

They all may have felt relief at dodging a catastrophe at sea, but the entire crew was getting sick of whoever was waging this war against CMPT Company.

The news of the attack also reached Jasper. In his office, Ginger stood next to the desk, a glum frown on her face. "Those idiots were only supposed to put a scare into the tourists so the bad press would cripple the company!"

"Did you ever think," Jasper began, "that if tourists became afraid of being hijacked on the *Satisfaction*, they might think *no one* is safe off the shores of Key West … including our operators?" The last sentence lingered, and Ginger felt the sting of his rebuke.

"If it had not been for the *Satisfaction*'s Captain and crew and how they'd played it all out, tourism on the island might have been sunk." He shook his head in disgust. "Along with our fortune and your inheritance. Had you even thought about that?"

Ginger remembered her fathers' response to her plan and now wondered why he had not mentioned his current opinion before the plan went into play.

Hypocrite, offered Proxy.

Ginger struggled with her response. "Our guy said they fired cannon balls at them. The *Satisfaction* is not supposed to be armed!"

Jasper shook his head. "Neither were your guys. You could have destroyed us all with your recklessness!"

Ginger scrambled, looking for anything to take attention away from herself. She felt like a rodent caught in a kitchen when the lights came on. She did not need to be the first rodent to hide, just not the last one left in the light. "Can't we do something about their cannon fire?"

"Perhaps," replied her father now pacing slowly around the room, still visibly upset. "But this has gotten outta hand. You're going to send us both to prison. I forbid you to do anything more against Chase Porter and his company, do you understand?"

As Ginger stared at her father her face darkened.

Oh, methinks you do, prodded Proxy.

Ginger bit her lower lip to quell the anger bubbling up inside. She held most of it down as she walked over to him and took his hands as she always did when she wanted to reassure him. Only this time, instead of softly caressing them, she tightened her grip until Jasper winced in pain. His hands buckling under her grasp, what little anger she let come out would be sufficient to make her point.

"Father," she began slowly, menacingly, "your plans so far have failed miserably. It's my turn now. These were minor setbacks. Minor. We will continue to follow my course of action to rid ourselves of this plague, not yours. Do you understand?" Jasper nodded weakly under Ginger's firm grip and even harder gaze into his eyes.

Proxy was gleeful. *Girl, don't forget about forbid.*

"And another thing, if you ever use the word *forbid* in my presence again ...." Her voice dropped off as her hands released his bent fingers, her message received.

"What do you want me to do?" he asked meekly, knowing he was no longer in control.

"Go see the chief of police." She walked around to the back side of his desk, pulled out his chair and sat down in it. Ginger had just taken over. "You have a complaint to file."

Like King, Chief Deakin was also not having much luck finding the arsonist. His original plan had his men working overtime to solve the case, instructing two officers to get the records of every cab, Uber, Lyft, bicycle, or other transportation company in Old Town working the evening of the fire. Now he sent the forensics crew back to the dock to find new evidence the police could use to link a perp to the crime scene, hoping Chase's theory paid off.

Next, he instructed Sergeant Willis and his team to scour the gas stations and convenience stores for a video which could prove helpful in figuring out how the perpetrator got the accelerant used for the ship fire.

The chief shook his head. Too many questions and not enough answers. He had never had a case like this before. Key West had been a quiet tourist town. The most troublesome aspects he had witnessed in his years as chief were the drunkards, domestic disturbances, or property damage. But arson? Never.

The more the chief thought about the crime, the more it worried him. It did not appear to be a random act, but a well thought out plan to destroy a single target. A target taking money away from the other tour boat operators on the island. The only way to return to the status quo would be to eliminate the threat named the *Satisfaction.*

Deakin also surmised the one person who benefitted most from this crime would also be the one with the wherewithal to pull it off because of the assets he owned: trolleys for transportation, B&Bs for overnight accommodations, and one other asset. A marina with gas pumps at his disposal. Now, the only question burning in the chief's mind; could he find the proof? While pondering the thought, he received a call from his sergeant.

"Willis, what have you got?"

"So far nothing from any of the convenience stores, but I did go over all the marinas, and I have appointments to go over their fuel records this week. You'll never guess who tried to put me off?"

"Jasper Cobb?" asked the chief.

"Yup. Says, they've been having issues with the pumps. They're getting them repaired and can't give us access till the following week."

"What about video?"

"No go there as well. Seems like the recording equipment broke down. Coincidence, eh?"

The chief shook his head in disgust. "Any luck with B&B records? Trolley receipts?"

"Sorry. chief, you know how easy it is to let someone stay in a room or hop on a trolley for free? The only way to pin something like that on a company is if an employee spoke up, and even then, it would be sketchy."

"Keep at it and keep a low profile. We don't want to make anyone a suspect until we find proof. Got It?"

"Got it, chief. I'll be back into the station after I talk to a few more folks."

Chief Deakin believed he had his suspect. He just didn't want to alert him until he had enough evidence to arrest Jasper Cobb so the prosecutor could make a conviction stick. What he did not expect, happened next.

"Hello, chief," Jasper said as he walked into the office. He had a sickly-sweet smile on his face that made Deakin feel a little queasy. Something about Cobb seemed a little off, but he could not put a finger on it.

"I'd like to file a complaint," said the not quite right Jasper Cobb.

SWABBING THE DECK

CHIEF DEAKIN REQUESTED Chase to come back to the station for yet another conversation about the firebombing investigation of the *Satisfaction*. He could tell Chase was not happy by the demeanor of the young man as he walked into the office. "Chief, we've gone over the story and tape so many times, I can recite it verbatim and relate the video frame by frame. What more do you need?"

"Sit down, will you Chase?" began Deakin, amused by Porter's frustration level.

"Chief, what more can I tell …."

"Wait," the chief raised a hand to interrupt. "This is something new. How about you tell me about your little pirate adventure out to sea yesterday?"

Chase only stared at the chief.

Deakin noticed how he toyed with the chain around his neck. The detective in him wondered. *Is he nervous?* "Well? You gonna sit there and stare at me all day, or are you going to tell me what happened?" The chief drummed his fingers on the table to add a little irritation.

"All part of our show," said Chase. "We were explaining about 18th-century weapons when on cue a boat approached and wanted to board us. We showed off our weapons, and they backed off. The crowd loved it."

"Part of the show, huh?" the chief asked, unsure if he bought this story yet. "And I suppose firing cannonballs are part of the show as well?"

"Now, chief," Chase responded, "you of all people know we only use gunpowder for show and besides, it's illegal to fire real ammunition, not to mention bad for the environment as well." Skirting the truth now became Chase's primary defense, and he was sticking to it. "But out of curiosity, who told you about our impromptu show?"

"Jasper Cobb. Said he had a complaint."

The chief observed Chase's head turn as if the question caught him by surprise. He also reached for the coin around his neck. "A complaint … from who?"

"Jasper said it came from one of your crew members." The chief looked for more signs of surprise.

"One of mine? I doubt that!"

Deakin waited for Chase to add to his statement. *This is one cool customer*!

"Let me reassure you, chief. I don't know where Jasper gets his information. You need not worry. Next time we'll use an attack vessel from the 18th and not the 21st century. You know what sticklers we've become for historical accuracy. This was a beta test to see the lubbers' reaction."

"And how did the test go?" The chief continued fishing for information.

"Great! However, until we have another ship of the same time period, we'll have to save our gunpowder for the sundown celebrations. Not that we have any plans for another ship, trade secrets and all."

The explanation placated Deakin for the time being. He knew there was more to the story than this. But there were no other complaints and he did not trust Jasper one bit. Time to put it on the back burner. No harm, no foul.

Deakin took a deep breath and said, "Chase, in my experience I've found there are some people who don't want the light shining on them. They play a game I call *Monkeys in the Tree*. When you start looking at the root of the tree—a metaphor for the issue that person does not want you to see—they start pointing to the monkeys in the tree, hoping to take your focus away from the roots. You just happened to be one of the monkeys. Seems like our friend, Jasper, has a few roots he doesn't want us looking at, doesn't it?"

"Seems that way. Do me a favor, chief. If someone other than Jasper comes forward, let's revisit this complaint. I'll address this with my crew to see if anyone has an issue with the way we operate the company. Until that time, we stop looking at Jasper's monkeys and get back to the root: who wants the Captain Morgan Piracy Tour Company out of business so badly he would resort to arson?"

Chief Deakin contemplated the young man. Calm and cool under pressure and adept at staying focused on the real issue. No monkeys in the tree here. Deakin liked the young man and decided Jasper had come to him with a complaint minus any real proof or witnesses.

The chief had only one question on his mind. *If Jasper Cobb was trying to get the law to look at monkeys in the tree, what is he hiding in the roots?*

The next day at happy hour, the Berth had a bar full of housekeeping staffers. Normally done with their chores in the early afternoon,

it afforded them some time for enjoying adult beverages at their favorite watering holes ahead of the bartenders and wait staffs.

For some reason, they were uncharacteristically thirsty. Add a handful of tourists to his regular customers and King had a surprisingly good afternoon cooking before his tour of duty on the sundown cruise.

Sharing the bar duties with him today was another bartender named Julie, who also lived in King's rent-controlled house. As King and Julie hustled drinks around the Berth, King kept his ears open on the outside chance he would hear some news leading to the firebomber. Time had moved along and so had the opportunity to get reliable information. Or so he thought. King was bringing Mojitos to two twenty-something girls at the end of the bar, when his patience paid off.

"It's the strangest thing," said the first girl with dark hair matching her complexion. "He sits by the pool, never saying a word to anyone. He has a cooler by a chair and pulls a beer out now and then, but he never gets into the pool. Then he'll go back to his room and hang a *do not disturb* sign on the door. I haven't been able to clean it for a few weeks. It's gotta stink to high heaven by now." She had been relating her story to her blonde friend with a ponytail, as they sat together at the bar within King's earshot.

"What did your supervisor say?" Ponytail wanted to know.

"She told me to never mind and stay away from the room."

King watched the dark-haired girl push the bangs out of her eyes and give an audible, "Tsk!" An indication to him she might have been perturbed by the slight.

"Rude. Do you think he's some celebrity or something?" Ponytail asked.

"Maybe," responded Dark Hair. "We see celebrities at the hotel from time to time but never at the B&Bs. Wonder what his story is?"

King shuffled drinks as fast as he could to get closer to their conversation as Dark Hair continued her story. "Funnier still, I checked to see what name he registered under, and he isn't."

"Isn't what?" asked Ponytail before finishing her drink.

"Isn't registered. The register has room twelve blocked off for repairs."

"That *is* weird," acknowledged her friend as she rolled her eyes.

Dark Hair shifted the conversation to the plans Ponytail had for the weekend.

King interrupted them with new Mojitos.

"We didn't order these, did we?" Ponytail asked as she accepted the drink.

"Nope, on the house for you two. You work at the … uh…uh…"

"Coconut Garden B&B." Dark Hair answered happily.

"Just like to take care of our hospitality workers," King explained.

"We work other places, too!" said Ponytail, hoping to plant seeds for future drinks on the house.

King smiled. *Patience is a virtue only when it pays off.* This payoff proved huge as the Coconut Garden happened to be one of the assets owned and operated by none other than Cobb Enterprises.

He pulled out his cell phone and called Rio. "I need a favor, and this old man needs a young man's legs." He told Rio where to meet him.

With the information he had just acquired, and knowing Rio was on his way to help, King went upstairs to his apartment and grabbed his digital camera off the dresser in his bedroom. As he passed the bar, he grunted a harmless lie to Julie about going *birding* with instructions to hold down the fort. Then he walked out the door towards the Coconut Garden.

It was past three p.m. when King arrived, walking into the alley between the Garden and an old mansion occupied only in the winter by an elderly couple. They had not yet moved down, so King snooped undetected as he looked for a vantage point to get a good shot of the *celebrity* of Coconut Garden. A large garbage dumpster provided the perfect platform to see into the Gardens' pool area. King just hoped his *celebrity* remained sitting by the pool.

A few minutes later, Rio showed up a little winded. "What's up?"

"Need some pictures, and I'm not as eager to climb as I used to be." King pointed to the dumpster and explained what the girls at the bar had told him.

"I love this cloak and dagger shit," Rio whispered, climbing onto the dumpster.

"Can you see anything?" King asked.

"Not yet, maybe if I climb this tree I can get a better view," Rio stepped onto a branch and disappeared into the tree brush. "I got him!" he whispered down to King who had managed to climb on top of the dumpster and balanced precariously over its smelly contents.

King could now see why Rio needed a better vantage point. There was an umbrella blocking some of the pool area. But in the distance, lounging in a chair sat a small, dark-haired man with plain features sitting by himself. Beside the man rested a cooler. He reached into the cooler with his left hand, pulled out a beer, opened it and took a long swig. He put the can next to his chair and looked up into the sun to tan his face. From within the tree branches, King heard the clicks of his camera as Rio began taking pictures.

"Make sure you get pictures of everything," King whispered. "*Everything.*"

"So, tell me. What did the chief have to say about Porter firing a cannon at poor, unsuspecting boaters?" Ginger asked.

Jasper scowled as he sat down in the visitor chair in front of his desk. He was angry his daughter had commandeered his comfy chair sitting behind his desk, but wary to challenge her.

"He said he'd look into it. I told him one of Porter's own people on board had complained. That should get the ball rolling." Jasper wriggled uncomfortably in the wooden chair.

"Good!" she said, smirking wickedly. "We need the heat on someone else while we think of what to do next."

Jasper, about to speak, stopped as he noticed the evil look on his daughter's face. He barely recognized her. *How reckless was this girl?* If he let her continue, she would ruin them both, and he was not about to let that happen.

The time had passed to call the doctor. Now frightened of this woman, he felt the need to be cautious, tread carefully and bide his time while he found the right course of action to get her under control. If she could plan those terrible things against Chase Porter, she could do dreadful things to anyone. Including her own father.

"Are they still on the wild goose chase? Pun definitely intended," Ginger asked, smiling at her own joke.

"What?" A startled Jasper stirred from his train of thought, derailed by her question.

"Chief Deakin and his dumbass deputies. They still out there looking for the arsonist?"

"Uhm, yes, they came snooping around the marina—" Jasper stopped mid-sentence at Ginger's use of the term *goose chase*, as if the cops were looking in places the arsonist would never be found. "They won't find him on the road, air or by sea … will they, Ginger?"

"Of course not, Papa," she said, obviously pleased with herself. "He's been chilling out at the Coconut Garden all this time. But don't worry, he'll be leaving shortly. Soon he'll be getting on a cruise ship and sailing to the Bahamas. The police are searching for transportation records *off* the islands, but I thought it prudent to keep him here right under their noses. Then spirit him away where they'll never find him. Smart, huh?" Ginger looked smug sitting behind Jasper's desk.

It now dawned on Jasper she was smarter than he gave her credit for. And a lot scarier.

"Can he be trusted to lie low?" Jasper asked, knowing her response, yet asking anyway.

"Of course. He's not registered at the B&B, and we blocked the room off as *under repairs*. The only one who knows is Marilynn, the manager, and she believes he's a celebrity who needs his privacy. It's a perfect cover, so there is no paper trail or suspicion."

"Looks like you've thought of everything, haven't you?"

Her look turned sour. "I have. And soon, we'll no longer have anything to worry about. Well, except what to do next. Any ideas, father dearest?"

Jasper shook his head. He had no plans to come up with any ideas which would drive him in deeper with this crazy person pretending to be his daughter. If he was to survive this mess unscathed, he'd have to come up with another plan. He knew of one called an *exit strategy* used in commerce when the time was ripe to leave a business venture behind by selling off its assets.

Jasper, certain the time to be overly ripe, decided to extricate himself from this mess by developing his very own exit strategy.

King recalled a saying about a picture being worth a thousand words, but the digital images on his camera left him more speechless than usual. He had several close-ups of the subject and a keen sense of Déjà Vu. *I've seen this guy before, but where?*

Maybe the girls at the bar were correct about the fella's celebrity status. A movie star, perhaps? No. He looked a little too ordinary to be a famous star. But King, feeling certain he had seen him before, just had to figure out where? *If I were this guy, what would I do if I wanted to burn down the Satisfaction?*

He began to check off a few items before the real answer soon became clear. To know the best place to start a fire, you would need to do surveillance. What better place to do surveillance than on the ship itself?

King stopped cold. He remembered where he had seen the man. He had taken one of their cruises, King was sure of it. The man had come on board alone; the reason King had noticed his face out of so many others in the first place. And, if he had taken one of their cruises, there might still be proof of it.

Happy with his deductive reasoning, King headed over to the retail shop in the hopes he would find that proof. He opened the shop's door and mumbled to himself, "Where do they keep the pictures people *don't* buy after our cruises?"

King hoped his subject had been one of those customers and with any luck, may have forgotten his picture had even been taken. If King could place the man from the Coconut Garden on the *Satisfaction*, it might be enough proof for the chief to bring him in for questioning.

King went through the door into the storeroom where he found a box filled with pictures of lubbers from past trips over the last several weeks.

He looked for a single man to match the picture from the Coconut Garden. He flipped through pictures of couples, families with kids, and retirees for about thirty minutes until he found one that was odd. It was a picture of a face blocked by a hand.

"Hell, that's no good," he complained, tossing the picture back in the box. He rummaged around for another when he stopped.

A guy trying to hide his face? Does he think he's in the witness protection program?

Curiosity got the best of him as he recovered the picture and inspected it more closely.

"Shit fire," he whispered, checking his camera's digital images until he found what he was looking for. A grin of recognition formed on his face. Rio had taken his advice and filmed everything. This would be better than any facial feature. And perfect for an arsonist. King had found his match. As he headed to the police station with his camera over his shoulder and the picture firmly in his grasp, he said, "Well, if a picture is worth a thousand words, both of these are worth a hell of a lot more and hopefully a prison sentence or two."

At the police station, the chief looked over the tour photo.

"I can't move on this evidence," he complained. "You can't even see his face."

Handing the chief the second photo, King explained, "You don't have to. Look at the back of the hand."

The chief's expression changed, registering his understanding.

"Willis!" he yelled. "I'll send the Sergeant over to the Coconut Garden to pick him up for questioning. Let's see what our friend has been up to in the national criminal database while we wait, shall we?"

While Sergeant Willis went to retrieve the suspect and Deakin ran the picture through the national criminal database, King headed to the *Satisfaction* to find Chase. He wanted to get him up to speed on the breakthrough in the case before they had to leave on the afternoon cruise. Unfortunately, King would not find Chase on the ship.

Or in Key West, for that matter.

Chasing Pirate Treasure

KING, RIO, AND Anne were scheduled to take the *Satisfaction* out for its regular tours while Chase had the day off. Rather than sleeping late, he got up early, excited to get a jump on the day because of the opportunity to dive once again. Chase got to the dock on time and met Captain Mark preparing his crew to sail.

"I heard you were coming out with us today. Hope you don't bring any of the bad luck following you," Mark said, greeting his friend with a joke.

Chase chuckled. He could not blame him. When someone meant you harm, it wasn't hard for those around you to also feel like a target. "I'm driving myself in King's boat. I promise I'll stay far enough away so you'll be safe... unless you keep coming up with those lame ass jokes." Both men laughed as Chase boarded the Grady-White.

"I do have a favor to ask."

Captain Mark eyed Chase suspiciously. "A big one?"

"Nah, just a few items I accidentally dropped off the ship the other day. I'll text you the coordinates if you'd be so kind to return them to me."

"Accidentally, huh? Ok, I'll see what my divers can find. But you owe me one."

Ain't that the truth. Chase reminded himself to retrieve the Bezoar stone and spoon from the reef and return them to Captain Mark. *That should make us even.*

The day turned out to be a beautiful, cloudless one with calm seas, allowing the surface to shimmer like glass. These were ideal conditions to dive, and Chase looked forward to getting in the water to assess his new rebreather. He knew he was breaking the rule of *never dive alone* but justified his decision knowing the stakes were high and he didn't want anyone slowing him down.

Besides, I only have the one rebreather.

Chase had a computer on his wrist to alert him when his sensors indicated low oxygen content. He didn't want to take the time nor the chance on details his monitor could handle for him. He wanted to find something of value today and wanted nothing to get in his way.

Chase wanted to further test his theory because he had a different path in mind. One he hoped would pay more substantial dividends.

At the site, he put on his equipment, excited to see how long he could stay submerged. Slipping below the water's surface, Chase found it as quiet as a library at midnight. He loved the tranquility but knew it to be a facade. The ocean carried its hazards. Wild things swam in the depths, currents were treacherous and unpredictable, and a storm above the surface could arise at any time. These were only a few items keeping divers on their toes. Chase had one more than most, his dead boy. But for the treasure hunter, the reasons to dive far outweighed the dangers, even if they were other worldly.

Chase swam towards the debris field. The *Mastery's* crew had found some items associated with the sterncastle in its arc, but that trail had gone cold and they had not found any other items since the Admiral's seal. Chase knew why. So, while the other divers were searching along the south to northwest arc, he planned on a southwest heading instead.

He knew it to be a long shot; treasure hunters take years to find things of value. Still, Chase had a sound theory, a rebreather, and what Rio might have called large cojones. He needed to make his search count as he could only be there for one day. Plus, Anne expected him for a late dinner. With the words, *Today's the day!* ringing in his ears, Chase headed southwest.

As he swam further from the Grady-White, Chase waved his right hand over the sand every so often, moving the small particles up in a puff. His hope mounted. Could the solution he worked through for the sterncastle turn out to be the right one and not just a wild goose chase? His ideas were based on sound research and a gut feel. The same gut feeling he had about leaving academia, starting the tour company, and preparing the crew for an attack at sea which had actually materialized. His gut had not let him down on those occasions and proved to be a strong force. Now, he just had to find the evidence.

The Pulse metal detector attached to Chase's left arm had a depth rating of two hundred feet. He looked at his wrist gauge and saw the present depth to be seventy-five feet and Chase hoped he did not have to go too deep or far from the Grady -White. The metal detector had an audio/vibration setting. Chase switched to vibration mode.

With the rebreather, he was prepared. He also carried a titanium dive knife on his right leg for cutting or digging. It would be useless in case he met up with an unfriendly shark. For that scenario he'd have to use his hands to bop it on the nose or pushing it away to make the animal understand Chase was not part of the menu.

He kept one eye on the metal detector and one eye on the depth gauge as he continued his path southwesterly swimming in a zigzag pattern.

Having been underwater for approximately one hour and thirty minutes, the rebreather would allow him a four-hour window. If he kept going, he would move out of range of King's craft and might not find his way back in time. He now swam at a depth of ninety-three feet, and nothing of significance had occurred.

Chase felt ready to turn around and head back to the ship when *negative* thoughts crept into his head: *What if my theory is wrong? Maybe I'm wasting my time out here when I should be working with all the other divers.* He understood why his theory of hurricane patterns or currents might be off. The theory of the lighter sterncastle floating away from the rest of the ship seemed crazy to him now. He still needed to pick up the submerged items for Captain Mark.

As he spun around, he was startled by a distinctive voice behind him. *This way.* Clear as the boy in his dream. He listened intently, but the only thing he heard were the bubbles from his regulator. He began to swim again. Chase had not made ten feet when he heard the voice again. *This way.*

Now it was unmistakably clear. He *must* be on the right path. He wasn't entirely sure until now. His dead boy had led him along the way and he was not going to let fear stop him from discovering what the boy wanted him to find. He began to swim in his original direction.

Until now, the Pulse detector had remained still. Chase had been occupied looking for any indication of the apparition when the vibration startled him. Stopping, he waved the Pulse over the area. It went off again. He dug his hand into the sand and pulled up a mound, letting particles sift through his fingers. A slight current moved the sand in a westerly direction. Nothing.

He dug several more times around the spot and still found nothing.

It must be deeper than I can dig, he thought, as he swept the vibrating Pulse over it once again. He registered the coordinates on his dive computer to refer back to them later.

He continued on despite no physical evidence. All he had so far was a single location and nothing else. And a hit could mean anything. A discarded piece of junk, a tool off a passing boat. Finding treasure in the ocean equated to looking for a needle in a haystack. But two hits and he might be on the right track.

He pressed forward, his zigzag pattern changing to a straight line. Thirty yards past the last hit, he got a second one. Excited, he brushed away the sand, yet felt immediately disappointed when he did not find anything. But that disappointment did not deter him.

Chase continued to swim southward; the Pulse stretched out in front. He stopped to look at a school of tropical fish as they swam by, marveling at their colors. He kept his eyes alert, head swiveling slowly from side to side, making sure there were no fish bigger than those he had just passed. The hits continued sporadically; the objects buried too deep to dig by hand. To retrieve them he would need Captain Mark's equipment.

Encouraged, he pressed on, marking each hits coordinates, and checking his oxygen levels. Another hundred yards south, Chase suddenly stopped swimming when up ahead he noticed a large dark mass. Cautiously, he swam slowly toward it hoping it would not turn out to be a shadow caused by something larger above. As he drew near, Chase discovered it was not a shadow.

An old barge rested on the ocean floor with barnacles and coral affixed to its metal hull. *What is a barge doing out here?* A small bridge sat at the stern, it's open windows allowing fish to swim in and out. The outboard motor that once powered the craft had been reclaimed long ago. Chase wondered if the craft had been in an accident or sunk on purpose. If there was a needle in the haystack, this was a pretty big needle. He swam around the length of the vessel when movement caught his eye in the bridge. The fish scattered out of the bridge windows as though someone was inside. Could it be his dead boy? *Stop calling him that.* He had a name. It was Riley. Riley Patterson. This had been the first time Chase had actually said his name since the accident and it had a profound effect on him. He bowed his head and said a little prayer hoping to ease the soul of the dea- of *Riley.* And to soothe his own from the guilt that haunted him.

Chase then swam up towards the bridge to investigate. He couldn't shake the feeling he was not alone at this depth. Peering into the bridge acknowledged his belief. There was nothing there. But it didn't eliminate the feeling he was not alone, in fact, it grew stronger.

Chase was convinced the young man had been trying to tell him something all along. To lead him to this spot. He knew it sounded crazy, yet here he was. He began his descent back to the hull of the barge, turning on his Pulse and waving around the base as he once again circled the craft, careful to steer clear of the metal hull. Chase had made his way from the port stern side all the way around to the starboard side with nary a blip. It seemed as though the only metal belonged to the hull as it settled in the sand. He looked up at the bridge with a plea. *Can I get a little help here? Riley, If you are around, can you point me in the right direction?*

Chase waited for an answer, but it didn't come. Looking at his dive computer, he decided it was time to leave. He turned away from the barge and slammed right into a large fish, the collision forcing him to let go of the Pulse, allowing it to settle at the base of the barge. Chase turned toward the fish, *Where the hell is it?* Try as he might, Chase couldn't find the sea creature anywhere. It had just disappeared. He regained his composure and went back to retrieve his tool slipping his arm into the rest and grabbing the handle.

It was vibrating!

Chase looked up at the bridge and gave a little nod in recognition. Perhaps Riley *had* shown him the way. With his help, concerning the haystack, it seemed as though the needle had found Chase.

The arsonist Barry Stallings packed his bags. After several long weeks, he felt glad it was time to get out of this town. The ship would leave the next evening and he was anxious to call a cab, get to the dock and board the cruise liner to make his escape complete.

He tried on the fake mustache, sideburns, and round-rimmed glasses. The disguise looked convincing enough. He also had purchased a straw Fedora hat with a black band to make him look like the tourist he pretended to be. He toyed with the idea of putting a small feather in the hat band but nixed the idea not wanting to draw undue attention to himself.

He had money and fake credit cards in his wallet and an Illinois driver's license with his new name to go along with his doctored passport. He also had access to an offshore account where his latest employer had generously paid him his fee even though the job had not shown the intended results. Evidently, his employer would rather have an incomplete job and a happy arsonist than an unhappy one who could create further trouble. Anonymously of course.

Barry, nee Donald, was nearly home free and feeling good about how they had manipulated the local police department into looking for the wild goose everywhere but in a Bed and Breakfast right under their noses. His employer had seen to every last detail making sure the job proceeded smoothly.

The plan had been so simple. Start by walking past the ship and the prying eyes of one single camera while avoiding all others. Check. Throw canisters. Check. Slip underneath the dock and crawl back to the street undetected. Check, check, check. Just the thought of having outsmarted the cops made Barry smile. He had just finished removing his disguise when he heard a knock on the door and a woman's voice called out, "Housekeeping."

"Damn!" Barry said under his breath. No one was supposed to bother with his room, the idiots. He hid his fake facial hair in his toiletry case and tossed it into his suitcase before closing it. As he opened the door, he began to rebuke the housekeeper, "I don't need any housekeep—"

Barry stopped mid-sentence. Standing behind the housekeeper were two police officers.

"Sir, I'm Sergeant Willis of the Key West police department. Do you mind stepping outside?"

Barry took one step outside the door before Sergeant Willis grabbed his left hand and turned it over. As in the pictures King had presented, a large burn mark covered most of it.

Willis continued his duty. "You have the right to remain silent...."

Barry slumped his shoulders as he listened to Sergeant Willis read him his Miranda rights.

Maybe these cops aren't as dumb as I thought.

The news of Barry's arrest reached Jasper within minutes. Marilynn, the manager at the Coconut Garden, phoned his office as soon as the police headed off towards Barry's room.

Jasper immediately called his lawyer, Trevor Stevens, and instructed him to go to the police station. While on his way there, Jasper called his daughter, his voice barely hiding his frustration and anger. "Ginger, the police found your guy at the Garden and have him at the station for questioning. I've called Trevor. He's headed over to represent him. I'm also going there to file a complaint about illegal trespass on our property. I don't know how they got to your man, but if we don't fix this now, I don't have to tell you what the consequences will be, do I?"

What Jasper *did not* tell his daughter was that he'd found Ginger's source of income used to pay the arsonist and attack crew. It had taken him a while to track where the cash had come from. He had to admit she'd been crafty. Having his daughter followed was not a pleasant task, but it had paid off in spades. Jasper made sure anyone looking over his books would find nothing out of the ordinary; a money trail back to him did not exist. Thankfully, Ginger had been discreet about her embezzlement. He was not sure how long she had been making the withdrawals, but he made damn certain she would no longer be able to continue the practice.

Ginger sat in her office, stunned, unsure what to say to her father except for a barely audible promise. "I'm on it!" She hung up the phone. The plan should have been foolproof. She had planned for every contingency, or so she thought. The guy had no idea who Ginger or Jasper were because she had used an intermediary and also used Marilynn to book him at the Grove.

Ginger began to panic. She knew if the arsonist flipped and gave up the intermediary, it would blow back on them. Confused and sweating, she tried to think, but fear blocked all her neural pathways.

Get a grip. You need to do damage control, said an equally shaken Proxy.

Ginger dialed her intermediary and got his voicemail. She planned on leaving a message, but decided against it, not wanting to leave a trail for the police. She hung up and dialed again but got the same result.

Should have purchased a burner phone, scolded Proxy. *It would have been impossible to trace the intermediary back to her if she had purchased one. So much for foolproof.*

Ginger's only hope rested on the premise the guy sitting in the police station would be smart enough to keep his mouth shut. If he was not smart, Ginger had one more plan up her sleeve. It was bloody, but she would execute it in the event things went south. It was now a matter of self-preservation.

You can't trust anyone these days, can you? Proxy commented.

Ginger got in her car for the drive north to Pine Key where no one would recognize her. She had to purchase a burner phone to call the intermediary in Miami again. She had to find out what the hell happened with the arsonist who was now in custody at the Key West police department.

Walking quickly into the store, she nervously scanned for anyone who might recognize her. Finding the right phone, she went to the checkout, fumbling with her purse as she looked for cash. She wore a wide brimmed sun hat and sunglasses to hide her identity from both the cameras and the clerk. At this point, Ginger Cobb could no longer make any mistakes.

Once back on the road, she drove to her office, calling the intermediary from the new burner phone, but once again getting voicemail. She left a message, "Your boy is now in jail cooling his heels. Beware he may flip on you. Call me as soon as you get this message!"

Ginger's anxiety ratcheted up, slamming her palms against the steering wheel and voiced a string of obscenities. The car swerved, but she quickly recovered. Slowing down, she decided against a repeat lest a local cop pull her over for erratic driving. Her breathing became labored as she felt a tightening in her chest. A million thoughts stockpiled in her head, each one worse than the last. Shaking slightly, she decided to find Jasper to explain the situation and tell him how she planned to fix it.

She would also call *another* friend in Miami. This friend contracted work no one else wanted to do. *Wet work.* They'd known each other for some time now socially, and she knew what he did for a living, but she didn't judge. She rationalized what one person had to do in order to survive should not impact her as it was none of her business. She had never needed this type of service before. If a choice had to be made between her going to prison or disposing of an arsonist, the answer seemed easy. Ginger Cobb would never stand for incarceration.

Besides, Proxy rationalized, *You'll be doing humanity a favor by eliminating the little vermin who likes to burn things.*

It was not Ginger's fault she had a weak father who did not have the guts to do what it took to eliminate Chase and company. Once she handled this last mess, Ginger would take care of Chase and his band of interlopers for good. Right now, she needed to focus on cleaning up one mess at a time. As she drove back into Key West, she dialed her 'wet' friend from Miami on the burner phone, and as it rang, Proxy made one last comment. *Let's hope this is one friend we can count on.*

STEINBECK WAS RIGHT

CHASE THREW HIS equipment into the Grady-White before jumping in. Turning the ignition, he pushed the throttle forward on the three Yamaha 300 HP engines and sped towards the Mastery.

As he approached the ship, he throttled the engines back from its full-throated roar, so Anne could hear his voice when he called, though he would still have to speak up. "Anne, it's me. Before I head back, I have—"

She cut him off. "Chase, they found the suspect who torched the *Satisfaction*. Seems the police have been sent on a wild goose chase looking for the arsonist leaving the Keys. King found the guy, who was still on the island hiding out. And you'll never guess where?"

"Would I be out of line if I said at one of Cobb's properties?"

Anne shrieked with joy. "Ding, Ding, Ding! Always one step ahead!" She relayed the rest of the story as Chase bobbed on the waves. "They picked him up at the Coconut Garden. He's being questioned now, and if all goes well, we could have charges filed in the morning. Isn't that great?"

Chase idled towards the ship to tie off. "Great news! I hope they string the bastard up. If they can tie this to Jasper, I'm going to… well, I don't know what I'll do, but I'll think of something."

"That's my pirate," Anne cooed sweetly.

"Oh, hey," he began again. "I'm going to be a little late. have an errand to run, so I'll be home later this evening."

"Aww, we were going to have a late dinner." Her disappointment evident to Chase.

"Can't, babe, but I'll make it up to you … I swear," Chase said, as he tied off to the ship and jumped out of the boat. Chase grinned, knowing Anne would grill him once he got home, but he wasn't ready to tell her his news. His information too important to relay to anyone except Captain Mark. He chuckled at what Anne thought at this moment. He could actually see the look of concern when he heard her lovely, but suspicious voice ask, "Chase Porter, just what are you up to?"

He ran up to the bridge and was told Captain Mark could be found in his quarters.

"Look what the porpoises dragged in," Captain Mark teased as he reached out a hand to shake. "You've been gone a long time. Almost called the coast guard."

Chase ignored the comment as he stood in front of Captain Mark's desk and leaned forward to talk quietly. He had a more pressing agenda. "I have a surprise for you," Chase said in a sing-song manner while he placed a bright green emerald on the desk and slowly slid it with his index finger toward the Captain. As it reached a wide-eyed Mark, Chase whispered, "I think I found your sterncastle."

He then dropped a few smaller emeralds, some silver Reales, and gold coins on the desk for effect, clearly breaking his father's rule … *Tell No One.*

Captain Mark reacted in wonder. "Where the hell did you find it?"

"I had some help," Chase answered, but was not about to explain the strange experience of a dead boy giving him directions. Who would believe that story?

"What do you mean, *some help?*"

"Let's just call it *Divine Inspiration* and leave it at that," Chase responded with a wink. He now believed Riley was responsible for gifting him the sterncastle location. The boy also took something from Chase in return. His guilt. Like the apparitions, it had totally disappeared.

Captain Mark rolled the beautiful stone through his fingers. "Do you realize the only two people to have touched this precious gem in four hundred years are in this room?" A look of concern crossed Captain Mark's face as he added, "What's this gonna cost me?"

"Not much. It's your find, but I do have a plan and here's how I see it." Chase proceeded to tell Captain Mark what he requested for his role in the discovery.

"Agreed," said the Captain. "But I can't fulfill my promise until you tell me where I can find the sterncastle. That's one detail you've left out."

"Right," countered Chase. "You know there is a sunken barge out there due southwest from here?"

"Of course. We've been over her a number of times and found nothing. The metal hull throws off our sensors."

"That's your problem," said Chase, a grin forming. "Instead of going over her, did you ever think of going *under*?"

Chief Deakin sat across the suspect he had ushered into the interrogation room at the Key West police station. For over an hour, he had been questioning the man to no avail.

"Is your real name Donald Sharpe from Illinois?" The chief had been grilling Barry without success but continued to probe. "Why was your room at the Coconut Garden listed as unregistered? We found a disguise in your bag. What do you need a disguise for?" All questions went unanswered. The chief did not know Barry's real identity because the man did not have any identification on him other than the one claiming to be Donald Sharpe. His image had also come up empty in the National Database. It was if the fella did not exist. Unfortunately, even the chief of police could not arrest a person for being a ghost. Fortunately, the suspect had not yet asked for a lawyer. He had not asked for anything.

Sergeant Willis entered the room and beckoned the chief to step outside. When they walked into the hall the chief told Willis, "This guy is a stone face. Can't get a peep out of him."

"There's been a development. Jasper Cobb is here screaming about illegal search and seizure crap, and he brought an attorney to represent your suspect. Did the guy ask for one?"

"No. So we are not yet legally obligated to make one available to him," the chief remarked while rubbing his chin. "So, Jasper hired a lawyer, did he? Hmm. Your guys find anything else?"

"Yes. First, I checked with the state of Illinois, and they have no record of issuing a driver's license to a Don Sharpe. But here's the really interesting part. Mr. Sharpe is registered for the cruise out of port tomorrow heading to the Bahamas. It was a smart escape plan, to keep him here under our noses the whole time. Other than a fake ID, we've got nothing we can hold him on, so if we don't find some way to keep him here, we're gonna lose him for good. Can't charge a guy for arson if we have no proof."

The chief nodded at his sergeant. "You're right, we can't. Any luck from the dock?"

"Forensics pulled partial prints and sent them to the lab with his. Haven't heard back yet if they are a match. Their attempt might be futile. It'll be murder to get anything else to stick if we cannot tie him to the crime scene."

"Wait a sec," the chief said interrupting the sergeant. "You just gave me an idea of how I can get our suspect to talk."

"Glad to help. You wanna tell me what I should do with Jasper and company?"

"Let them sit on their heels a bit longer. I have a suspect to break. Here's my idea: A crime suspect can only be held for twenty-four hours of questioning without positive proof. If a suspect asks for a lawyer?" The chief waited for his sergeant to respond.

"We have to allow for one," answered Sergeant Willis.

"Correct," the chief continued. "If the suspect retains a lawyer, what one thing has to be made clear?"

The sergeant thought for a moment, the answer making him shake his head in understanding. "His identity. Smart. Having this info will make our job so much easier."

The chief instructed Sergeant Willis, "Inform Jasper and his lawyer they have to wait to see their client while he's being *processed*.

Willis laughed, "My favorite police term aka our *stall tactic*."

"If they ask for more information, give a vague answer. Wish I could be there to see the look on Jasper's face. Good work"

While Willis went to stall Jasper and his lawyer, The chief walked back into the interrogation room.

"Mr. err... Sharpe," he began, "I've asked a lot of questions, and you have not answered any of them. I have one last question, and I hope you'll answer it. Because you threw a firebomb on the *Satisfaction* where two people slept onboard, you endangered their lives. It is no longer a case of mere arson, but now a much more serious crime. How do you feel about an attempted murder charge?"

The suspect turned towards the chief, his eyes widening with fear. Deakin knew his perp was about to talk so he kept up the pressure. "Let me see, an arson sentence would be three to five years. Attempted murder carries up to twenty-four years behind bars." The chief mentioned this fact casually, knowing the man sitting across the table might react to the sentence. Barry did not disappoint.

"I want to talk to a lawyer," the man claiming to be Donald Sharpe demanded. If the suspect was finally going to talk, the chief was pleased these were his first words.

"Sure. You'll get your lawyer. In fact, Jasper Cobb has one for you outside in the station, will he do?"

The quizzical look on the guy's face showed no recognition as to who Jasper might be.

"There's a lawyer out there now? To talk to me?"

"There is. The owner of the Coconut Garden sent him."

"Yes," replied the perp. "Send him in."

"You'll get what you want." The chief smiled. *And I'll get what I want.*

Attorney Trevor Stevens was escorted into the interrogation room where he began to talk in hushed tones to his new client, Donald Sharpe. Soon to be known by his real name. "Do you mind if I speak with my client?" the attorney asked the chief.

When Deakin didn't move, he asked with a tone the chief interpreted as one of irritation, "Alone?" Stevens turned to Barry and whispered, "They have no evidence to link you with the arson attempt. As long as you stay silent and let me do the talking, I can get you out of this."

Chief Deakin had a different plan. Willis had returned and handed him a report that just arrived compliments of his forensics team. He read it slowly before commenting, "Sure, but before I go, I need to tell Mr. Sharpe something important." Turning to the perp, he said, "We have evidence putting you at the crime scene."

"My client was nowhere near the crime scene," the attorney spoke up. "You have no proof he was there. Absolutely none at all."

"But we do," claimed the chief, waving the report in front of the attorney's face. "We have fingerprints matching your client." As expected, the perp's face went white.

"Impossible!" the attorney protested as he read the report.

"No. It's not impossible." The chief eyed the perp as he set his trap. "You took your gloves off before you crawled *under the dock*, didn't you, Mr. Sharpe?" He reveled in the way both men squirmed at hearing the news. "And now, we're adding attempted murder to the arson charge." While the chief enjoyed the show, he knew it was about to get better … much better.

He watched in silence as Barry looked at his new lawyer, then back at him. The suspect's expression began to show panic, unsure of how his attorney could extricate him from this development. "I want to make a plea deal," Barry announced, disregarding his attorney's *Keep your mouth shut* advice.

"Do you know who I am?" Jasper yelled. "I am a well-connected and respected member of this community. This is not a police state; it's America!" He barked at the desk sergeant and anyone else within earshot. "You cannot, for no good reason, just go waltzing onto someone's property, break down doors and arrest a guest at one of my establishments!"

No matter how much he protested, Jasper was not allowed in to see the prisoner.

The attorney he had hired, on the other hand, had been allowed to meet with the detainee.

Running out of steam, Jasper sat down on a bench and plotted his next move. He would wait for another fifteen minutes.

If his lawyer did not come out by then, there would be more to the story.

In the meantime, Jasper polished the story to explain his presence. The police executed an illegal search and seizure at one of his properties. He leapt into action to defend his guest from the overreaching arm of a corrupt legal entity failing in its duty to protect and serve. He would continue to play the outraged business owner looking out for his guests.

He realized the ploy would also play well for his business. Come to Key West and stay in one of Jaspers properties. If you get into a scrape with the law? He'll stand beside you. He tried the saying out in his head. Even for bullshit, it sounded good. Jasper would no sooner stand by one of his customers than give anyone free passage on one of his tours or trolleys. For now, the story suited his purpose.

Jasper contemplated how to use this incident to his advantage. The Key West Visitors Bureau would not like the negative publicity he could generate. If he played his cards right, there might even be money to be made in a lawsuit against the police for their gestapo entrance and unlawful arrest. Yes, this could work out nicely and profitable to boot.

As he sat congratulating himself, his cell phone vibrated. Checking the caller ID, Jasper walked outside and pushed the green button to accept the call. "Where are you?" he asked flatly.

"Hello to you too, Padre. I'm calling to tell you I have a call into a friend in Miami about fixing our minor problem." Ginger said.

"Fixing? You have fixed enough for my liking," Jasper growled. "We're in this thing deep enough as it is without any more of your *fixing.* Stay out of it. I've got it handled. Call off your fix and do it now!"

Ginger had made a mess of everything, and he'd be damned if she'd make it blow back on him. About to disconnect the call, Trevor Stevens ran out of the police station and grabbed him by the arm. "C'mon Jasper, we need to go." The attorney began to pull Jasper down the sidewalk.

"Stevens, get your hands off me, who in the hell do you think you are?" Jasper struggled to break free. When they got to the car, Trevor opened the passenger door and pushed Jasper inside before getting into the driver's seat.

"Your arsonist is going to flip despite my protestations, so I am no longer his lawyer. As for who the hell I am? I'm the guy who has to keep you out of prison," barked Trevor, as he sped off in the direction of his office.

While Jasper pondered that development, his anger grew. He could taste the acidic sourness in his mouth as he thought about his enemies … *those pirate wannabes.* This mess was all their fault. As Trevor drove down Southard Street, Jasper realized in another block they would pass the Berth. As they got close, he told Trevor to stop the car.

"Drop me off here. And leave the car running. I'll only be a moment," he said through clenched teeth.

"Jasper, this isn't the time or place for a drink. Your freedom is on the line. If the arsonist is going to spill his guts, I don't want you anywhere near the evidence."

Jasper grunted and exited the car, heading for the Berth's door. His attempt to barge into the bar failed miserably, managing to slide past the big oak doors feeling like a worm slithering through a crack in the foundation. He pushed the thought from his mind. He was not the worm. Chase Porter was.

"This is all your fault!" Jasper screeched at Chase, trying to catch his breath. "You came into this town, my town, and with your band of miscreants, turned everything upside down!"

Chase spun around on his stool but did not get up.

King came from around the bar but Chase raised a hand signifying for him to stop. The big man complied but stood next to his friend. Rio stood on the other side. Chase spoke calmly, "Jasper, you seem upset. Come and sit down and we'll talk about it."

"There is nothing to talk about!" Jasper strolled toward the bar, his face scrunched in hate, a finger pointed in Chase's face. "You have gone too far this time, accusing one of my guests of being the arsonist who set your ship on fire? What proof do you have? None! And the police barging in on my property with an illegal search, abducting my guest then carting him off to jail! It's a travesty, and I will not stand for it. It's all your fault and when I get through with you and your band of buffoons—"

King interrupted Jasper. "Chase, if this guy says one more word...." King did not wait for the word. Instead, he grabbed Jasper by the back of his shirt and the seat of his pants and lifted him into the air.

"Put me down, you cretin!" Jasper spit. "I'll have you arrested for this!"

Rio ran to the door and pulled it open, allowing King to toss Jasper out of the bar and into the street. Jasper muttered a string of obscenities as he flew through the air ending up sprawled on the sidewalk.

"Looks as if you've wanted to do that for a long time, eh King?" Chase commented.

"Good thing it's trash day," joked Rio. "Here come the collectors."

The squad car pulled up behind Trevor, and the chief got out.

Trevor scrambled from his vehicle. "We're on our way to my office now," he murmured helping a shaken Jasper up off the sidewalk.

"No. You're not!" ordered Chief Deakin. "We'd prefer to question Jasper at *our office*. You can follow us there if you'd like."

Trevor frowned without saying another word.

Jasper, on the other hand, continued his obscenity-laced tirade while being dumped into the squad car and driven away.

HURRICANE GINGER MAKES A FINAL PASS

KING AND CHASE watched Captain Mark on television as the news of the sterncastle discovery broke. He began with a definition of the sterncastle and its importance. Yes, he had a crew already working on the new debris field, and some finds were confirmed from the ship's manifest. No. The discovery was not near the original *Atocha* debris field. Yes, the salvage rights of the original find of the *Atocha* had been extended to the sterncastle debris field.

On a table, Captain Mark displayed the artifacts. A few Muzo emeralds, several coins, and a few pieces of silver flatware surrounded the Bezoar stone. He did not mention to the reporters how his divers had set out for the barge as soon as Chase had left the ship, nor that anyone else had been involved in the discovery.

"I can't tell you exactly how we found it. Trade secrets and all," he fibbed to the reporters. "Let's just say we did a lot of research on weather, ocean currents, and wave patterns. Add to *that*, a little luck helped us locate the remainder of the lost *Atocha* treasure. There are more secrets to discover, and we'll be sharing those as we uncover them. Right now, I need to get back to work. Thank you all."

With the news conference concluded, King turned down the volume on the bar television and looked at Chase with a wary eye.

"What's that look for?" Chase asked. "You've got something to say for a change?"

"Trade secrets my ass," King said over his shoulder as he walked into the back room to change an empty keg.

Chase's cell vibrated, and he saw it was Captain Mark. "Nice press conference, Bud. You should consider a career in television… Oh, wait. You should buy the network instead. Now that *you've* found the sterncastle and its riches."

"Funny. You got time to visit an old friend?"

"I think I've got a few hours before our next tour if you've got any Scotch."

"Fresh out. What I do have is a six pack of beer and the items I promised. When can you stop by?"

"I'm on my way!" Chase left the bar and strode down Southard to Duval Street and made another left onto Greene street where Chase met Captain Mark, who ushered him into his office. Mark opened a small cooler and produced two beers. "Lime?"

"Nope, I drink my beer fruitless. So, what's up."

Captain Mark took a swig from his bottle. "Have you found what you're looking for?"

"I have," Chase replied.

"Do you have a timeline?"

"I do."

"So, let's complete the transaction as per our plan, shall we?"

Finishing off his bottle, Chase tipped it towards the captain. "We shall, but first, I'll have another."

Captain Mark grabbed a cold beer and placed it in front of Chase. He opened his desk drawer and pulled out a leather pouch, untied then upended it, spilling the contents onto the desk.

"Take a look at these."

Chase's eyes brightened. He was impressed. They were perfect. Just as he had asked for. "And the other request?"

"I had to send it to a friend in Miami who's a real artist. Don't worry, it will be ready by the time you return."

"Are you sure you don't want to come with?" Chase had pestered Captain Mark to come along with him on his next errand needing an extra hand.

"Would love to but can't. However, a few of my deck hands volunteered," Captain Mark offered, opening a beer for himself.

"Really? I could use a few more hands on this mission. You sure you can spare them with the new find and all?"

Captain Mark nodded. "I can. They need some downtime. Been working them like dogs."

"Great, I'll welcome them aboard," Chase said as he returned the items to the leather pouch.

"By the way," Captain Mark said. "I collected something else you asked for."

Chase furrowed his eyebrows wondering what Mark meant. The captain pointed in the corner. "You shouldn't leave these things lying around the ocean floor. They're illegal, ya know."

In the corner sat the chain shot, cannon ball and several four pound balls from the swivel guns from the deck of the *Satisfaction*.

"I'll hold 'em until you're ready to come pick 'em up." Captain Mark winked and finished his beer. Chase followed suit, grabbed the pouch, and stood to leave.

He loved it when a plan came together.

Trevor had come to speak with Jasper in the Key West police station, where he was held for questioning. Unused to the accommodations or the nefarious company he found himself keeping,

Jasper paced back and forth in the cell as he waited for his attorney to arrive. Thanks to the suspicion of guilt surrounding him regarding the crimes committed against the CMPT Company, he had become a guest of the town's correctional facility.

"You look like shit, Jasper. Are they treating you okay?" Trevor asked.

Jasper, still angry from his encounter at the Berth, barked. "I wanna sue that horse's ass for throwing me out!"

"Whoa, champ. Let's take it one legal argument at a time. Stay focused with me on this one, will you? I'm more concerned with your freedom, not your ego. Is there a way you can prove you had no knowledge of this?"

"They have to find Ginger," Jasper announced, still irritated. "*She* had the connection. I had nothing to do with hiring either the arsonist or the boat attack."

"Let's not even discuss the latter, because that's not even an issue. It has not been reported as a crime, so please don't bring it up again. What's important is how we distance you from your daughter's actions. Do you know where she is?"

Jasper thought about where she had traveled lately. "Miami," he stated. "She's probably headed to Miami. She's made a few trips up there lately meeting with the franchisor for our new restaurant. Check it out with them. You can get the contact info from my phone."

"The police already anticipated she would drive up towards Miami. In fact, they stopped her car on the Overseas Highway out by Islamorada, but she was not driving the car. One of your employees was behind the wheel. Said Ginger told her to drive to Miami to pick up someone."

"Which employee?" Jasper asked angrily, believing when he got out, he would have the great joy in firing those employees who went along with Ginger and her schemes.

"They won't tell me. All hush-hush. Part of the investigation they say."

Jasper guessed what kind of person was to be picked up. Again, Ginger's recklessness showed. Imagine sending an underling to pick up a hitman? Fortunately, thanks to Jasper, the employee would have returned empty handed since there were no funds to pay her lethal passenger.

Jasper had shut down his daughter's fraudulent accounts just in time. Enough charges were pending against them, murder for hire would not be one of them.

"So, where is Ginger now? Is she still on the Island?" asked the lawyer.

"Trevor, I don't know but I have to tell you," Jasper began in a fatherly tone, laying it on thick. "Lately, Ginger's been exhibiting symptoms similar to those of my ex-wife. Irritability, narcissism, lack of empathy, manipulative behavior, even violent tendencies. I'm no psychiatrist, but I think it might be Antisocial Personality Disorder. I'm hoping they'll find her so we can get her the help she needs." *And make a case for mental incompetency in court.* Jasper kept this thought private until it was necessary to use.

"The authorities have not been able to locate her, Jasper. If you have any ideas, now's the time to tell me. I'm doing my best to get you out of this mess. I can't do it alone."

Jasper thought carefully about what to say to his lawyer. He had a good idea of where Ginger might be hiding and if she got away, he'd take the fall for her misdeeds. For Jasper, there was a fine line between business and personal matters. But when it came to accountability, the issue remained clear. There were no lines. She had put their business and their future in jeopardy. Arson, piracy, and embezzlement? Not to mention attempted murder.

He found it difficult to think his only child had gone so far down a terrible path to get what she wanted. But Jasper knew the decision he had to make would be best for both the business and Ginger. She was too dangerous on the loose and he needed to corral her before she did something they would not recover from. Once again, he put on his best fatherly act. Sighing heavily, he began to talk, pausing as if struggling whether to tell of her whereabouts. Finally adding the piece which would have landed him a Best Actor Oscar had it been a movie instead of real life. "Please make sure they are gentle with her, she's a sick child and probably scared."

Trevor jumped out of his chair and banged on the door to inform the chief … Ginger was on the water attempting to flee and may be unstable.

Jasper smiled for the first time all day. *You may have just dodged this bullet.*

Soon he would get out of this hellhole. When he did, Jasper would turn his attention to that brute, Sam King. He would not stand for the physical violence perpetrated against him. He could not wait for the day when he would be able to exact his revenge on King, Porter, and the rest of those miscreants. They had made his life a living hell. It would take time, but he planned to return the favor … soon.

Ginger felt the blood rushing to her cheeks, embarrassed by the way her father spoke to her and tired of him telling her what to do. She was ready to assume control over the family business until she overheard the end of the phone conversation loud and clear. Barry was going to flip and tell the police everything.

If that happens, Proxy volunteered, *Jasper might be able to walk away from this. But we certainly won't.*

"What do we do?" Ginger ached with a fear that gripped her. The realization hit her for the first time. She was truly vulnerable.

First, get a grip on yourself, Proxy instructed. *We stick to the plan to silence the rat before he exposes us.*

"Then what?"

I'd suggest not getting found by the po po...

Her plan in shambles and with only one piece of the puzzle left, Ginger left Key West on the *Ginger Snap* and headed north. Fleeing seemed the only option; she still hadn't heard from her contact concerning exterminating the rat arsonist. Something told her she never would.

You can't count on anyone these days, said Proxy, as if she were talking about an auto mechanic and not a hitman.

Ginger had tried to buy some time by sending her assistant on a drive to Miami, hoping the cops mistook the female for her.

Clever diversion if I say so myself, said Proxy.

Ginger found herself in no mood. "Shut up, will you!" she screamed. "I am so sick and tired of everyone giving me their two cents. God, it's so annoying!"

Take it easy, will ya? Proxy was clearly unfazed by her outburst. *There are other options.*

Ginger calmed down enough to listen to Proxy's argument. There was another option to this dilemma. One that didn't include fleeing. The police and Coast Guard were out looking for her and would eventually catch up with her. Jail did not suit her so Ginger thought through what this final option would entail.

She could not get to Barry due to his stay at Hotel Incarceration, but Ginger could create a little havoc among those freaks who caused this whole mess in the first place. The mere thought of Chase, Anne, and especially Rio made her want to vomit. She could feel the anger rising in her throat, as a clear picture of what she must do materialized.

Ah, is there mayhem afoot? asked Proxy.

"There is indeed," Ginger said, through clenched teeth. She turned her craft around and headed south toward the Conch Harbor Marina with malice on her mind.

Once in Key West, she sped into the harbor and moored the craft haphazardly, then hurried to the CMPT store and burst in on an unsuspecting employee. "Where is Rio!" she screamed at the girl.

The frightened girl squeaked her reply, "He's on board doing a tour." Then added, as if it might help, "It's Tuesday, his usual day onboard." It didn't.

Furious, Ginger knocked over a display stand on her way out the door then found herself standing face to face with Anne.

They stared at each other like two alley cats anxious to claw one another.

Anne snarled, "What do you want?"

"Nothing you can give me, you wretched cur." Ginger grabbed Anne by the shoulders, shoving her toward the edge of the dock. Anne's legs became entangled in the rope barrier, forcing her to lose balance and tumble into the water.

Ginger did not wait to see if Anne rose to the surface, too intent on revenge as she raced to her craft, untied it, and sped out of the harbor ignoring the *No Wake* buoys.

She now had one mission: find Rio. As she sped out to sea, Ginger formulated her next step, knowing it would not end well. She popped in a Rolling Stones CD, the perfect mayhem music. Singing along, her voice rose with her intense anger. "I CAN'T GET NO... SATISFACTION!"

Oh yes you can, Proxy whispered, approving Ginger's intentions.

The *Satisfaction* sailed swiftly across the calm seas. Chase marveled at how they all had overcome adversity and hoped that today would be uneventful. He wasn't in any mood for any more surprises. Hadn't they seen enough? The thought had just finished when Tom Garrity up in the crow's nest signaled to Chase. A vessel was coming towards them at a high rate of speed. Chase bowed his head momentarily and whispered, "Damn," then jumped into action, his adrenaline kicking in. He gave Crunchy the signal to slow down and motioned for King to head to the battery. He ran to the port side looking over the rail in time to see the blue and white yacht speed dangerously close to the ship before veering to its left and speeding away. Its wake splashed water up on deck, drenching him. Wiping his eyes clear of the salt water, he saw the name on the stern of the yacht: *Ginger Snap*.

Everyone on board who recognized the craft looked up at a stricken Rio on the poop deck. The fear in his eyes was evident as if he had seen a ghost.

The training from the first attack meant the crew was prepared for another sea assault, but no one would have guessed it would come from Ginger Cobb. Chase realized her provocation could turn ugly in a short amount of time so he began barking more orders aware there would be no attempt to trick the lubbers into believing this was part of the show. He needed to prepare his crew and everything else took a back seat.

Except for the lubbers. They lined up front row against the port side staring at the boat as it turned around and headed back towards the *Satisfaction*. They'd find out soon enough this attack was no stage play.

Signals flew around the ship as all hands prepared for the assault. The *Ginger Snap* was speeding on a course toward the ship. It soon became evident Ginger was aiming straight for the poop deck ... right where Rio stood.

Turn, dammit! Chase wiped sweat from his brow.

Below in the battery, King awaited his order to fire. "Hold," Chase yelled to him as the boat continued on its path, not reducing speed. Chase looked up at Rio now staring as his ex-girlfriend sped toward them.

"Hold," Chase yelled again to the crew.

To the approaching boat he said, "C'mon, break off!" The last thing he wanted to do was hurt another human, but he had a duty to protect a ship full of passengers and his crew.

The craft continued to track for a collision with the *Satisfaction*. It was a few meters out when Chase commanded, "Crunchy, hard port!" The ship banked left as the *Ginger Snap* reached its stern, harmlessly grazing it.

"What the hell is she doing?" Rio yelled, looking as confused as the rest of the crew.

Undaunted, Ginger's craft sped away and made a long arc before turning around. Chase tracked the craft and it became clear her intention was to ram the ship again.

Chase knew what to do. "Rio," he yelled, "come down here!"

Rio came down from the poop deck and now stood next to Chase in the center of the main deck. Ginger adjusted her course, aiming her bow directly at the two. Chase felt no maneuvers would stop her now, but he knew King could. He now had a straight on shot.

"Lubbers! Head up to the higher decks!" commanded the captain.

To John Garrity, he motioned to get ready to evacuate the ship, prompting the young man to descend from his perch.

Yelling down to King he ordered, "Cannon, On my mark."

Chase did not want to open fire on the woman, but if she got much closer or did not slow down, he would have no choice. Ginger held her course on its path directly towards her ex-boyfriend.

"Hold!" Chase ordered, waiting until she came near enough for them to take the closest and most deadly shot. The *Ginger Snap* was moments away from a meeting with a cannonball or the broadside of the *Satisfaction;* either way, Ginger would lose.

"Ready!" Chase commanded.

The order to fire was on the tip of his tongue when Tom Garrity yelled down, "Cap'n, hold your fire!"

When Chase looked up, he saw Tom holding on to the rigging with one hand and pointing behind the stern with the other. Chase turned back to the rail in time to see a second craft speed alongside the *Satisfaction* and crash into the *Ginger Snap's* bow, sending the noses of both boats along with bits of boat parts high into the air before splashing back into the sea. The second craft was King's Grady-White.

Chase now watched in horror as Anne was thrown from the Grady-White into the water, making a smacking noise like a slap across the face. He reacted quickly, grabbing a life ring, and diving overboard. Swimming quickly to her landing spot, he navigated around boat parts looking for her, but she was nowhere to be found. Panicked, he released the ring and dove under the water, searching frantically. He came up for air and dove back under the surface to try and locate her, disregarding the water that burned in his nose and throat. Once again, he had to resurface.

Just as he was about to dive again, she popped up to the surface spitting water. He began to swim toward her but she held up a hand. "I don't need a man to save me. What do you think this is, a fairy tale? Just throw me the life ring." Chase did as he was told. Evidently, Anne noticed the hurt look on his face.

"What I meant to say was thank you," she said as she swam.

Chase followed her back to the ship just in case, a smile plastered across his face. They were helped aboard by crew and lubbers alike. Chase didn't miss Anne's wince as she was helped to the deck, holding her arm against her side. "Hold still," ordered King.

"Did I stop her?" Anne's voice squeaked.

"Yes. You did," explained Chase. "Everyone aboard the ship is safe. You're a hero."

But how did you know she was out here?" Rio asked.

"Woman's intuition," she answered. "That and she pissed me off when she pushed me into the water. Could not let her get away with that shit, could I?"

"No Ma'am," King answered wearing a broad grin on his face.

"I'm sorry about your boat, King," Anne apologized.

"No worries. It's insured."

"Chase?"

He bent down closer to listen to her soft voice.

"I think I'm gonna need a few days off. Whatever will you do without me?"

"We'll manage," Chase responded, feeling relieved; her sense of humor was intact.

"We'll manage."

The Grady-White's bow stuck to Ginger's boat like a remora attached to a shark. Her craft kept spinning in circles to nowhere. Cursing loudly, she shut off the engines. She was still cursing when the Coast Guard arrived.

RATS SINK THE SHIP

WHILE THE COAST Guard brought Ginger back to Key West to her new accommodations at Hotel Incarceration, events that signaled her undoing began to take place without her knowledge.

Once the police provided evidence showing Barry Stallings had been at the arson site, he gave up the name of his contact in Miami. A gentleman by the name of Freddy Garcia, who was now in the custody of the Miami Dade Police Department.

Freddy, in turn, had given up evidence concerning one Ginger Cobb. He included her cell number, the number of times they talked, and where they met. Upon further investigation, the authorities discovered video evidence of Ginger walking into the bar where the meeting had taken place. They had no evidence Freddy Garcia received any payment from Ms. Cobb. His defense attorney stated Freddy knew a guy named Barry looking for a girlfriend. He further claimed he had no knowledge Barry was a criminal, let alone an arsonist. He insisted Ginger had been looking for a date.

Under intense police interrogation along with Barry's testimony, the ruse failed miserably. Because Florida's conspiracy laws do not require the defendant to have done anything in furtherance of the crime itself, Freddy Garcia found himself under arrest for conspiracy to commit arson and quickly changed his story in order to cooperate with the authorities against Ginger Cobb in exchange for a lighter sentence.

The employee driving Ginger's car to Miami was pulled over by a sheriff south of Islamorada and ordered to turn back to Key West. Authorities questioned her to determine why she had been headed to Miami. The employee, a Ms. Debra Gage told the authorities everything she knew. She had been instructed to drive to a parking lot in downtown Miami and wait for a cell phone call. Her only other instructions were to bring someone back to Key West with her and put the guest in room twelve at the Coconut Garden. Debra Gage gained her release but was ordered to stay in Key West in case the police had further questions. Her cell phone confiscated as evidence, the authorities awaiting the Miami call in order to trace it. It never came.

Jasper told his lawyer everything. Well, almost. He discussed the plans to buy the business from Chase to partner with him, buy the marina to kick Chase and company out of Key West, all to enhance his own business interests. No one could find a crime in those actions. He then turned on Ginger, disavowing any and all knowledge of arson or any other illegal activities. Jasper claimed "shock" and "embarrassment" at the claims made against his daughter and said he would do everything in his power to cooperate with the authorities. He also had Trevor Stevens present the Antisocial Personality Disorder claim to the court with the intent to use mental incompetence as her defense.

The judge ordered Ginger to be evaluated by a team of experts to verify whether a diagnosis could be determined before they proceeded to trial. What Jasper did not tell Trevor, or anyone else, was where the money had come from to pay off the arsonist and the attack boat.

It seemed Ginger was not the only one adept at playing chef with the company's finances. Over the years, Jasper had had a few lessons in cooking the books himself. He did not need any additional cooks in his kitchen. There would be no paper trail.

If the arsonist had not flipped, Ginger might have gotten away with the crime. Trying to ram a frigate out at sea with scores of camera-wielding tourists was a different matter altogether.

Both her car and the remains of the *Ginger Snap* and the Grady-White were impounded, all overwhelming evidence against Ginger. The expert analysis on her mental health found her competent to stand trial stating if her symptoms worsened, medication would be prescribed.

Ginger was found guilty on a conspiracy charge to commit arson with a ten-year prison sentence likely. Because they found no evidence of conspiracy for attempted murder of the two people aboard the *Satisfaction* on the night of the fire, that charge was not presented.

Barry stared down a five-year sentence and a fifteen thousand dollar fine for arson and blinked. His attempted murder charge against Chase and Anne dropped for lack of evidence and because he had cooperated with authorities. Not entirely out of the woods yet, now that the authorities had his identity and fingerprints, old investigations of arsons would be re-opened.

Freddy Garcia faced only a three-year sentence for his part in the arson conspiracy, helped by Barry Stallings claim to have never heard of Jasper Cobb.

Ginger Cobb tried several times to implicate her father in the crime but contradicted herself under police questioning causing her testimony to prove unreliable. It didn't help that she exhibited erratic behavior, occasionally carrying on conversations with herself.

The district attorney found no physical evidence implicating Jasper in the conspiracy to commit arson and found it likely Ginger acted alone. Jasper was never charged. On the charge of second-degree felony attempted murder as she tried to ram the *Satisfaction*, those lubber videos and pictures were gathered and used as evidence against her. She was found guilty and sentenced to a minimum of fifteen years.

As an officer led Ginger out of the courtroom, Jasper heard his daughter's pitiful cries, her voice cracking pathetically as she called out to him. "Daddy? Daddy!"

He walked out of the courtroom without looking back, a stone cold expression on his face as he strode to his lawyer's car for a return to his office. There was no longer a need for an exit strategy. Ginger had used hers instead.

The *Satisfaction* left port with another load of lubbers. Chase and his team all breathing a sigh of relief knowing the threat was finally over. The tour bookings remained strong, allowing the four partners to continue their business expansion plans even if it did put a crimp in Rio's resumed amorous activities. "Hopefully, there will still be enough pretty ladies around by the time we pay off *the old lady*," he said, referring to the *Satisfaction*.

"You can always rely on those old ladies for comfort in your advanced years," Chase chimed in, turning the gigolo joke around on Rio for a change. "As a famous cartoonist once wrote, *Bravo for life's little ironies.*"

The afternoon cruise headed out past Sunset Key. The sunny weather combined with a westerly breeze proved perfect for unfurling the sails. The lubbers were in a buoyant mood and who could blame them? It was the start of the week when most tourists had just begun their vacations, looking forward to several days of rest and enjoying the treasures Key West had to offer. For some of them, sailing aboard the *Satisfaction* was a first.

Chase turned to gaze at Anne. They were both happy to be planning another trip to the Bahamas in *Brains and Braun* soon after the tourist season ended. Who knew how much time and energy would be spent once the next season began? They wanted to get in a vacation soon, or it would be a long time before they could take any time off again. But first, she had an arm to heal. While no bones were broken, she did bruise it. Today, Anne was just along for the ride.

"No work for you," Chase commanded as he tenderly checked her sling.

The cruise held no danger or extracurricular activities, just a normal excursion enjoyed by all. As the *Satisfaction* sailed back towards Key West, Rio summoned the lubbers to the midship for Captain Porter's speech.

He took his customary place on the quarterdeck, looked out over the lubbers standing at attention below him and began his story about a pirate by the name of Charles Vane … a man who eluded capture for years. But, like all pirates, he was finally caught and hanged on the dock of the harbor. A cautionary tale to pirates that a similar fate awaited them.

The *Satisfaction* entered the bay as Captain Porter emphasized his last point about piracy by extending his index finger towards land. "Look there on shore, past the naval station."

All eyes gazed at a dock sporting a wooden pole. It rose upward with another attached at the top reaching outward and resembling an inverted L. At the end of the L, hung a chain attached to a metal cage containing what looked like a skeleton whose tattered garments swayed gently in the breeze. "For pirates caught, their price to pay," he finished.

An audible gasp arose from the crowd, the intended effect he counted on.

Chase loved to see the crowds' reactions and always felt good he had entertained them in a way no one else did on the island.

It gave him personal fulfillment. He wanted to use the story at precisely this time, making a direct connection between the pirate and Ginger Cobb. Both had committed terrible crimes. Both got away with evading justice briefly but were eventually apprehended and made to pay for their transgressions.

They may not have been able to prove any guilt of conspiracy, but Chase and his team were convinced Ginger included Jasper in every move she made. The snake in him had managed to slither his way out of all charges, leaving his daughter behind to rot in a cell.

The coincidence was not lost on the crew, either. Especially Rio. "You had to use that story today of all days, didn't you?" he asked Chase. It was the day Ginger Cobb was in court awaiting her sentencing.

"Let's call it poetic justice, shall we?" Chase answered. He felt a wave of happiness come over him for the blessings he'd received. Friends, family, and work he loved. Smiling broadly, he looked back to his pilot. "Crunchy, take us into the bay for the sunset celebration!"

There was one last reason to be happy. Since his sterncastle find, he had no further nightmares concerning Riley, the drowned boy. It had occurred to him that taking responsibility did not mean *being* responsible for the mishap. Chase hoped that Riley had found peace, as he had.

As the ship sat in the middle of the bay, everyone's attention turned to the setting sun and the anticipation of King's cannon fire. A gentleman sidled up to Chase and asked for a moment of his time. Warily, Chase surveyed the stranger. Given what had transpired the last few months, he stayed on the cautious side.

"My name is Derek Holt. I work with the Discovery Channel, and my job is finding new talent for a television series we're trying to launch. After discussing my ideas with the folks here in town, they all suggested I speak to only one man. You come highly regarded for this project I'm planning, Captain Porter. And if what I've seen today is a glimpse of what my audience might see, I have a feeling they are going to love it!"

Chase took a long look at the man before answering. "Sir, I appreciate the kind words, but I have a good thing going here, and we're very busy. So, I can't even think about taking on any new roles, even if it is in an advisory capacity for a TV series—"

With a wave of his hand, Mr. Holt interrupted. "I'm sorry if I haven't been clear, Captain. I'm not looking for you to *advise* me on the television series. I want you to *star* in it."

At that precise moment, King started his round of cannon fire as the sun dipped below the calm waters off Mallory Square to the cheers and applause of the people aboard and on shore.

Chase, dumbstruck at the man's offer, heard none of the noise going off around him.

Sometimes one had to separate business with their personal life. For the first time, Jasper felt he had to sacrifice his daughter to save his business. It was time to pick up the pieces and move forward.

Even though he had been exonerated of any crime, the stigma of being associated with his daughter's crimes did hurt his business. Contacts shied away from him. Bankers refused him credit. Boaters looked to Conch Harbor and other marinas for berths. His water taxi and tour reservations dried up and the B&Bs had vacancies even during high season. And finally, his franchisor pulled their support from his restaurant project, killing the venture. Jasper Cobb, whether he liked it or not, could now add *Pariah* to his list of accomplishments.

Bent, but not broken, Jasper vowed to rebuild. He had the drive, planned exceptionally well, and it did not hurt to have control of Ginger's offshore account. When he finished rebuilding, he would take the time to exact his revenge on the people who now ruined him. The best part of the plan? They would never see it coming.

Jasper immersed himself in reorganization mode. No longer wanting to think about his daughter and her lengthy prison term, he needed to stay busy. His first task was to assess his business units, which ones were making money and which ones were failing. His B&Bs were paid for, but the taxes in Key West were astronomical, so he put a few up for sale to garner some cash flow.

The trolleys still brought in a decent revenue stream and with little competition in the area, he chose to keep those assets. The Ghost Tour, while labor intensive, had no physical assets. Still, there were always people willing to work at night, so finding low-cost employees remained stable. The water taxi business had indeed dropped off, but there would always be a need for the service, so he believed it would bounce back.

As far as the water tours were concerned, Jasper felt it time to sell his tour boats. He had floated the idea to Chase to buy a new ship. Even if that had happened, he felt his water tour business would have sunk anyway. He approached the other water tour operators and liquidated his fleet to them, not receiving the payout the boats were worth, yet enough to keep the other operations going. Despite open berths, the marina was still a good revenue generator making the "keep" list, but he might need to lay off a few employees. The last piece of the puzzle was the cottage on Sunset Key. It was apparent the wealthy cared more for their comfort than about Jasper's financial problems. He decided to keep the property…unless he got an offer to sell for the right price.

Now, operating as a smaller yet leaner enterprise, Jasper would be able to focus on cash flow, the key to his own exit strategy.

Grow cash reserves, then liquidate everything until he had more than enough to live the rest of his life comfortably off this cursed island. He would find a place to live in obscurity where no one would ever find him.

Jasper had one other plan. To build a war chest and using the funds to exact his revenge against Chase Porter and company. But the timing would have to be just before he fled Key West. Until then, he would act like a model citizen. And the first test of being a model citizen would have to start with an apology. He would let everyone know Jasper Cobb was on the straight and narrow. Remorseful, humble, and modest. A ploy to disarm all until it was time to open the war chest for its intended purpose.

At the end of the day, why build a war chest if you don't plan on going to war?

MORE UNREALE
DEVELOPMENTS

"**K**ING, HAVE YOU seen Chase? I've been looking all over for him. We were supposed to meet on the *Satisfaction* this morning to go over the numbers, but he didn't show. I'm not gonna lie, I'm a little spooked."

King looked across the bar at Anne. She sure looked worried, and if Anne worried, there had to be a problem. She kept biting her bottom lip, her eyes looking as if she might cry. King put a beer in front of her and said, "Maybe he's running errands?"

"That's what he told me when we spoke Friday. Said he'd be back soon. It's not like him to miss a meeting, and when I call his cell, it goes straight to voicemail. Just because one threat is gone doesn't mean there are no others out there." Anne took a sip of the beer and asked for a shot of rum. "But just one. Beer alone won't cut it today, King."

"How's the arm?" he inquired, trying to see if she was still on pain medication.

"Getting there. The physical therapy is doing its job." Reading King's expression she answered, "And yes, I'm off the meds so I can have alcohol."

He chuckled, thinking Anne knew him too well. "Did ya talk to Rio?"

"Not yet. Thought he might be here. I'll call and have him come over." Anne called Rio and they had a brief conversation. She hung up and relayed to King, "He's around the corner and he'll be here in two."

King nodded as he set the shot of rum in front of her.

"It's not like Chase to be incommunicado. That's what's so worrisome," Anne said before downing the shot.

King took the shot glass away just as Rio entered and joined the pair at the bar. "Any word?" he asked. "It's not like Chase to up and leave like this. It's as if he disappeared into thin air. You don't think—"

King cut Rio off. "STOP!" He opened the bottle of rum and poured a shot for Rio. "He'll be here when he gets here."

"*If* he gets here is what worries me," lamented Rio, before downing the rum. He pushed the empty glass in front of King for another one. "If Chase is going to keep us all waiting, then I'm going to keep drinking." Rio's attempt at humor had the opposite effect as his two compatriots frowned at the joke.

King tried to stay busy while Anne sat on the bar stool and kept checking her phone for text messages.

"It'll beep if he texts, ya don't have to stare at it. Won't do any of us any good." Rio shook his head. "Probably got drunk with Captain Mark, and they're both sleeping it off."

"Stop," King said again but spoke softly. "Please, just stop." He knew Rio was trying to lighten the mood. "We all have a job to do tomorrow, so take it easy on the sauce. He'll be back soon." Despite his own words, King was not convinced. He wanted them all to be ready for tomorrow's cruise so he put the bottle of rum behind the bar.

The door to the Berth opened slowly, and their heads turned in anticipation of Chase's entrance. Instead, they spotted the loathsome Jasper Cobb as he tried to slide into the bar.

Clearing his throat as he walked towards them, he said, "I do hope I'm not interrupting?"

Rio spoke up. "What the hell do you want here, Cobb. Why don't you high tail…"

"Please?" Jasper raised his hands. "Let me apologize to you for the trouble my daughter caused. I must admit, I did want your company for my own. But I can honestly say I had no fore knowledge about the arson plan nor any other. And her attempt at crashing her boat into your ship? Horrible. I'm at a loss for words … it was all Ginger's doing. I would never do bodily harm to anyone. It's against all I stand for."

King, Rio, and Anne remained open-mouthed, staring at Jasper Cobb now standing in the Berth making apologies?

"By the way, where is Chase? I wanted to apologize to each of you personally."

"Chase ain't here," said King gruffly.

"My, that is too bad, Mr. King. Please pass on my apology, and when I see him next, I'll do so in person. If there is anything I can do to make up for this debacle, please let me know."

As Jasper took a step to leave, he turned to address King directly. "Mr. King, I also owe you an apology for the other day. I was a bit out of sorts and wrongfully blamed you for Ginger's issues. I hope it was no cause for concern on your part. You had every right to throw me out of your establishment. I hope you'll accept my apology."

Two apologies? King's face opened as if he had witnessed a miracle. One apology was unbelievable but two? That was down-right inconceivable.

"Again," Jasper's head lowered as he pulled at the Berth's door, "if there is anything … anything at all I can do. Isn't forgiveness the gift we give ourselves?" he said before he stepped outside leaving the three alone again.

"Ain't buyin' it!" barked Rio.

"Thought I was gonna puke on his *forgiveness* crap," said Anne.

King decided to open up. "Something I have to tell you two. I suspect Chase's disappearance has something to do with the recent sterncastle find."

"What makes you say that?" Rio asked.

King debated whether or not to disclose his thoughts on the subject. "Ah Shit fire," he said, giving in. "Did you see the news conference?"

"I did," Anne said. "Captain Mark stated he and his divers found it but not how. Trade secrets."

King shook his head. "Not sure that's true. Someone else found it. Didn't want anyone to know."

"Who? And why would they want to keep it a..." Rio stopped. "Chase?" he blurted out. "Chase found it, didn't he?"

"I think so," King said, nodding. Anne and Rio began peppering him with questions. Specifically, why would Chase let someone else take the credit? And what did this have to do with his disappearance? Were there other people out there who wanted to harm Chase?

They pondered the answers in silence. It did not make sense. Chase had always been transparent with them from the beginning … until now. As they sipped their drinks, the questions faded to only one.

Where the hell was Chase Porter?

Chase wasn't in hell; he was on a mission.

Before finishing the Dry Tortugas run on Thursday, Chase had made plans with Rio to work for him on Friday. Rio obliged, giving Chase Friday and Saturday off from working the *Satisfaction* runs.

On Thursday evening, Derek Holt met with Chase for a drink at the Green Parrot, a Key West tourist bar not frequented by Chase's partners. Over drinks, the two made plans for Derek to pick Chase up early the next morning to drive to Miami and meet the show producer, Jamie.

The meeting went well. The three discussed the concept, and the role Chase would play, accepting some suggestions he brought to the table. Chase would work with salvage crews up and down the Florida coastline, doing research on the shipwrecks using his own system: Wave currents, NOAA historical hurricane patterns, logs from the times of their sinking, and a little luck to help the salvage teams. One unearthly search tool that wasn't mentioned would remain that way.

He would also weave in pirate stories or those about sunken ships and the treasure they took down with them. A second crew would film selected tours aboard the *Satisfaction* for color.

Asked how he planned to juggle the TV show with his business, Chase explained the decision to initiate a new protocol to cross-train employees on various parts of the business from how to work the retail store to becoming a cast member. Several employees who showed a flair for the dramatic were allowed to play the more significant roles. While only the rare few were chosen to represent the Captain on deck, fewer still would pursue their Master's license in order to relieve Crunchy.

Chase ended up by saying, "This will also give us additional actors should we need them for this television show."

"Chase," Derek asked with a hint of surprise, "Do you always think of everything?

"My crew tells me I like to stay one step ahead."

Chase noticed Jamie smiling at Derek several times during the meeting indicating Derek had been right, Chase Porter *was* the right man for the job.

"I believe we have all the information we need right now," Jamie said, still smiling. "Anything we missed, or you need from us?"

"As a matter of fact," Chase said with a sly wink. "There is something I need. I have one more chore to do, and now I'm the one who needs a few right men for the job."

"Still a step ahead, eh?" said Derek after Chase explained about the TV man's upcoming role.

"Yup, and this is a secret mission, so shh!" Chase put his index finger to his lips, the universal sign for *tell no one*. Chase hoped he could explain this rule to his friends to understand why he had been so secretive.

On Sunday afternoon, Chase strolled into the Berth and sidled up to the bar ordering a beer, sans lime as if he had been gone a half hour and not two and a half days.

King stared at him. Anne ran over and threw her arms around his neck and kissed him.

Rio angrily chastised him, "You're gone for a few days without a word, and all you can say when you get here back is, *Can I have a beer?*"

"Maybe I should have asked for a lime to go with it?" Chase tried to look innocent but the mischievous twinkle in his eye would not allow it. "If I knew I'd get this kind of reception, I would have come home sooner!"

"You ever do this again, and I'll kill you in your sleep!" Anne gave him a mock-punch to his arm with her good one. "We were so worried! Where were you?"

"I had a little errand to run with a few surprises. Here's the first one." Chase pulled out a small leather pouch tied with a string. He untied it and poured out the contents. Four necklaces identical to his lay on the bar. Chase used his index finger to push one toward each of his friends.

"So," started Rio. "You give us all heart attacks about your whereabouts and all we get is a lousy UnReale necklace?"

"Yeah. About that," Chase began. "Seems I have not been straightforward with you. See, mine is actually a real Spanish silver coin ... and so are yours."

King chimed in, "You mean?"

Rio finished his sentence. "They're *real* UnReales? Really?"

"Really," Chase said. "And this is our little secret. We want to keep people thinking they're replicas. They're really from Captain Mark. A gift for my help in discovering the sterncastle for him. Oops, there's another secret out of the bag."

"I knew it all along! TRADE SECRET my ass!" King barked, repeating what he had heard during the news conference. "So, who's the fourth one for?"

Chase picked up the last necklace. "I'm full of surprises today because this one belongs to him." Chase raised a thumb over his right shoulder towards the door where Daniel stood.

"Me! It belongs to me," Chase's father said, walking up to the bar. "This guy had me fooled for twenty some odd years. The least I could do is get one as well, right?"

"Daniel!" Rio shouted out to him, "Why didn't you let us know you were coming?" "Rio," Daniel said, shaking his head. "Are you still unaware of how loose lips sink ships?"

"I thought storms sank ships?" Chase chided his father.

"Don't start with me." Daniel said, smirking. "Now, where's *my* UnReale?"

Chase handed the necklace to his father while King placed beers on the bar. Anne spoke up. "Wait a second, What else have you got up your sleeve?"

"Thought you'd never ask." Chase took a small box out of his pocket. Opening it in front of Anne. Inside a brilliant diamond sparkled, two Muzo emeralds flanking the gem.

"Will you still marry me even if I don't get on bended knee?" Chase gave his best impression of the pirate pose, his left leg propped on the bar rail, right hand outstretched offering the box with the beautiful ring inside.

The guys laughed as Anne sat with a stunned expression on her face until King whispered in her ear. "You are supposed to say *yes …*"

Anne jumped into Chase's arms and through her tears mumbled, "Yes. Yes, I'll marry you!"

"Get a room!" heckled Rio, as everyone congratulated the couple.

While Anne cried tears of joy, she still managed to one-up Rio. "That will come later. We have a lifetime to practice."

"And I'm looking forward to it!" Chase added.

An embarrassed Rio had nothing to say.

King pulled out a bottle of rum. "Drinks on the house!"

"After those embarrassing comments, we'll need two or three!" Daniel laughed.

King poured four shot glasses but stopped before pouring the fifth and frowned.

"Hold on. I'm doing some simple math in my head, and something does not add up. For one, it should take longer than a few days to get the real UnReales put into fake settings or get the ring settings done. And two, from what we've been told about the sterncastle findings, they're counting the value of the treasure into the hundreds of millions. They won't split the find until the division party. So, where did you get the cash for the ring and what did you do for the two days you were gone?"

Everyone at the bar stared at King in disbelief. Other than playing his character on the tours, this had been the longest sentence the man had ever spoken. Still, he made good points.

Anne and Rio joined King to stare at Chase as they searched for answers. Daniel stood waiting. Loose lips sink ships. Indeed.

"Yea," Rio said, finding his voice again. "Normally, you would be fondling the real UnReale around your neck and worrying what to do next."

"I can't," Chase joked, disregarding the word *worry*. "I have a beer in this hand…" he lifted the bottle with his left and took a swig. "And my *fiancé* in the other." Anne kissed him passionately at the mention of the word.

"Well!" Chase began, regaining his composure. "There were a few things I wanted to accomplish. First, I had help with the ring and Unreales. Captain Mark handled those tasks. He also provided an advance on my part of the sterncastle treasure, so I paid off the note on the *Satisfaction*. We now own her, free and clear, and before you all cheer, let me give King congrats! The bar is once again all yours, my friend."

"Then," he continued, "I invested in another lady. With all that went on, we never had time or the money to get a sister ship for our fleet. Well, no more. I purchased her, had her brought to Miami, and then sailed her, yet unnamed, back to Key West where she now rests comfortably in Conch Harbor."

Rio's brow wrinkled and he interrupted Chase to ask, "Where did you get the crew to sail her back? Our people were all out with us yesterday or working their regular jobs."

Chase smiled again. "That's where the next surprise comes in. Last week a guy from the Discovery Channel took the Tortuga run and pitched an idea to me for a television show. They want me to star in it, and the plan is to shoot the pilot in June right after the end of tourist season. I told them if they wanted me, they had to help, so a few came aboard the new ship and with the assistance of a few of Captain Mark's men and my dad, we all sailed here together. Upon getting into the harbor, I told the television guys, I would accept their offer only if my partners were agreeable." Chase raised his glass. "How would you guys like to be on television?"

The questions came in rapid-fire succession, but Chase would have none of it. "Whoa, we can work out the details later. We're a team. Right now, are you in or out? We make this decision together. I will not do it without you."

Anne stood and raised her good hand. "Aye Aye, Captain!"

The other two followed right behind her and even Daniel joined in.

Chase nodded. "It's settled. We still have two more pieces of business." All eyes were upon their captain as he took a final swig of his beer before placing the empty soldier on the bar.

"My next visit is to stop by Bill and Mary's place to let them know after the division party, we'll soon be able to settle with them for the balance on the marina."

The three looked on in amazement as Chase turned to the man standing *behind* the bar.

"And for the final surprise, you better set us all up again, King. This is the last one for me. Moderation and all."

Anne smiled demurely. "Moderation refers only to alcohol consumption. Not our sex life," she whispered.

Chase regained his composure before continuing. "You know both Rio and I belong to the Loyalty Rewards Program. What you don't know is over the past few years, I've been investing not only into the program for myself … but for each of you as well. This year, you are now aware, it will pay off rather handsomely, so as part of the program, you also get a part of the treasure. It may not be enough for you to retire on, but it should be a nice nest egg towards the goal. And speaking of which, I believe we should start a 401k and health benefits program for the full-timers at the company. They're going to need it if we're going to be shooting the television series. A need to retain good talent. Just goes to show, loose lips may sink ships. But hard work, a sound theory, plus a little luck, can raise them up again."

Everyone began speaking at once except for King, who leaned against the back of the bar wearing a goofy grin on his bearded face. Reaching behind the cash register, he produced a box of cigars and handed them out. More shots were poured, beer bottles opened, and plans discussed amidst the hazy smoke. Chase kept his promise and switched to soda.

Rio downed his shot and said, "What are we waiting for? We have a new ship out there to inspect!"

Everyone turned towards the door to leave.

"No!" barked King, then softly, "Savor the moment." The big man cleared his throat before continuing.

"We're all chasing something in life," he began quietly, cigar smoke curling from his beard, reminiscent of his famous pirate character.

"Daniel has been chasing treasure and its history for years. Chase, you've been chasing adventure, and by all accounts, you've found more than your fair share. Anne here has chased and found love … first Key West and then the *Satisfaction*. And now with you. Rio chases skirts and the good life, sometimes catching more than he bargained for." This last observation caused head nods and chuckles. Camaraderie enveloped the crew like a comfortable sweater on a fall afternoon.

"Me," King continued, "I chased down leads to help us catch the bad guys. And I take a beer chaser with my rum." He took a drag from his cigar as if to let the thought drift in the air like the gray smoke he exhaled. "Separately, we've all chased different things. Together as a team, we chase only one." King paused and took another long draw on his cigar.

Chase asked, "Well? We're waiting. What are we all chasing?"

King let out a mouthful of thick smoke. Drifting up, it enveloped his head and framed the sneer on his face. In his best Blackbeard voice, he boomed, "PIRATES!"

Anyone within a block of the Berth would not have been able to miss the sound of raucous laughter on that lovely afternoon under the bright Key West sunshine.

EPILOGUE

CROWDS GATHERING FOR the nightly sundown celebration along Mallory Square were treated to a few new experiences. The first showed not one but *two tall ships* in the harbor, the well-known *Satisfaction* and a new vessel recently added to the CMPT fleet.

The second treat, a celebration on both ships as Anne and Chase were to be married aboard the *Satisfaction* on a beautiful Sunday evening. King applied online for and received his license to perform the ceremony. He now stood proudly before the happy couple. All the guests waited to hear what the man of few words would have to say about joining his two friends and business partners in matrimony.

Rio stood by Chase's side as best man. Because there were so many friends and family in town, they brought out the new ship, recently christened *Anne's Revenge*, to accommodate everyone. Rio chose the name for the new vessel as an homage to the bride to be, and as a side joke concerning the life Chase was about to embark upon.

While Crunchy captained the *Satisfaction* and Captain Mark piloted *Anne's Revenge*, both Garrity brothers were promoted to

Master Gunners to fire the cannon at sundown in celebration of the nuptials.

The wedding party all dressed in authentic pirate gear; Chase as the swashbuckling hero dressed in all black complete with a bandana around his head, spit-polished boots, and cutlass by his side. Anne opted for a feminine look with a white bustier and smart jacket combination with a lilac behind her ear complete with only one earring, stretch pants and white knee-high boots. The sling finally off her arm, she also carried her cutlass. "For protection on my wedding night," she joked to a round of bawdy laughter. All UnReale necklace-owners wore them with pride. This day, all would go untouched.

In attendance were Bill and Mary Hemmings, Chief Deakin, Sergeant Willis, and members of the Key West's Police and Fire Departments. Anne's family, of course. Her father proudly giving her away. Also, Derek Holt was on board dressed in his own pirate fashion.

"These people are going to make great television!" he announced enthusiastically to the news cameras.

Daniel stood up with Chase and Rio, beaming with pride. The only one who could not be there was Chase's deceased mother who all agreed would have loved Anne as a daughter and been so very proud of the man her son had become.

King, reprising his role as Blackbeard, began the service performing well. In fact, some would say quite eloquently for a bar owning pirate. Coming to the final part of the service, he asked the crowd, "If there be any scalawag who objects to this marriage, let him speak now...." Pausing for any responses, King pulled out both pistols from the belt across his chest. Holding them in the air, he finished with, "Or forever hold your peace." Hearing no objections, he replaced the pistols to their rightful positions, put a hand on each of their shoulders and stated, "By the power invested in me by the pirate code of the Conch Republic, I now pronounce ye man and wife and let no man tear asunder, be he pirate, Spaniard, or BRITISH ROYAL NAVY!"

It must have been an interesting sight to observe two old frigates full of wedding guests dressed in pirate attire turn their heads and spit in unison.

Then, and only then, did Chase kiss his new bride. But no one could hear the cheers from the wedding guests on either boat or from Mallory Square, because as the sun set on the moment the bride and groom touched lips, the Garrity brothers began filling the air with smoke and the sound of cannon fire.

About the Author

Brian DeLaney is a former advertising executive with years of sales, management, and creative messaging experience and is a member of the Atlanta Writers Club. He writes because he likes to use his imagination to entertain readers. His first novel entitled "A Good Mourning" was published in January of 2022.

Brian lives in Alpharetta, Georgia with his wife Cynthia, near children Kelly, Kirstie, Samson, and their families. Together they enjoy traveling and frequently visiting their grandchildren. Brian also enjoys camping, kayaking, yard work, and playing his guitar. He is working on several new projects. *Chasing Pirates* is his second novel.

For more information go to: www.briandelaneyauthor.com
Contact: bdvpfg@briandelaneyauthor.com